PRAISE FROM
PHILIP K. DICK

"**Junction** is where Ursula LeGuin's **Lathe of Heaven** and Tony Boucher's "The Quest for Saint Aquin" meet . . . and yet it's an entirely new novel, a good one, an exciting one, and even an important one. . . . It delightfully deconstructs your notions of time and space and reality in ways I myself never thought of—but would have liked to. Rather than saying that Dann has based **Junction** on my work, I think I'll say that I may very well be basing some of my future work on **Junction**. I don't usually react to the writing of other s-f authors with such pleased satisfaction. . . . It's daring, it's original, it's fun. Dann does not rely on any clichés; he is inventive and creative, and most of all, he can think. . . . If you have a good mind, a mind that loves intellectual adventure, this novel is for you. It kept me away from the TV set for a good long while; can I say more?"

JACK DANN

"One of the most admirable authors to emerge in the '70s . . . SF could use a lot more writers as good as Dann." —Michael Moorcock

"Jack Dann is a reality magician. Like Castaneda, like Lewis Carroll, like Philip K. Dick, he is a master of nothing-is-what-it-seems-and-everything-may-or-may-not-be-seeming viewpoint." —Roger Zelazny

"A major science fiction writer." —Ben Bova

"A true poet who can create pictures with a few perfect words." —*Library Journal*

"Jack Dann is a serious, artful writer, who blends bizarre images with a deep concern for human beings. His nightmares are all the more frightening for being subtle." —Gregory Benford

Author of
JUNCTION

"A dazzling trip through strange Heavens and stranger Hells, *Junction* is a bawdy, vivid novel that mixes the insight and humor of *Tom Jones* with freewheeling speculations on metaphysics, religion, and cosmology, as baroque and packed with wild new ideas as anything by Charles Harness or A.E. Van Vogt." —Gardner Dozois, editor of *Best SF Stories of the Year*

JUNCTION

JACK DANN

A DELL BOOK

Published by
Dell Publishing Co., Inc.
1 Dag Hammarskjold Plaza
New York, New York 10017

Dell ® TM 681510, Dell Publishing Co., Inc.

ISBN: 0-440-14416-7

Printed in the United States of America

First printing—January 1981

For Bev Evans

All of the characters in this book are fictitious, and any resemblance to actual persons, living or dead, is purely coincidental.

*But I shall not grow too old to see
enormous night arise,
A cloud that is larger than the world
And a monster made of eyes*

—G. K. Chesterton

Part One

JUNCTION

1

Ned Wheeler was caught again by the edge of Hell. Standing in the tall grass, perspiration running from his armpits, soot on his face, a milky weed stuck between his teeth and protruding from his mouth at an odd angle, he surveyed the black kingdoms before him and the desolate umber and ocher deadland below. Half asleep on his feet, he stifled a yawn.

Before him, beyond the tundra that extended from the grassy plain to provide a dividing line between two realities, a mountain grew. It pushed itself out of the ground silently, belching amorphous rock, forming new mountain chains, proclaiming a new geologic era. Snow-capped peaks reached into a slate sky colored with blue streamers of cirrus. Ned waited for the mountains to dissolve, merge with the robin-egg clouds, or explode into a shower of hypercubes to provide fourth-dimensional moisture. Anything could happen in Hell.

Behind him was Junction, still the same: prim, pretty, full of foul smells and fine citizens. Today it was a bit noisier than other days; only a thin whisper reached Ned, a grumble. The Desert Midland Bank reflected the afternoon sun like a nightbeacon flaring for sailing ships and shamelessly showed Junction's teeth to the creatures of Hell.

Junction was a democracy. So elections were being held and ale being drunk and the whores were working overtime. President's Day was a time for hymns and good pot, a time to jump and scream and not be jailed or whipped or clamped in stocks or thrown into the urine pit. But today Junction was too noisy for Ned, and everyone would be using his favorite whores. If he stopped at the Congress Bar, which smelled of perspiration and soil, they would probably put him to work. So here he was, hand in his pocket, awed by nature freaking out before him, thinking about Hilda's heavy hips and Sandra's tiny breasts. He thought about his mother, whom he had never known except as a presence when he was a babe. She had walked into Hell during the happy time of Whitsuntide and never returned. As she had been claimed by Satan, so Ned's father gave up his life to prayer. The old man never wearied of telling Ned that he was "a pea from the pod," just like his mother in looks and temperament. He wondered what his mother had found out there and why she had stepped off the edge of the world. He felt the draw of Hell and shivered.

"You should be ashamed of yourself, Ned Wheeler," shouted Forester, the church featherwaker, as he pushed his way through the tall grass behind Ned. He was a small, nervous, bald man with a red, freckled face and arched, bushy eyebrows.

Ned started, as if he had been jolted out of a dream; he was cottonmouthed and groggy and annoyed. But Forester had no authority here, and Ned would not give him the satisfaction of recognition. Even now, when he was off duty and merely another placid citizen of God's only city, Forester affected the vestments of the clergy—the carycoat and overhood; but he had taken pains to make his clothes much fancier than the humble priests. Embroidered edging and a blood-purple chasuble told everyone that he could afford, albeit just barely, to buy an acre of Heaven.

"You're being drawn into Hell, and none too slowly. A perfect example you're setting for the children.

. . ." He stopped beside Ned, pulling grass away from his coat, and turned his back to the tundra and Hell. "You're turning into a dybbukdevil, if you're not one already. Have you nothing better to do but suck up the effluvia of Hell?"

Drop dead, Ned thought, but still he ignored Forester.

The children shouted, whooping with excitement.

"See," he said, "they are here, just as I thought. And you just let them be, didn't even chase them away from the hands of Hell." Forester turned around, shielding his eyes with one hand and crossing himself with the other.

Ned watched the children playing in the gray scrub of the Helltundra. It would not do to tell Forester that he had not seen nor heard the children before, that Hell had soaked up sight and sound into its unholy patterns.

A whore's daughter, blond and buck-toothed, hiked up her skirt for Handler, Small Henry's youngest son, who was shouting, "Bugs, bugs, it's probably full of bugs."

Ferris Angleton's daughter, Flora, joined him immediately, shouting, "Bugs, bugs, I see the bugs."

The little girl pulled down her skirt and then started to laugh. She walked toward Handler, swinging her hips in an exaggerated fashion, and then grabbed for his crotch, screaming, "I've got the worm."

Handler blushed and Flora lifted up her dress to prance around singing, "I've got a worm and it's bigger than his, it's bigger than his, it's bigger . . ."

"Listen to them," said Forester. "They're being swallowed by Satan. You'll get a day in the stocks for this, and if I have anything to say about it, you'll be thrown into the pisspit."

Ned watched a mountain melt and grow again in Hell.

"Get out of there," Forester shouted at the children. "Come up out of that Helltundra at once."

The children walked toward them, crying and clasping their hands against their chests in innocent shame. Forester lectured to them, his rouged cheeks puffing in and out as he worked his mouth around words he barely understood, words he had learned from the whores in study-sessions. The children bowed their heads, probably thinking about tonight's dinner they would not get and the beechwood thrashing sticks hanging ominously on the kitchen wall.

Ned had heard Forester's lectures before in the church; they were all basically the same—pompous and filled with words no one could understand. They were too shrill to have effect. Even the children squinted and pulled in their cheeks as his sandpaper voice splintered the surrounding sounds into coughs and shrieks. But crying was in order, and the children did that well, although they managed to give Ned a few well-formed dirty looks and stick their pink snake tongues out at him.

He pretended that Forester's voice was a huge waterfall crashing into the rocks below, spurting foam into the air, filling everything with a dense mist that could not blunt the roar of clear water. His attention wandered, seduced once again by Hell—he was frightened by the growing black mountains; they were great bears lumbering toward him, mouths slavering, needle-teeth glinting under a black sun. (Ned had never seen a bear, had only read about them in a golden book found in a dank cellar.) But he was still drawn to the edge of Hell, fascinated by its landscape of nightmares. For everyone else, especially Ned's father, Junction was a holy haven; for Ned it was a trap.

"*That's* the will of God," Forester said, pointing toward Junction. "And that"—pointing toward Hell with its new mountains—"is the will and the way of Satan.

Are you coming to church and wash these sins away before Satan sucks you in?"

Say yes, Ned told himself. For all Forester's shrillness, blind faith, and silly pomp, he was right—Junction was the way, the glass church was—or should be—his beacon. As Ned had been told: "Glass to let in the many eyes of God. A transparent mountain of perfection." Yet he was still transfixed by the kingdoms of Hell.

"Well?" Forester asked. "We're leaving this minute. I can feel this place draining my strength, filling me with sin. Come along."

"No!" Ned shouted, overcompensating with his voice for his fear and anger with himself. But he couldn't leave yet, and certainly not with this buffoon who had somehow managed to steal God's love and happiness, and now made everything soggy with it.

Ned's silence broken, Forester smirked and said, "Then let Satan have you." He pushed the children to get them moving. Flora turned around after about five paces and gave Ned the finger and a coy smile. Soon they became a rustle in the high grass, a screeching memory that would refuse to fade. Ned would almost prefer Hell to the reception he knew he would get in Junction. How could he face his father who was praying with tears and chestbeating for the return of his prodigal, the misfit who drew life from his seed?

Ned was ashamed that he could not see Heaven. He cried for his father, felt the guilt of the church upon him, but was compelled to stand on the edge of reason, on the perimeter of God's hope. This, he thought, was true perversity. It was as if by just standing here on the edge, he could enter a dream, and he was certain that his nightmares were connected with the stuff of Hell. And if the dream-scrims would part for only an instant, he would be able to see what really lay outside Junction—not the shades of Hell, but another world.

He watched Hell's mountains and began to dream.

As Ned had been told—"And to punish sinners, God sundered cause from effect." And he believed it; he was watching it. The mountains, growing and sometimes collapsing, looked real in every detail: snow-capped peaks, lowland vegetation straining up ever-increasing inclines, becoming sparser in the cold, high regions. The earth colors were soft browns and greens stippled with black and ocher—all the shades of Junction reality reflected in a slightly curved mirror. In those impossible regions time could be speeded up, stopped, or merely distended like a balloon ready to burst. Out there, only the presence of Hell's black sun was predictable; everything else could, and would, change. Ned had often before dreamed that the sun was a terrible pit with no bottom, a hole in the sky. And out of this hole flowed the very stuff of Hell.

Something moved just beyond the tundra.

Ned felt a chill crawl up his spine, a shudder that silently cracked in his throat; yet still he dreamed. He tried to turn and run toward Junction Road where he felt he would be safe, but his body stood immovable, fixed to the worm-ridden soil as any of the grasses swaying in the slight breeze.

He could barely make out a creature running toward the tundra. It seemed to run faster and faster, just reach the tundra, but it could not cross over. It was small, but, like a swimmer in a still pool, its shape kept changing, swirling into vagueness, as if it were trying to shift from one reality to another.

Ned was certain that a creature from Hell could not reach Heaven, nor Heaven's holy outpost. Even Forester could not deny that, although he would probably like nothing better than to watch the creatures of Hell smite the sinners in Junction. But the creature would not give up; it was still running, never quite reaching the grayness of sand and rock and plain. The sun was shadowed by clouds that drained the landscape of color, leaving only ash waiting to be dissolved in bright light. The creature shrieked and crawled and begged, but the distance was too great. Ned tried to make out its words—if, indeed, that's what they were—but they were too jumbled, and he could not be sure that they were not just sounds in his head, like the noises he could hear when no one was about and it was absolutely quiet.

He thought again to break free, but the roiling dreamstuff of Hell leached away his will, dampened his screams, stilled his movement, and transformed his fear into cold bridges of thought. What if this raging Hellbeast did break through Heaven's bounds? And then it would be free to swallow Junction and vomit it up again—a new city, dripping with the saliva of sin, drowning in Satan's sperm. He studied the monster and tried to make out its features. Was it a woman? Did it have pointed teeth? How many arms and legs? He couldn't tell; its shape changed so quickly. But it seemed to him that it might be a bird. Was that a yellow beak protruding from a faceless face? An intuition told him that was right.

The clouds had scudded across the sky, leaving the sun alone to burn in a clear blue ocean. But the snow-peaked mountains in Hell reflected no light. They seemed to absorb it; what was left became constant twilight. Above the mountains, the black sun was a dead ember in Hell's firmament.

Perhaps the creature was a bird of Heaven trapped in Hell? Ned thought about that, trying to recall a phrase from the Book. Ezekiel the Wisherman saw in a vision beasts with wings that were called angels. That was in the Book. "And they were full of eyes round about them." He didn't quite know what that meant. If only the monster trying to escape into Junction was a bit larger. Then he would be able to make it out.

He thought of Saint John the Diviner and remembered his father, who could memorize anything, recite: "And before the throne *there was* . . ."—he would raise his hands above his head at this point—". . . a sea of glass like unto crystal: and in the midst of the throne, and round the throne, *were* . . ."—he threw up his hands again—" . . . four beasts full of eyes before and behind.

"And the four beasts had each of them six wings about Him." Father breathing with difficulty, looking to the ceiling. "And they were full of eyes within, and they rest not day or night, saying, 'Holy, holy, holy, Lord God Almighty,' which was, and is, to come."

Full of reverence, he strained his eyes to see the creature. It might be a lion—he knew that wasn't right—but a lion couldn't run upright. It was too small to be anything but a small animal or a bird. If its shape could change, then so could its size. Perhaps it was a combination of monsters: lion and bird, snake and lizard, spider and bear—or, worse yet, perhaps it was an ephemeral monster cobbled out of Ned's fears, only real for Ned. Real enough to eat him, but not true enough to last. And if it was a creature of Hell it could (and probably would) devour the infant mountains and drink the river. The river was fed from Hell; it was an abomination, an anabranch of Satan's piss coursing through God's land and then back into the Hellsump. But Junction wasn't Heaven yet and thus had to be fouled. It was a busy little Purgatory, full of reminders of the sins of man and the glories of God, closed in—and in fear of—Hell in all its black magnificence.

Eyes straining, Ned could see it now. The creature was crawling, growing; its yellow wings were flapping wildly. Its henna and stammel eyes were blinking as if they were regulated by God's clock. Ned could see every detail: yellow beak, claw feet, and the hundred eyes of Heaven, or Hell. So it was a bird. He had been right, but the details blurred with his illumination; his eyes strained to plot the creature's course and shape—and could do neither. The vision was in his mind, or at least magnified by it, a dream that he had soaked up from Hell.

He stared at the earthly terminator that divided Heaven's possibility from Hell until his eyes burned and welled with tears. Go home, he told himself, and pray with Father. But he could not stand the thought; his father's love seemed to be driven by hate.

Again, he saw the creature. It jumped into the air and rolled into the tundra. But it couldn't escape from Hell, Ned thought.

Hell's mountains turned to glass, reflected the black rays of the sun.

Ned screamed as bright images flashed in his mind: his father growing old in a mirror, Sandra changing into someone else, a bridge into Hell, tunnels and God's locomotives, and a desert of red sand, tuff, tundra, and stone churches.

He tried to fight his way out of the dream.

But he seemed to be in the grip of the hand of God.

I repent, he thought; but he had no voice. He was still trapped as securely as Satan had been in the icy center of Hell.

I repent. . . .

The creature from Hell was drawing near. It was coming to claim him, the sinner. But perhaps it was an angel from Heaven sent to help him. Could this only be a vision, a vision of conversion? An angel that had escaped from the torments of Hell—that, it was said, had happened before. Leland had escaped from Hell to present Christine with the rosary, the beads of life, the prayers of eternity.

The monster lumbered across the tundra, wings folded across its back, eyes blinking.

But which monster did he see? Was it only a figure of his imagination or was it tangible, a new addition to Junction reality? It became larger as it bridged the distance, investigating new ground.

Ned found he could close his eyes—that was better than facing it. "Coward," he called himself, but his eyes, now blinded inside his head, refused to open.

How close is it? he thought.

"*As close as your dream,*" said a voice inside his head, a not-quite-voice that was more like noise, like the thunder or static he heard in his head when he was alone and frightened and thought he could hear angels rustling their wings and whispering amongst themselves.

"*I've come to take you. There's much ahead for you to remember.*"

Ned found his voice and screamed, but it was as if he was listening to someone else. When he stopped—his ears ringing and blood pounding in his head—he thought he heard another voice, a real voice cutting the air with breath and spittle. But that, too, seemed to be coming from the monster. Could it have as many voices as it had eyes?

"Hello, hello. Are you Ned Wheeler? Don't be afraid. . . ." The voice seemed to be swallowed by the very air. It was a voice he could barely understand, for it had no nasal twang, but he could certainly make out his own name.

"*Come now or run. It's no difference to me. Work it out. But I won't leave without you. It's already done.*" Then static, the rolling of drums, birdscreams, the coughing of broken lungs.

"Leave me alone," Ned shouted.

And he was free, released from the dream. He turned and ran through the high grass to Junction Road, looking back only once—and found nothing but grass and a sunny day behind him. The creature had disappeared or perhaps had never been there in the first place. Ned was still trembling. This might be a vision of conversion, he thought. That meant the angel would not leave until Ned held God's hand. That's better, he thought.

He did not stop running until he reached the moss-covered cobblestone road. This northernmost part of Junction Road was not cared for and was overrun with weeds and white flowers. It was a nursery for insects and noisy things that scratched and squeaked and jumped through weeds and grass. Spiderwebs glistened in the sun. Ned's fear began to ebb as he sat down on a stone, leaned over, and carefully tore the heads off near-by flowers. He rubbed his hands with them until he could smell their pungent aroma mixed with his healthy perspiration—the sweat of physical exertion concealed the fetid sweat of fear. His breathing returned to normal; his head cleared. It was as if Ned had just awakened. Even as he tried to remember, the vision began to slip away, almost as if it had never been, to be replaced by vague whisps of thought and feeling. But as Ned savored the warmth and color of Junction's eternal summer, he remembered one of his father's favorite sayings: "How soon we forget the teaching of the Lord."

It was probably a revelation, he thought. A waking dream. A lesson. But Hell plays tricks on the eyes and mind. And he was much too close to Hell, not even a mile away from its borders. But why am I drawn here? he asked himself. It is a magnet for evil thoughts. He felt a twinge of guilt, but, as always, it turned into vague sexual desire. Perhaps my mother draws me here, he told himself, but could not believe that. Many folk had walked into Hell to die by its various engines. Why, Sam Sense had even watched one of the greasy women from the Faubourg beyond the wall step into Hell, only to break apart like shattered glass. And Sandra had told Ned stories about Hell, how one might melt like wax or turn to stone. Perhaps I'll end up broken in Hell, Ned thought, feeling as if he would be forever alone.

Gaining courage, Ned walked back to investigate. He took his time, considered turning around several times, but continued on—at least no one would think him a coward. He followed his path of trampled grass to the edge of the field, to the border of the tundra, and looked into Hell. He searched for his mother's face as if it might have become part of Hell's body.

Before him, the mountains of glass had turned to gelatin and were shaking and melting. Hell was melting, turning into primordial ooze.

He could not find any monsters. Everything was calm. The sky was bright, the clouds full and luminescent. Hell had turned to mush, its foundation and reinforced reality pulled away to reveal a bare stage ready for new props and sets.

Although he was awed by the religious moment, he still couldn't repress an urge for some good grass, a touch of spider brandy, and a good fat whore—after all, he rationalized, it would be a long walk through the grass, woods and wastes, commons, meadows, and lammas lands. But friends and whores would not satisfy him, and his grin seemed to be pasted on his face.

As he turned away from Hell, he heard a noise in his head, a rattle he couldn't shake away, an almost-voice that was there to stay.

Junction consisted of two great streets running parallel with each other between the hillside and the river—which was fed from Hell. All the other foul, narrow streets fed into these two avenues at right angles, forming a "rib" pattern and creating the tidy, unnatural lines of the city. Both streets wound their way closer to each other and almost came together in the Portus Park section, an important parcel of cityland populated originally by guildsmen (*after* God raised Hell and knocked everything down), but now a center for all craftsmen and artisans, artists, seers, poets, and other frowned-upon iconoclasts. A strange melding—one that produced a respectable amount of brawls and folktales.

It was around and about Main Street that the Old Desert Midland Bank, now a glorious church, and most of the popular whorehouse bars could be found. Riverside Drive, a hated but still used name, was a market and residential street, although most of the market stalls could now be found on Main Street and in the Portus Park area, where the fiercest bargaining occurred and the loudest voices could be heard. In the middle of Main Street there survived, against town law, a large farmhouse with all its agricultural and pastoral appurtenances: horses in the stalls, chickens pecking for food, a sad-eyed old bull about to drop dead, and a dung-heap of gigantic size in the front yard.

That house, known conveniently as "The Stone House," was the President's residence. The horses and bull were displayed as symbols of power. Before God raised Hell, the house had been a rich man's home, a museum and cultural center, and a synagogue.

Since a president could only serve—or be served—for one year, Thomas McCall, the incumbent, a tall, long-faced, muscular man who disliked Ned for his whoring, but used the same whores himself, was moving out. He would return to his house in the bowels of the Portus section and resume his old trade as a mason. McCall was still enfeoffed to Ned's father, and had once banged Ned on the head for trying to collect his father's rent.

On the southeast perimeter of Junction stood the ruins of a town wall that had never been completed. It was to encircle all of Junction, but—so the tales had it—the workers had quit for religious reasons. The wall was to be two meters thick and eighteen meters high, an insurmountable object for the crawling beasts of Hell. That, of course, was never believed. It would cast a shadow fifteen meters on either side—Hell's reflection of walls, gates, and towers. The wall was begun on the side farthest from Hell and represented the weakened will and fear of its builders, for who would willingly stand near Hell and coax its monsters?

It was said that the strident word of the church had once more carried its people into Heaven and, more mundanely, lessened their workload; for town law had it that such civic duties were to be scheduled so as not to interfere with the normal workday. That meant civic work had to start at about three in the morning—serfage, tradeswork, and the many services that awakened the city for another day of toil would begin at dawn.

Beyond the southeast wall were farm and fallow lands, Sky Forest, named for a lake that had mysteriously dried up long ago, a few small villages and settlements, and the inevitable borders of Hell. The Fauboughers who lived on the farms beyond the wall, were infidels, backsliders, misbelievers, heretics—too afraid of Satan and not sure enough of God to trust in his beneficence and be sheltered. The church of Junction fought the Fauboughers with slogans—hatchets of God they were called—since country trade and commerce were too important to lose, even for religious prejudices. There could be no *jihad* or crusade with fists flying and heads rolling.

Bridgehead, the northwest corner of Junction where Ned had seen the monster from Hell, was almost surrounded by Hell. It was cut off from the mainland by Sticksveiller River, which ran down the northeast side of Junction before changing its course. Bridgehead boasted the finest smoking-grass, provided the leafy crop was carefully tended, but it was too close to Hell and its fatal miasmas to be inhabited. In fact its smoking-grass was said to contain the smoke of Hell.

Built over Sticksveiller River, Bild Bridge was the only way back from Bridgehead—unless you were going to Hell or were willing to follow the narrow band of duskland that was sometimes swallowed by Hell, sometimes by Heaven, to Crocus Bridge, a wooden cut-across that rocked and swayed and squeaked when stepped on. Bild Bridge was forty meters high and had circular masonry arches. But it was dumbly humbled by the skeletal remains of a great steel bridge that had collapsed under God's shaking. Like a Roman bridge of similar plan, which had spanned the Tagus River near the Spanish-Portuguese border for two thousand years, Bild Bridge might last the years if it could stand God's shaking and if Satan did not pull the cover of Hell over it.

Ned had a recurring dream that always began with Bild Bridge, but he could never quite remember what happened—the bridge, indistinct figures, mountains growing in his hand, tunnels yawning before him to turn into crawlways were swallowed by his screams which would tear through layers of sleep and push him into wakefulness. He would find himself sitting up in bed trying to remember, eyes still pulling against the dream, as he fell back into deep water and passed through the warm thermoclines of sleep. But his dreams were always nightmares; in these dreams he was always trapped or isolated from his friends and father. In dreams he could not open doors or even make himself known. He was a ghost, or a dead thing. And always, there was something drawing him, waiting for him.

All that was far away from Ned now. In the middle of a warm afternoon, dreams became like childhood memories, unreal, transparent things—dust dragons swept away by noise and motion, whispers lost in a forest. Although he tried to remember his vision, it slipped away, as if it were sand spilling out of a child's tightly cupped hands. Noise filled everything up, blotted out memory, created a bustling, all-important now. By the time Ned reached Junction proper, he was sweating. He thought of his father, who would be waiting impatiently for him in church. He felt the pressure of being forced into Heaven by guilt, and slowed his gait.

The streets were crowded with election day celebrants. Dressed in Sunday best, courteous to one another, singing, laughing, giggling, the townsfolk were all walking to church or a bar or a lover or favorite whore. Men dressed in cardboard stiff carycoats and loose-fitting frieze pants lifted their caps to the ladies who had not bathed in weeks but were dressed in multi-petticoated finery. All wore the neatly powdered, and by now slightly sticky, look of celebration and humility. Their Victorian faces possessed certitude and thin-lipped righteousness.

Of course, the street people and "serfies" were strident and ragged and earthy and full of sin and momentary happiness. Drafts of cheap brown beer and an occasional poke of rough-cut grass turned prayer day into holy holiday. The whorehouses helped, too. They proclaimed love for everyone and offered the necessary edge of sin and guilt to the righteous and cheap fun for the poor, for on holiday everyone paid what he could afford.

Ned felt alone, isolated from the crowd. A man without a shirt, chest covered with ashes, winked at him as he passed. Ned had seen him at the Congress Bar a few times, quietly sipping a drink and waiting his turn. Ned bowed his head at a group of ladies prancing by, but he wasn't interested. They giggled and pointed at him, their pungent smells preceding them. The youngest one, a saucy blond, scratched at her crotch and Ned looked away, wishing for a swim and a smoke. Ned was of marriageable age and very eligible. When not working for his father, he spent his time whoring and Hellwatching—and the only women he befriended were whores. That made him very desirable. Although he had little money now to support a pink-cheeked wife, he would later inherit his father's privileges and estates, receive his due of revenues from Faubougher and Freemen alike, and by then be a fine example for his young children. But he had often said to his friends that he would rather marry a whore who could think than a respectable babymaker from the northeast section of Portus Park. That was good for a laugh and a tumble with the girls.

Ned thought of the whorehouses just ahead; but something buzzed inside his head, spoke gibberish and words he couldn't understand. He felt the touch of a dream and stopped walking, oblivious to the crowd flowing around him. He fought the dream, told himself that the voice was his conscience or his thoughts that had been confused by Hell.

I must stay away from Hell, he thought. I won't go back again, he resolved.

But the voice whispered to him, and Ned felt drawn into the dream, tied into something larger than he could imagine. But what?

He screamed, remembering the birdbeast, discovering that it had found its way into his head.

"Leave me alone," he shouted.

And the voice was silent, as if it had never been. Again he felt disoriented, as if he had just awakened, trying to remember. . . . Dreams dissolved, were replaced by passers-by, who gave Ned quizzical looks and shook their heads.

Embarrassed and sweaty, Ned began to walk quickly. He would go to church and pray for true conversion.

The church was several blocks away. There were not very many vendor stalls in this area, and most of them were closed—the proprietors were either praying or whoring or politicking. He passed "The Hanging Tree," a small, ramshackle, sidestreet whorehouse that was doing a good trade today. But the girls were not up to par, Ned thought. They were jealous of the Congress girls and were always starting fights. Ned remembered a skinny redhead named Reisel who painted her toothless gums and had given Sandra the long pink scar that ran across her face. It had been a good fight: Sandra had knocked out all of Reisel's teeth and was about to kill her when Ned broke up the fight. But that had been years ago, when he frequented every house in town.

Ned sighted a piece of glass in the gutter and stooped to pick it up. That would bring good luck—glass had taken on religious significance. It symbolized grace and the all-seeing eyes of God. Since the shaking, when man fell from grace and lost the privilege of doing God's handiwork, it was forbidden to cast glass. But the Book promised that after the Last

Days, men would be cleansed and "stand upon a sea of crystal." Most of the church glass that had once littered the immediate vicinity of the bank had been picked up, but Ned could always find new pieces around—it was as if the precious stuff regenerated itself right there in the street. Although some of the glass had been donated to the tabernacle, most was kept for luck and private prayer. It was a very valuable black-market commodity.

Much of Ned's whoring money had been made by selling these sharp trinkets. There were as many rumors that Ned was dealing with Satan as there were that he was chosen by God—luckily, the conflicting rumors negated each other and he was left to himself. That gave him a freewheeling entry through Junction's stratified ways.

Ned had slipped the sliver of glass into his handkerchief and put it into his pocket—sure that it belonged to the bank and was holy.

"Hello, Ned Wheeler," shouted Miss Jenkens, a squat old woman wearing a faded black dress and a veil. She was Ned's old schoolteacher. She caught up with him and asked, "Are you off to church?"

"Yes, mam," he said, walking a bit faster, hoping she would fall behind.

Puffing, she said, "Your father's worried about you. Do you know that? Do you know that he's in church praying for you right now?"

Ned nodded, visualized his father crying and praying for his son's darkened soul, and hurried along the street; but Miss Jenkens kept apace with him like a hungry dog.

"He's a good religious man. And he's worried about you, worried you're going to walk right into Hell. 'The sinner will be cast into Hell.'"

Ned looked around the street; there was no escape. He did not see a familiar face. He would just have to wait it out—she would have to stop talking when they reached the church.

Miss Jenkens's favorite project was the true conversion of Ned. That would surely wing her into Heaven, erase the simple sins of her youth, and turn Purgatory into a short vacation. She had begun teaching Ned the true way when he was a little boy. Now she was his veiled fury, a self-righteous Hydra with enough talk and gossip for seven heads, a peek-a-boo Thomasa, always waiting, watching, counting up his sins as he forged them with sleep and compromised women.

"I saw you pick up a piece of holy glass," she said. "Don't you know that's a sin—and probably the work of the devil, anyway. You're not allowed to touch it. Your fingers will burn in Hell. And it's against the law, only a clergyman is pure enough to touch it. What if I told on you? What then? Are you going to give it to one of your whores?"

Ned sighed and said, "No, mam." He quickened his pace, but the old woman was vigorous and undaunted. Already he was beginning to regret his vision and possible new conversion.

"Aren't you worried just a little bit about being poisoned in Hell with your whoring and singing and smoking and drinking?" At best she could be sententious, at worst, her conversation would consist of wheezes, coughs, and long misquoted passages from the Book.

"Yes, mam, I am," Ned said. And he meant it, although he dreamed about Sandra and some good grass, dreamed of sweaty company and a smoke-filled room. He wanted to tell Sandra about his dream in Hell—what he could remember of it; perhaps she could interpret whether it was holy vision or chimera. He wished he were singing songs in the Congress, making up new words to old refrains while customers sang off-key and clinked pennies into a dish. But he was thinking of sin again.

"Ned Wheeler, if you're really going to church, I won't tell." She had a fit of coughing, spat up yellow phlegm onto the back of her spotted hand, and reached for a handkerchief.

"Thank you, mam," Ned said after a pause, hoping she wouldn't cough herself into Heaven. But she kept up with him, pace for pace. There were horses and wagons in the narrow, cobbled streets. Ned kept to the carriage side of the road so as not to be splashed by garbage. A bag fell from a third-story window-hole and exploded beside Miss Jenkens, who was still quoting from the Book. She covered her mouth with her hand, pressing the veil into a mask against her skin, and suffered the putrescent smells that were immediately picked up by a warm breeze and wafted down the street. A Faubougher, roughly dressed, passed by them. Miss Jenkens turned her head away; Ned averted his eyes. There was something vaguely familiar about the wiry haired, tight-faced peasant.

They skirted the north edge of Commons Green; in the green the joys of good company could always be had on a Hanging Saturday or after dark on a Sunday.

Ned could hear laughter coming from the Congress Bar, a two-story frame building, garishly painted in red, white, and blue, and—as usual for holiday—filled with celebrants. It faced the church, which was on the other side of Main Street. It equalized holiness with sin, a perfect Manichaean match. This year the Congress Bar could boast a cellar full of electors and party prompters demanding girls and beer and grass and music so they could better make decisions. There would be good boasting, old remembrances, fine fellowship, a few fistfights, and party politicking.

There was a small crowd milling about in front of the building. Ned thought he could hear Hilda's husky voice over the din. He remembered how she loved to laugh and bite when she trembled—a fair furrow for his member, a heavy, lazy woman who camouflaged wit and intellect with silliness and truculence, a freethinker—too impatient to be respectable, too loose for a static society.

"Well, if you're going to church rather than that whorehouse, I'll walk along with you." Miss Jenkens handed him her bible and took his arm.

"Your sin will be on me," she said, "but I think I can better stand it than you. Perhaps now God will see to look into your soul. As the Book says . . ."

The crowd standing in front of the Congress Bar shouted at a group of Fauboughers, chided, spoofed, and catcalled.

"Hey, Fau Fau. Go back to the woods."

"Watch out for Satan. He's close by Bridgehead. He'll squeeze you and eat you."

Ned felt a chill as he remembered the monster breaking out of Hell. He thought of his mother, imagined her being pulled apart by Satan's tentacles. Afraid of being pulled into another dream, Ned concentrated his attention on the familiar sights and sounds around him. Gooseberry that she was, Miss Jenkens was an anchor to the here and now, to comfortable afternoon reality. He pulled his elbow to his side, tightening his hold on Miss Jenkens's arm.

Freemen stood on the steps of the church and watched the Fauboughers. Children shouted but were quickly quieted by parents, for the church must be kept holy. If one side of Main Street was full of bawdry and laughter, the church side was heavy with prayer and the sobbing of penitents. Well-wishers nodded to the Fauboughers who filed past, ignoring everyone. Inside the church, voices rose to the melody of a psalm, and Ned imagined that his father had been standing in prayer for at least several hours—he had spent the previous night praying alone in his pew, and had not left the church all day. Not only would his father be praying for his son's conversion, but he would pray for the impossible—for the return of his wife from Hell.

Ned climbed the stone church steps slowly, his schoolteacher hanging on his arm. He tried not to look at the Congress Bar on his left. The side door had become the official entrance to the church; only children used the front entrance. The church was the highest and grandest structure in Junction, a glass and metal box that had somehow survived the shaking. Much of its holy glass still remained, although the western wall, once as transparent as God's eye, had to be bricked up and closed to the gaze of the sunset until enough glass fragments were acquired to open two "eyes" in the wall just below the roof. The western wall became "Wailing Wall," a place to gnash at old sins with teeth and tears, a place to cry and pray for the almost dead, the suffering, the children, oneself. Especially oneself. Although the walls and windows were cracked, they had been mended and pasted together, reinforced with mesh and wood and brick.

Some of Ned's friends called to him from across the street. He didn't turn around.

"Hey, Ned; you're missing a hell of a party."

"Hilda's been asking about you. She misses you. And Ma Fishbine wants you to sing for the customers."

"Going to church with Miss Jenkens. Ned's got religion. And he's using the side door, too."

Ned felt his face flush. Miss Jenkens said, "Come along. Pay them no mind."

A catcall from the second story, a strident voice was shouting, "Ned, honey. Going to church? Come back soon, we're having an election party."

That was Hilda's voice, Ned thought as he opened the door for Miss Jenkens and then followed her past the stairwell and study-rooms into the temple, his heels clicking on the faded red and blue parquetry. But I have no friends, only acquaintances. Even Hilda is a shadow. An image of talking bones and hanging flesh passed through his mind. He could hear the congregation praying and singing, his father's gritty tenor the loudest of all. Just now, he felt that only he was real, that the congregation, his father, Miss Jenkens were shadows. Or perhaps you're the shadow, he told himself.

Quietly, he opened the door to the temple. It squeaked and a few heads turned around to look, but most of the congregants were engrossed in their Books. He followed Miss Jenkens to her seat in the first pew.

Hilda must be taking a rest, Ned thought. But not for long, not on a holiday. He imagined Hilda turning around from the window-hole to face another customer. A fat frop or a skinny eel—no difference, he told himself. They all hold coins. Am I not so different? Sometimes he felt that he knew Hilda only a little better than did her customers.

He could smell the mold of the pulpit carpet in front of him. A heavy man with thinning hair combed up into a pompadour was leading the services. The notes of "My Country Tis of Thee" echoed in the open vaults where Ned used to play hide and seek and had once banged the carpenter's daughter. At the time, the carpenter had been president, and his daughter was, indeed, a prestigious prize. Ned paid for it with a whipping.

Miss Jenkens sat down and patted the seat behind her, motioning Ned to stay with her. But the smells and her devotion were too much for him, and he was anxious about meeting his father. He excused himself, saying, "I should really find my father. He would be angry if he knew that I was in church and didn't sit with him."

Dreamlike, hidden in his thoughts like a twine of black thread in a dark cloth, the ghost-voice gabbled inside Ned's head. The voice was giving him a headache, yet it was softer than a whisper.

"You're probably going to sneak out the front and run across the street. Your friends are probably calling you. Isn't that right?"

"No, mam," he said as he watched her breasts rise and fall as she breathed. He tried to imagine her frail pumps working to eke out enough oxygen to keep her alive for another few seconds. But they could collapse at any time, and Miss Jenkens would deflate, sink into the chair like an empty sack. And her bones would crumble to ash: the leavings of an abandoned hearth. At one time, it was rumored, she had been a beautiful woman with a full face and long black hair. She had had a few lovers, one of them his grandfather, or so he had overheard his father say. But her shriveled skin was too old to remind him of anything but death.

"Well, all right. Go look for him, if you must," she said, rubbing her left eye. "At least you're respectful. Could I borrow your handkerchief for a minute? I've left mine at home and I think I've got something in my eye." She took off her hat and veil. Her hair was dyed red and she was slightly bald in the back. A bug crawled to the surface and then disappeared again into her red forest which had been patiently stiffened and combed.

"Well?" she asked.

So she still wants that little bit of glass, Ned thought. Payment for paradise. He laughed a bit too loudly and he felt everyone watching him as he walked toward the door. Then up two flights of stairs, past the sitting room—which was the drinking room—and down the hallway onto the balcony. The balcony was accidental: the second floor had given way years ago, and the masons had simply smoothed the ragged edges into an oval and the carpenters strengthened what was left. Wooden supports and roughly finished

plaster-work contrasted with old glass, delicate parquetry, and the sleek finish of the walls—hands could
not compete with machinery. Fine art had given way
to rough craft.

Ned's father—a well-built, stocky man with thick
gray hair, a wrinkled forehead, shadowlines running
from nose to corners of a thin, stern mouth, and deep-
set blue eyes like Ned's roofed with black, pencil-line
eyebrows—was praying, left hand holding the Book,
right index finger pointing out the lines to whomever
might be interested: he was very proud of his reading
proficiency. Sitting comfortably in his special chair
near the balcony rail—a traditional place reserved for
the older and most religious men—Ned's father was
easily the youngest man in the "Book-whackers" section. But he was a magistrate, and that good office
gave him special rights and responsibilities. (Older
judges had claimed that it was a shame that a man under sixty should have to judge others; but God's finger had been laid upon him.) Ned always felt uncomfortable in the presence of his father's peers, these
foul-smelling, coughing, lupus-faced men who held up
the ceiling of tradition, orthodoxy, and religion for the
rest of Junction.

Squeezing between his father and Mr. Brownlaw, a
city official and most fervent churchgoer, Ned sat
down. He repressed an urge to run out of this fetid-
smelling room filled with the almost dead and the
most holy. Behind him was a large window that overlooked the street and the Congress Bar. His father,
without even looking at him, handed him a Book, and
Ned held it open while his father stood up and prayed
silently, rocking back and forth on his heels and wiping his eyes with a clean handkerchief. Feeling the familiar pangs of guilt, Ned waited for him to sit down.
Mr. Brownlaw—a small-boned emaciated old man
with a full shock of white hair and brown parchment
skin—remained seated and mumbled his prayers in a

singsong, occasionally sneaking a peek through the window behind him.

A half hour later, after all the young men were happily seated, Ned's father sat down. "Why did you bother to come?" he asked. "It will be over soon."

Ned knew that there would be at least eight hours left—twelve, probably, for his father. "I had a vision of Hell. That's why I came."

His father was suddenly interested. He brushed back his gray hair and picked at a mole on his forehead. Where his father was ruggedly handsome—features sharply defined and body well kept—Ned was overweight and his face was soft. He had long blond hair that stuck to the sides of his face, small teeth set in a large jaw, a rather large, sensual mouth, and dark blue eyes that lightened to cerulean after he ate or made love. He resented his father for more than his hard good looks, but the whores liked Ned. And he was three inches taller than his father.

"I told you to stay away from the tundraland. You shouldn't even go near there. You've got your mother's blood." He sighed, looked toward the front of the church as if he were looking once more at the face of his wife, and said, "Tell me about your vision."

Ned told him what he could remember, and his father nodded and smiled, as if he had experienced that vision many times before. Mr. Brownlaw buried his face in his Book, but had stopped turning the pages while Ned talked. But even here, in God's temple, Ned could feel the face of Hell pulling at him, drawing him away. It had always been like that. He thought of it as darkness inside him, a dislocated part of Hell that would always be charmed back to its source.

"I'm still waiting. Time enough."

The voice of the Hellcreature spoke very clearly inside Ned's head. Ned felt throat-choking fear and revulsion, but they passed before he could scream, for the voice and all its whispers and gutturals were now familiar and woven into his thoughts, like dreams from which he would awaken with only a vague unease.

"Haniel, Kafziel, Azriel, and Aniel," his father said. "You saw one of the monsters from Heaven. A wonderful sight. And you found nothing when you went back. Well, visions are only to see once. I knew this would happen one day. Sit and pray. I'm very proud and happy." He turned the pages of Ned's bible to the correct prayer and began intoning the words. But Ned felt listless, drained of will and spirit; it was as if everything he had told his father was a lie, just a nightmare that had broken loose on a warm afternoon. He listened for a voice in his head, but found only his thoughts.

From where he sat, Ned could see the pulpit and a quarter of the main-room congregation. Readers dressed in Sunday finery, priests in coarse black, high almsmen, a serfage worker, and a woman with her first born—a baby gurgling and laughing inside his rag blankets—stood stiffly on the dais, mouthing words from a book most could not read, speaking the holy words with trepidation—for each word mispronounced was an extra eternity in Purgatory. Listeners leaned forward in their seats to catch every word, to be the first to shout, "Misstag." Each "misstag" corrected pushed Junction a step further toward Heaven.

Simon Forester, the featherwaker's son, was needling the less alert congregants and making too much of a fuss over his temporary position—a position he held while his father rested from his duties. A featherwaker could rouse the congregants to prayer in any manner he saw fit, and Simon's father had broken more than one man's knuckles with his "waking stick." The son was the image of the father, but with more hair and less energy. Simon would only pester in spurts, then he would open his Book and rock back and forth to quicken the interminable rise of his prayers into Heaven. Soon he would make his way upstairs.

Ned stared at the true Book and remembered that it was Miss Jenkens who had taught him to read it. She used to have a classroom habit of raising her eyes to Heaven whenever she said an important word. Once, on a dare, Ned had looked up her dress as she embraced the sky and said, "Amen." He had nightmares for weeks about that unholy place, which, according to Baldanger, was a nest for maggots and worms. She used to scold him when he went to the Old Library south of Portus Park to read the other old books. She had told him about "trash" and why the old books didn't count or work any more. "That was before God punished us and raised Hell to Earth," she had said. The library was now used as a stowbin and dump—it was a place for heretics, a dark room fit only for garbage and old tools. There were very few books left: most had been burned or just rotted away, leaving a musty stink and a few dead worms. It was said that the Fauboughers had great quantities of books hidden, although Ned did not think any Faubougher had ever read them. But the books in the library, soiled and yellowed as they were, promised the secrets of antiquity. Since Ned could understand very little of what was written in those books, they remained mysterious and wonderful, unsoiled by comprehension and objectivity.

Still thinking about the old books, Ned forced himself to read the bible and pray—his father had begun to get nervous and kept turning Ned's pages and underscoring important passages with his finger. Ned's bible had seen too much wear (it had been passed around in two families for three generations) and was falling apart, but, then, it had only been made to stand up to normal use. The binding was torn, the parchment pages were yellowed and cracked, and the script was smudging. Upon closer inspection, Ned could see that it had been transcribed in haste; many words were misspelled and the letter-hand style was crabbed. Scribes were notoriously sloppy, so quality was compromised by quantity, although Sam Sense could still make a fine Book, one that could stand up to Hell itself. Ned might have become a fair scriviner, but he hated the work, for it was slow and boring, and his father had chided him, saying, "One must be worthy of inheritance; only boys and men of holy demeanor could be ordained to scribble in God's Book or work in the court." But Sam Sense had taken Ned to the cellars where he worked and tried to teach him the trade. He had even shown Ned an old time bible made of thin paper, its pages still white as a child's teeth. Although Ned still wrote private letters each day for townsmen and ladies, his talents were better put to carving and cabinetwork.

He turned a page in the Book; he did not mind the tattered binding and loose thick pages. A second-hand bible was considered by some to be holier and luckier than a new one; it lent the blessings of past prayers to the present user. So, of course, a second-hand bible was more expensive than a new one—and the more battered the better. Through the years each succeeding bible became slightly thinner as proclaimed authoritative councils decided what prayers were to be considered true and correct.

Remembering his vision and the mountains of Hell, Ned worked at his prayers, mouthed the words, tried to find meaning in the many cyphers. He sang and smiled at the congregation, but it was all empty gesture; he remembered vague bits of his vision and listened for the voice to speak inside his head. His head ached all the more, and he had a sudden, terrible thought that Junction and Hell alike were dreams, and he had mixed them up. The fixed reality of the church seemed to be melting, and Ned had an intuition that he could step from one dream to another. He glanced at his father, who had turned his head to sneak a peek out of the window behind him. The second-story window-hole of the Congress Bar was just visible. On the pulpit below them, the mockministers had donned white garments and pointed conical caps. With arms outstretched and fingers parted to form the sacred sign, they blessed the congregation and prayed to hold back the advance of Hell.

The congregation turned away from the pulpit, closed their eyes so as not to witness the holy sign, and beat their chests. Civilized, well-modulated voices became jungle wails, cries for old ghosts and better days. Ned's father clapped his chest the loudest and cried as he sang. Mock tears, Ned thought, for a formal occasion. Feeling suddenly guilty, he tried to imitate his father.

It became warm and stuffy; Ned could smell the pungent odors of old men. And the services went on. Ned's father was so happy that he wouldn't sit down. Whenever Ned would sit, his father would knit up his eyebrows in disapproval. And Ned would sigh and stand. As the hours passed, the glass behind him seemed to draw his face. And every turn of his head that brought him closer to God's glass, ironically, brought him closer to Hell.

Sandra was hanging out the window-hole of the Congress Bar. She had a finely featured face, black hair cropped short at the ears, and almost translucent skin. Her blue caryrobe was loosely tied to expose her small breasts. Ned turned and saw her, but could not hear her shouts. At his father's glance, he turned toward the pulpit and said a prayer, already feeling the old discontent of being forced into God's lap. The chair, although more comfortable than the benches downstairs, was beginning to hurt his buttocks.

Word had passed that Forester had returned and was coming upstairs to see if anyone had fallen asleep. That could only mean trouble. With Forester's approach everyone nudged his neighbor and sang louder. Forester's bald head was polished with perspiration; that's why he had acquired the nickname "Chromedome."

But what was chrome? A strange way to say shiny, Ned thought. "Another mystery of life," his father had said.

"There he is," said Simon, Forester's son, in a loud voice. Forester nodded pompously, pulling his lips tightly together, and walked over to Ned's father. Simon followed and stood near the window.

"Do you know that your son has been corrupting young children in Hell today?"

Ned felt his heart quicken and his face become hot, but his father ignored the featherwaker. He began to sing loudly.

"That's why he sits with you, begging forgiveness—now that it's too late."

Ned's hands were shaking, but he smiled; it was a defense reaction. He felt his grin freeze on his face, turn into a muscle spasm. Forester was lying and building up his own sins just to harass Ned. That took a strong faith and a belief that the end really justifies the means—for Forester probably knew the exact number of days he would spend in Purgatory, or even Hell, for this unholy diversion.

"I denounce him in front of this congregation and before God. I accuse Ned Wheeler of corrupting small children on the banks of Hell, I accuse him of having commerce with Satan this very day, I accuse him of defiling God's House. Everyone knows that he spends his hours with whores and on the rotting shores of Hell." That said, Forester took in a sharp breath and seemed to hold it.

"Liar," Ned shouted, looking down toward the pulpit, then facing Forester, meeting his eyes. Ned felt as if his heart was too frenzied to remain in his chest and had made its way into his throat.

The temple was silent; a sudden hush, every face within sight turned toward Ned. The mockministers below had stopped praying—they removed their conical caps and held them in their arms like ancient Torahs. To denounce someone in God's church before a congregation was an act of excommunication.

"I denounce him."

A pause, and then a few of the other congregants below repeated the phrase. A mere majority assent could pull the church from Ned, turn him into a social leper, require his father to pronounce him dead and mourn for him. The tension ebbed and then grew, each congregant anxious to add his word for a promise of Heaven.

Ned's father looked around at the congregation and, still ignoring Forester, motioned to the mockministers to begin. They shook their heads. He stood up, stared down Forester, and then turned toward the congregation and addressed the mockministers. Standing straight and tall on the balcony, he looked like one of God's shouting prophets, all strength and holy spirit. "I once judged this man to be stiffnecked, and I do so again." His voice echoed in the church. "He indulges himself in pride and jealousy even in the House of God. You all know that children sneak off to play in the prohibited places."

"Then why didn't your son send the children home?" shouted a guildsman from below.

Ned leaned over the balcony rail and said, "Because I didn't know they were there until Forester came looking for them." But his father gave him a hard look, as if this was not Ned's fight at all. And, indeed, Ned felt that he was a stranger here, a visitor who paid no fee for his pew, who brought nothing to the church, who took nothing from its good office.

"What were you doing in that unholy place?" shouted Forester.

Looking past Forester, Ned's father addressed the

congregation: "The boy goes to the edge of God's land to mourn for his mother. He goes to wonder and rend his clothes." Shaking, his face flushed, he tore open his blouse and said, "I denounce Forester the featherwaker." Without a pause he began singing the Mitleid Anthem and Ned joined him. Ned had to make a stand, sound his voice, let his father know he was a true believer, and prove the accusation false.

"I denounce him," Forester repeated.

But Ned's father's voice was strong—there was not the slightest tremolo of fear. It was a brass horn calling back the shepherds. Following his example, the old men began to sing, echoed by a chorus from the pews below. The mockministers and other pulpitmen (and another woman with her baby) were still silent. Their voices would claim the truth, for church purposes, and pragmatically bend the scales.

One could almost hear the buzzing of thought as the mockministers tried to reach a decision.

"And *I* denounce him," said Forester's son.

I'll surely be called dead now, Ned thought, truly afraid of being ostracized. He was already trapped inside himself; if the world also became silent, it would be worse than blindness.

For all his petty faults, Simon had a strength about him. He had chosen to stand with his father, even if it meant losing the church—and that was something that he claimed he loved more than himself. But Simon's words were too late: the mockministers had donned their caps and were addressing the congregation with *Dominus Vobiscum*. The congregation joyously followed with raised voices and holy signs drawn in the air. They were now freed from decision and sin and could resume their posturing toward Heaven with prayers and innocent play.

Now, for a set time, Forester could not be recognized, not even by his son, whose lesser sin of association required prescribed debasement and isolation.

They would be forbidden to work or pray in the church, for they were no longer to be considered church citizens. Everyone ignored them as they left the church.

But Forester still had his faith. He would probably just consider this another burden to be carried for the Lord. If he received no recognition for his martyrdom, that would be all right, too. There could be no recognition for an overdressed featherwaker. But, like Job, he would let the world pull him apart for his faith.

The services continued as if nothing had happened. Ned's father sang, stood up as much as he could, and pointed out to Ned important passages in his Book. Ned listened for the dream-voice again, but he could hear only outside noises—prayers, chants, and the coughs and wheezes of old men.

An hour passed. It was getting dark. Ned wondered if the mountains were still growing out of Hell. There, it would probably be as sunny as noon. Remembrance of his vision brought prayers to his mouth, although even now he wasn't sure of it. He mouthed the prayers. He would have to repay his father with piety. It was a grand debt. But his prayers were forced; they were just unfelt words repeated over and over in the hope that repetition might lead to meaning. Ned tried not to fight his father's will, but found himself staring into space, his Book open to the wrong page. He could feel the wires of Hell and hear his father say, "Stiffnecked still. Still choosing Hell."

Ned stood up with his father for the Standing Prayers, but the glass pulled Ned around just in time to see Sandra open her robe and dangle her tits at someone below. She glanced at Ned and winked. Although she wasn't his best lay, she was his favorite girl. He had once thought he was in love with her, but that died quickly. An awkward friendship remained, as did the psychological walls that Ned thought he would be able to lift. She sucked her fingers and Ned sat down again, covering his lap with the Book. His father raised an eyebrow, but it did no good: Ned would not stand. His face flushed as his father prayed.

Another hour, and dusk had lapsed into evening. The church candles and street lamps had been lit. Behind Ned it seemed that the entire town was trying to squeeze into the Congress Bar where a closed meeting was being held in the wine cellar—the traditional room for caucuses and political brawls—to decide who would be the next president. Of course, the president had no power—that was reserved for the clergy. It was rumored that the president really did hold power, but every president denied that.

Ned had to go to the toilet, but it was considered unholy to leave the church during services on a prayer day—and the old bathrooms had been bricked up long ago, for bodily functions were considered an unholy necessity not to be acknowledged in church. In church everyone was by definition pure. Ned could see Sandra still hanging out the window-hole as she looked for customers. She had pulled a jacket over her robe to counter the night chill, but expediency forced her to expose her breasts. Looking at her only strengthened the feeling of fullness Ned was trying to hold back. He did not so much want her physically, as he wanted her assurance and the security of her, naked beside him.

He turned around and prayed with his father. He stood up, sat down, mouthed all the words, made all the holy signs, until he could hold himself back no longer. Without asking permission, he stood up and left his father, ignoring the murmuring in the pews. I'll return, he thought. After all, did his father expect him to become a complete convert in a day?

Ned relieved himself in the small alley between the church and a Central Guildsbuilding. There was a cool breeze, and the street smelled of sweat and good food and urine. Behind him the great windows of the church were yellow with flickering light from the candles. A candle for each sin, the flame of penance. His father had already lit one for him.

He forced himself to walk back up the stone church steps. His father had not, would not, ever learn. As long as he could stand and pray, he would badger Ned with religion. He forced the faith upon him, would not let Ned find it himself. Ned could never be religious enough to satisfy his father—not even now when he wanted to, when he needed to believe more than ever, but could not resist his own pressure.

Make him happy, Ned thought, inhaling deeply, pretending he was smoking some good grass and lying with Sandra and Hilda. Stay with him tonight, he told himself. He stood by you. The vision was true. You're converted.

"Hey, Ned," shouted John Seawall, one of the town smithies, a big man of about thirty with a dark, wrinkled face and no teeth. He used to joke that the girls liked him better without any teeth—and so did the boys. He was standing on the porch of the Congress Bar, trying to hold his place in the crowd. "Come on, Ned. Party, party, party. They're thinking up the next president in the cellar. Aren't you interested in eavesdropping?"

"No thanks," Ned said, but he stopped on the stairs. Something was pulling at him. He stood still to resist.

"Everybody else is using up Hilda. Must be thirty guys jumped on her belly today, you've no time to spend a penny to give her a rest. You're up there praying with your highfalutin father."

"Shut it."

"Come on," shouted Baldanger, the shoemaker, from a second-story window-hole above the porch. "We see you, Ned. Everything's just about started, and who are we going to tumble the whores with? Old Herman trying to bounce long enough to come?" Baldanger whistled past a chipped tooth as he spoke.

"Come on, Ned."

"Wait," Ned said. "Shut it." Something awakened inside his head and began to speak again. But there was no background noise this time, just an overpowering stillness waiting for an echo.

"Can you hear the mountains? They lie on the other side of your face. They're for you. Waiting for you."

The words echoed in his mind, as vapors of dreamstuff settled over him.

"Let me alone," he shouted, but he was not sure if any words had left his mouth. Staggering out of the alley, he fought his way out of the dream. It was a spiderweb prison of thoughts and colors and ringing sounds.

Ned woke up in a cold sweat several seconds later; he was still standing. He had a sudden fear of death and wildly wanted to live. If monsters were waiting for him, Ned would have to face them shortly. Something irresistible was trying to take hold of him. But Ned would not give in. He promised himself.

The evening air chilled him—sharp little breezes picked at him like cold memories of things that had not yet happened. Behind him was a glass cathedral reaching for Heaven, shimmering yellow to relieve him of sin, its money vaults now collecting alms and prayers for the poor.

And before him, the devices of Hell—but human device was more comfortable than the dark mountains of Satan's mouth, or even God's love. . . .

3

Ned leaned out the second-story window-hole and watched the revenants promenading along Commons Green, west of the church's "Wailing Wall." A central bonfire raged under the silvery panoply of stars overhead and provided light and warmth for the cool night. The figures looked grotesque in the flickering firelight. Like intelligent moths they circled the fire in ranks of two's and three's. Ned tried not to look at the church, for he would see his father praying for him, the "almost convert." By now his father would be in a frenzy, forcing his ecstasy, making his last prayers count, for they were the most important. Soon the candles would be extinguished and he would be forced back into a less substantial world of grime, mud, and whores—a world contrived for lesser pleasures.

Ned wondered about the birdbeast, tried to recall the holy vision in its every detail, tried to isolate the sights, sounds, and sense of that time; but his head was aching with frustration, filled with thoughts he could not quite grasp, memories that would vanish just as he brought them into focus. He had seen a vision, but it had been too much a dream, and even now he was afraid that he was fooling himself into God's hands. Something is out there, he thought as he looked at the bonfire. Lest he slip into another dream, he tried to keep everything in focus; it was fear that kept him alert. The fire snapped and spat like a trapped beast. Ned was naked and the sharp night breezes chilled him.

"Is this for me?"

Ned turned around and saw Hilda examining a shard of holy glass before a candle. The glass sparkled, as if it had caught the flame. "I always know when you have glass by the way you fold your handkerchief," she said. "This is a pretty piece, it looks green at the edges. How come you always find the glass? It seems to grow out of the dirt wherever you walk, do you charm it out of Hell? Baldanger never finds any."

"Give it back, you pocket-thief. It's for the church." Ned would offer it as an expression of contrition for past and present sins.

"Come on, honey. You've got another piece of glass, give that to the church. I've earned this for all the free tumbles and drinks and grass when you said you didn't have a dollar."

Ned stood up and felt dizzy; he was exhausted, still fighting away inevitable sleep and dreams. Hilda ducked out of reach, layers of fat jiggling as she moved, thick auburn hair hiding her flushed face. She wore her hair long to distract customers' eyes from a rather plain face that would be bloated in a few years if she wasn't careful. An abundance of flesh, freckles (and an occasional pimple) gave her an earthy, homey appearance. She was Ned's favorite lay—a perfect combination of nervous passion and endomorphic laziness.

"Come on, Ned, a new position for the glass." She lay down on the floor, legs spread and raised in the air.

Suddenly, Ned wanted her, but not because her tricks excited him. He wanted to screw her until she screamed and pounded the floor with her fists. He wanted proof that he was alive.

"A fuck for the glass, a fair trade," she said, raising her head, looking at him through her legs. "You owe me a present, anyhow."

"Hell I do," he shouted, and jumped on her, straddling her wide stomach. She laughed and kept her arm out of his reach. Ned would screw her for the glass—and pry open her hand when she came. That little piece was for the church.

"If you had not become a whore, you'd find glass," he said as he wrestled with her.

"So whores are unholy. Then why did your friend Reisel find such a piece of glass in the woods? And if you put that thing into me, you'll be unholy, too."

There was laughter from the door. Sandra and Baldanger, arm in arm, were hooting and shouting.

"And look," said Sandra, "Ned with a hard-on. Very unholy and impolite."

Ned quickly lost his erection.

"Hilda's too strong for you, Ned," Baldanger said as he looked around the room. He had not been able to find his clothes and was wearing one of the girl's robes. He was a lanky man with a deep tan, a scruffy, light brown beard, and thinning blond hair which he combed over his forehead.

"Stop it," Sandra said. Her blue robe was open to expose small breasts with black fuzz around the nipples. The delicate network of veins was clearly visible on her throat and chest. "Give Ned whatever he wants and listen."

Hilda gave him the piece of glass and curled up in the bed to sulk. Ned felt drawn to the window, but he forced himself to stay with his friends.

"Have you seen my clothes?" asked Baldanger.

"Shut up," Sandra said and turned to Ned. "Word finally got out about your hassle with Chromedome. It seems you weren't the only one to leave the church early."

"So let Chromedome talk," Ned said. "He'll be talking to himself soon enough." Ned felt guilty enough about his father—he didn't want to think about Forester and his son.

"He won't talk about it," Sandra said. "I don't think he'll try to talk with anyone—he'll accept his punishment as God's gift and wallow in it. And his son will do the same. That's why this place wasn't buzzing with the news four hours ago.

"Anyway, you've made a few more enemies. Ferris Angleton is madder than hell. He really believes you corrupted his ugly daughter and he's talking for blood. Small Henry was upset when he found out that his son was out there, but I laughed it off and gave him a free squeeze. He was more upset that his son would be corrupted by a whore's daughter than he was about Hell."

"Ferris Angleton was downstairs, higher than a son-ofabitch, and telling stories," Baldanger said, curling his lip over his chipped tooth to stop the whistle—it didn't work. "He said he saw a monster that looked like a bird running across the northwest pasture. Christ"—Baldanger made a sacred sign by waving his hand in the air—"he even brought in his daughter, Flora, to say she saw it, too. He didn't stay long, though. Some of his friends carried him home; he was too drunk to walk."

Then the vision was true, Ned thought. He shivered and crossed his arms over his chest, as if to assure himself that he was real. He thought about the monster that was haunting him. He would have to face it, struggle with its filthy eyes that were focused on Hell, listen to it talk inside his head and grow inside him. It was surely a creature from Hell, not Heaven, he thought; and he felt a deadness resting on him like a shroud. It was as if he was butcher's meat and Satan's demon was devouring him from the inside out. His skin prickled, his hands were clammy.

"I heard something about a monster," Sandra said, "only from Alex Eitrides. She's one of the whores in "The Hanging Tree." It was her daughter that you saw playing with Flora and the little boy on the Hell-tundra."

"What do you make of all that?" Baldanger asked. He sat down on the bed beside Hilda, and Sandra, looking tired and draggletailed, leaned against the door-post.

Ned didn't answer. He did not want to talk, for they were interested in gossip, in turning a phrase and laughing and playing. He felt estranged from these people who thought they knew him yet didn't know him at all. He was drowning in his thoughts, unable to express them. He was still alone, even among his friends. He felt uncomfortable in the sparely furnished room. Two beds, foul smelling and damp, had been pushed against opposite walls to leave enough center floor space for play. Several blankets as damp as bedsheets were strewn about the floor to protect knees and buttocks from splinters. Ned's clothes were draped over a high-backed chair in the far corner of the room.

While Baldanger stuffed some green pot into his pipe and passed it around, Ned dressed. A stiff shirt and stained pants made him feel less vulnerable. He pulled the chair beside the bed and took the pipe Baldanger handed to him.

"The bed's big enough for you," Hilda said.

Ned propped his feet on the bed. They felt as heavy as gravestones.

"The Southsiders are making trouble downstairs," Baldanger said. "Politics. They're screaming corruption and squeezing our whores. And they're saying you suck Satan and pray with Fauboughers. The usual crap."

Ned's face reddened.

"Well, that got a rise out of him," Baldanger said.

"Forget the Southsiders," Sandra said. "Let them curl up with beggars and Fauboughers. Relax, Baldy bought the room. We're free for the night."

"So what," Ned said. "It's my room, anyhow."

"Only to sleep," Sandra said. "But Baldy spent all his money so we don't have to twist our backs for a crown and worry that the next whorehopper won't steal an hour's dollar."

"They'll be knocking on the door," Ned said. "It's holiday."

"Let them knock," Sandra said. "Old lady Fishbine's been paid—let her share the other girls with the cocksmen."

"What did you pay her with?" Ned asked.

Baldanger smiled and said, "I used a piece of glass you gave me."

Thief, Ned thought. I should have stayed in church and pissed my pants, he told himself. His father was probably beating his chest, accusing himself for his son's false conversion—Ned's sin was worse than misbelief: it was blasphemy. At least I have one piece of glass to throw on the pulpit—the other feeds the whores.

"Do you know who's in the cellar?" Sandra asked. "Well, from what I hear, there's almost no Southside representation. It's all Central and Westside." Sandra peeled back a broken fingernail, pausing for effect. "Old Herman is down there, and Stan and Freeglass and practically everybody but you and Baldy. You've got us to yourselves."

"What about Eastside?" asked Ned. "*They* must have people down there."

"Yes, they do," said Baldanger. "But not as much as last year. Reverend Surface had first choice on electors, and he probably figures it was only fair that we get more representation after what happened last year."

"I'm surprised he got away with it."

"He's strong now," Sandra said, "especially after last year's fiasco with the stinking Fauboughers deciding the election."

"Either way, it didn't matter," Ned said.

"That's right," Hilda said. "It's just empty rules and pride."

"Did they let the Fauboughers in again?" Ned asked Baldanger.

"They had to. They only let five in, though."

"It's still one vote."

"But it won't matter this time," Baldanger said.

"They shouldn't let any of them in—church rules or not," Sandra said. "Let them stay by themselves." Her face looked pale in contrast to her oily, unkempt, black hair. Her scar was a threadline from cheek to chin. She had a fragile bone structure, and at the moment she looked brittle, as if her face was a stiff parchment mask and her hazel eyes, rouged mouth, and scar had been painted on as an afterthought.

"Who cares," Hilda said. "Let the stinking Fau Fauws play too. What do you need political parties for, anyway?" She twisted her hair into knots as she talked. "Eastside, Westside, what are they but an excuse to get drunk and slide between our legs?"

Everyone ignored her. There was a loud knock at the door and someone shouted for a whore in a thick voice.

"See," Hilda said.

"Go away," Sandra shouted. "We're used up."

Mama Fishbine's voice boomed from behind the door. "Don't worry, girls. All fixed." There was a scuffle and more shouting.

"She'll take that cockeyed cocksman downstairs and feed him another whore," Hilda said. "But Mama will be back, as soon as she thinks you're sleeping and smiling. We're not done for the night, you can be sure of that." Baldanger chuckled and pressed closer to Hilda.

"It's a fraud," she continued, moving away from Baldanger. "What do we need a president for? He has no power, doesn't do anything, lives off the public tit like a Goddamn lord for a year, and he's elected by a bunch of drunks. Everyone respectable is over there in church." She pointed toward the window-hole. The church was brightly lit with candles and tallow lamps.

"That's not true," said Baldanger. "Hell, the Reverend's down there. The altarmen are covering for him at the church."

Ned ran his thumb over the surface of the piece of glass he had taken from his pocket. He tried to enter into the spirit of camaraderie. Looking around the poorly lit room, he began to feel more secure. But he thought of the birdbeast stalking him through dreams. There was no place to run; that he knew, for he couldn't run from his thoughts. "Nobody knows if the president's got any power because they never tell," he said. "Even Sam, after he finished his term, would only smile when anyone asked him about it." Ned made a fist around the holyglass, even hoping it would cut into him as punishment for his sins; but there would be enough punishment later, he thought, if Satan's demon could wrestle him into Hell.

"And look at all the old presidents, Ned continued. "They've all been smart, even if none of them had any education. As drunk as the electors get, they always elect someone smart. And how come there's always some clergy down there? Did you ever think of that?"

Hilda chuckled and tapped her fingers on Baldanger's bare leg. "Ned's going over to the other side."

"He was in church most of the day," Sandra said, "turning around, just like his father, to look at my tits."

"Shut up," Ned said. "The presidents have all had something to do with religion. Even old Sam was going to church three times a week when he was in office."

"That's because he had to," Baldanger said.

"That's right," said Ned. "The president represents tradition and religion. Remember the presidents used to rule over everything—no one could be more powerful except the church. So what does that mean since God changed everything and put Hell all around us? It means that the president rules Hell and Earth. And Junction, whether we like it or not, is Earth."

"Do you believe that God put Hell all around us?" asked Sandra in a low voice, as if God might hear her blasphemy. "Maybe the shaking was just a natural event. Maybe the same is true of Hell. Only we don't know the reason. After all, the stories conflict. How long ago was the shaking? Five hundred years ago? A thousand years ago? There aren't even any records."

"The shaking marked the end of the old life," Hilda intoned.

"Now we live for God and His church, and only the true Book holds meaning," Sandra said, as if finishing a prayer; but there was a note of sarcasm in her voice.

A hush filled the room, a strained silence. They had all been taught—and believed—that the church had to be permanent and eminent. Otherwise, all would fall and Hell would bury Junction. While Baldanger filled the pipe again and gave it to Hilda, Ned lit the tallow lamps on the wall. Twice he scraped steel against flint to ignite the tinder. The candles in the room were low—a measure of the holy candles burning across the street. Had Hilda or one of the other whores lit the candles as a mockery? Ned wondered. If so, everyone in the room would have to absorb the sin. But, perhaps, the candles were lit out of guilt. Everything looked soft and yellow. Ned could hear the chatter of the congregants as they left the church for home and clean living. The girls would soon be working overtime.

Ned passed the pipe to Sandra and watched the smoke curl in the yellow light. A breeze wafted into the room through the window-hole, circulating the bad air and banishing the smoke. Baldanger played with Hilda and Sandra. Sandra protested that she'd have to go downstairs soon and pee, but she leaned against the wall, her leg draped over Baldanger's crotch, and seemed to enjoy the company.

Deciding not to join them, Ned sat down in front of the window-hole and watched the congregants below. Were they waiting around for the electors to decide? he asked himself. But that would take all night. And what did he care? He did not want to face his father tonight. Ned knew everything the old man would say; it would all be true. Ned would stay here until morning. He dreamed of the church and the smells of the pulpit and traced his father's face in the street out-lines—shadow and line, a sparkle of glass, the holy building before him, to remind him.

As he stared out of the window-hole, he became afraid, but it was a quiet morbid fear. The church could not save him from the demon growing inside his head. He was alone, as he had always been. Angry with himself and circumstance, he resolved to fight the creature from Hell.

Sandra got up from the bed and stood behind Ned. Hilda and Baldanger were screwing noisily. Sighs and whispers were interspersed with groans and yelps—it was an old argument, a sweaty fight, and was becoming louder and more frenzied with every jab. Ned concentrated on the dying candles in the church. One by one they were slowly going out, substituting grayness for each yellow halo.

"I had a strange dream last night," Sandra said, massaging Ned's neck and back, probing and kneading one small area, then another, until he relaxed. "I went to see Alex Eitrides about it—she's supposed to be good with dreams and amulets—but she just told me she'd have to think about it. She said she had the exact same dream, and so did some of the other whores. When I went back there this morning, she'd gone, probably to the Faubougher Wall to think and read sticks. But I wasn't going to follow her there."

"What did you dream?" Ned asked as he watched another church candle burn out. The bonfire was low and would soon die unless more wood were added. The park seemed to shrink in the darkness, only the dying fire, candles, and tallow lamps held back the dark hands that waited to cover everything. Those who still remained in the park squatted around the bonfire or sat in the grass. Some brought blankets and food. Guildsmen talked to guildsmen, vendors talked to vendors. There were even a few Fauboughers on the lawn, but everyone else gave them wide berth. Boys with open shirts and girls with high skirts (it was too dark for the elders to see very much) were drinking and smoking and laughing while the old men slept and snored beside them.

"I dreamed about you," Sandra said. She told him her dream, carefully filling in every detail she could remember, taking her time with the vague parts, reeling it out until she was out of breath—and there it ended.

"Yes, I know," Ned said. "I had the same dream. I've been having it for a month, only I couldn't remember it until now." A breeze wafted into the room, tickled his face, chilled him, and carried in the familiar sour smells of smoking-grass, wine, sweat, and urine. Holiday stenches and fresh air mingled with the sickly sweet smells of lovemaking—Baldanger's musky, foul armpit odors and Hilda's heavy sweetness and garlic sweat. Ned remembered his dream—the bridge, indistinct figures, mountains, tunnels, crawlways, a great cavern, *and a creature made of eyes.*

He looked away from the dark church in fear. Its great windows had become black mirrors filled with fire. The bonfire burned in cold glass. Mirrors were Satan's invention, another ploy to "sack our souls," as Ned's father would say. God would have evil company in his church tonight, Ned thought. He trembled and daydreamed as Sandra massaged his back and whispered to him. His dreams were tempered with stained glass, fear, and wet lovemaking: Hilda screaming when she came. Baldanger grinding his teeth. And mountains of glass, polished and holy and transparent. Glass to walk on and slide on and touch. Glass to draw blood and sleep on. Glass in his pocket. Glass in the window-hole. All the glass in the world.

He dreamed of a birdbeast made of glass, its windowglass wings beating against the walls of Hell.

"What about the monster that Ferris Angleton saw?"

"It was a drunkard's dream . . . that will swallow the world soon enough." Ned was isolated with his hatred and fear of the birdbeast. It was too late to tell Sandra about his vision.

The bonfire was almost out. The voices below were hushed. Ned could see the fire reflected in the churchglass. Another sin, he thought, as Sandra led him to bed. She, too, had fallen asleep by the window-hole. But Ned was afraid to sleep again, even with Sandra comforting him. Tonight the dream would change. Later, he would remember what he dreamed, but then it would be too late to go back: the tall spires of glass and cement would be standing over him, just as in the dream.

"Wake up, Ned. You've got company." The room was filled with people who were shouting and laughing. The electors had not slept and were still drunk. They had been followed by the girls, townsfolk, and clergy. The strong morning sunlight streaming through the window-hole revealed the starkness and shabbiness of the room and the blanched faces that only rest could restore to life.

Ned was in Hilda's bed, arm propped up against the wall, leg resting on a pile of damp blankets. He awakened with a start, reached for his clothes, and shouted, "What the Hell is this? Leave me alone." Hilda lay beside him and snored. In her hand, unbeknown to Ned, she clutched the shard of holy glass. Sandra had left during the night to work another one of Mama Fishbine's special customers, but Baldanger was there, sleepy-eyed and grinning. Unable to find his clothes, he stood beside the bed and pulled Hilda's robe around him.

A tattooed whore pinched Ned's buttocks and shouted, "Out the door, out the door." Ned slapped her. She was a friend of Reisel's, the skinny redhead that had clawed Sandra.

"And don't forget his whore," a red-faced farmer shouted.

With that, Hilda awakened. She screamed at the crowd, then became quiet, as if bemused.

"What do they want?" Ned asked. His eyes were still gummy from sleep; and, even with the crowd around him, he felt groggy, exhausted from yesterday's vision.

"You're the Goddamn president," Baldanger said, trying to hold his ground in the crowd. People were pushing to get into the room for a look at the new president. "Watch them, they'll tar and feather you."

"Ned Wheeler," shouted a woman's voice. "Look at yourself. Whorehopping in front of the clergy. So that's what you did with the holyglass." Ned groaned— it was Miss Jenkens, flanking the crowd for a better view, wiping her nose and fondling her tattered Book.

"Ned Wheeler, King of the whores."

"The sleeper's a president."

"Life to the President."

"Sinner."

"Filth."

"Enough of that," shouted Reverend Surface, a short, stocky man with freckled skin, prematurely gray hair that covered his ears, and a broken nose—"Broken twice, in two different places," he had once told Ned on a President's Day. Rumor had it that Fauboughers had beaten him up for blessing them with clenched hands. "Remember the rules," he said to the crowd. "Holy humor—that's the law."

The room was sticky and full of smells: farts, sweat, decaying teeth, human odors mingled with stale perfume; they covered Ned like a blanket. He tried to move away from the people around him, congratulating him, poking, jabbing, laughing. The noise was like static. Ned shut his eyes for a second and the voice inside his head, as if waking up again, said, *I'm still waiting.* And then buzzing, inside and out. The crowd's noises completed the senseless, cacophonous song. Ned's head seemed open on all sides.

"Leave me alone," he cried. He had a bitter metallic taste in his mouth. He felt helpless, suddenly certain that there was no chance working here; his future was predetermined. It was inevitable that he should be made president.

"Go away," Hilda shouted. Baldanger lay back in the bed and laughed. Today would be a party, for all except Ned—he would take himself (and his office) seriously.

"Hey, look, the whore has a piece of glass for the church."

"It's mine," Hilda shouted as she was picked up and passed out the door by strong hands that playfully squeezed her soft parts. After a few seconds, her shouts changed to yelps and giggles. For the moment, she was the center of attraction on a holy day. She was not yet impatient with her devotees, impressing her, for the first time in her life, into religious service. Whores had often shared the fools-laurels on President's Day. She would become the president's giglet.

"Give me back that glass," she shouted.

Most of the people standing around Ned were his friends. He could see Baldanger, Herman and Stan, Sam Sense, Reverend Surface, and, of course, all the girls—all except Sandra. Ned wanted her to be there. She was probably at the Faubougher Wall, talking to the women who read sticks for the wealthy. He caught a glimpse of Alex Eitrides, the whore who read dreams and sticks, with her daughter. Even Small Henry, vexed with Ned for "corrupting" his young son, managed a tight-lipped smile. Most of the people in the crowd would play the happy roles of President's Day, but there were a few unfriendly faces.

Ferris Angleton, still bleary-eyed, was there with a few drinkers who hated Ned.

"Filth," shouted Fairchild Laylow, a slightly built man wearing a discarded guildsman's cap. He tried to knuckle Ned in the neck, but John Seawell tripped him. The crowd took over, pushed him aside, and blocked his way. Laylow had been a Central City party prompter—an empty title which bestowed no privileges other than political grace—before he defected to the Northside to become an elector, another lifeless title (you had to have priority to be counted), but supposed to be a step up; at least it gained him access to the cellar on President's Eve. His brother Cravett, who outweighed Fairchild by at least fifty kilograms, had a more difficult time just staying abreast and was kneed neatly in the crotch by Sam Sense while the crowd concentrated on the new president and his whore, deaf to Fairchild's hoarse shouts. As Cravett doubled over, Mama Fishbine let out a shrill laugh and pushed him into the crowd, burying him in a forest of legs.

"I never liked that sonofabitch, anyway," she said to Sam Sense. "For a skinny, bald-headed twirp, you have a good kick."

Fairchild called to Ferris Angleton to help his brother, but Angleton, hands pressed tightly together in a gesture of humble passion, could only look on quietly.

For all his pain, hate, and frustration, Fairchild's swearing and shouting were only harmless additions to the carnival atmosphere. This was a time to call the president "boob" and "cock" and "muntzer," a time to get back at authority by smearing its symbols, a harmless exercise, but only in fun—that was the rule. So Fairchild, still not playing the game, became just another clown jumping out of a burning house to the audience's raucous laughter.

The crowd, all smiles and leers and grasping hands, carried Ned and Hilda downstairs, past the bar which smelled of strong toilet soap, vomit, and ale, then out the front door, turning left on Main Street, and on to Commons Green. It was no use fighting the crowd; Ned would follow tradition and be passed from hand to hand. That was certainly better than being tarred and stoned. He could see Hilda several paces ahead of him. She sat atop the crowd like a burlap queen, Queen of the Whores, Queen of the fingerstickers that goosed and squeezed her. But the crowd held her for Ned; she was his lady in waiting.

Where was Sandra? Ned asked himself. She could be anywhere in that crowd. But if she was about, she would show herself. As Ned watched Hilda being happily tortured, the static and grinding noises in his head turned into words: *"You'll see Sandra again. But not this one. You've got to go back; you're being dreamt by the past."*

"I'm not going anywhere," Ned shouted, trying to drown out the voice; those who carried him paid no attention for they thought he was yelling at them. "Help me," he screamed. He prayed and stared into the cloudless blue sky above. He had a sudden thought that the sky was the clear eye of God, and he was a fly being devoured by a spider. "Help me," he cried. But God only watched.

Everyone on the green was shouting and waving at Ned. The crowds spilled onto Main Street which formed a circle around the park. The church looked on blankly with its broken glass eyes. Further down the street—which was roughly paved with cobblestones, but fouled with mire and the accumulation of garbage thrown from the adjacent houses—the shops were closed, although a few vendors were talking business, oblivious to the festivities occurring up the street.

"I won't do it," Ned shouted at the crowd, but he knew he would—he would do it for his father, as a penance for yesterday's (and tomorrow's) sins, and to purge himself, exorcise the demon that inhabited his mind. It was a church duty—for the state.

"Oh, come on, Ned," shouted Mama Fishbine. She had forced her way through the crowd—no mean task—and found a good spot next to some guildsmen wearing red and blue uniforms. Her gray hair stood out in a hundred pigtails and her sallow face was dirty. "And look after my girl, Mr. President. I'll be needing her back." With that she broke into laughter, long wheezes followed by snorts and sighs. The guildsmen pinched her.

A high-pitched voice shouted, "Speech, speech, give us an inauguration speech."

"Yes, a speech from the newly elected President."

They all began to chant, "Speech, speech, speech." Flagons of ale, mead, and hydromel had been taken from the taverns, for the Central City Party people were drinking and waving cups and mugs.

The electors, backed up by the crowd, pushed Ned and Hilda up a crude stairway onto the stocks platform in the middle of the park, where a hangman's tree and an assortment of wooden stocks and whipping posts served as warnings to any would-be offender.

It's like a hanging day, Ned thought, alarmed even to be on the platform—he had seen too many men die there. "Hanging Saturdays" always drew large crowds to the park. Little boys would climb onto the platform to play and eat candy while the gallowsman, dressed like a priest, pranced around, made faces at the crowd, mimed out the dance of death, and made a good Saturday show. When he was very young, Ned used to love Hanging Saturdays. He fancied that the condemned men were puppets and he loved to watch them dance and dangle. Now Ned stood on the platform, shaking as they did, angry and frightened and frustrated that he was being manipulated by shadows and dreams. Ned remembered many a picnic with his father and friends in the cemetery. As his father had said, "The soul is cleansed by the horrors of death. You must yearn for that scourging, see and smell the putrefaction of the flesh."

From the platform Ned could look over the heads of the crowd and almost see the length of Main Street. Houses and shops were scattered along the route downtown, clumped together to form subsections of the central village, their tiny roofs sloping toward the road and crowned with chimney pots in which swallows and swifts built their nests. Before Ned stood the glass cathedral, the tallest building in Junction. He looked up at the tall oak tree beside him, wishing he could climb it into Heaven and be done with all this.

"You're not done yet." Ned shook his head, but the

voice sounded like gobbledygook words and the soughing of the wind.

"Say something," Hilda said. "They're waiting for you to say something."

"That's right," said a young guildsman with a pimply face and a large mouth. "Do something. You're the body of the state."

"Scapegoat the faggot," said an old woman holding a wicker basket.

Ned started to speak, faltered, cleared his throat, and began again. He could not think of anything to say, so he just said whatever came to mind and hoped that the voice inside his head was not speaking. He looked over the heads of the townspeople at the church, stared into a small unpaved alley behind it. The alley was full of garbage—streetbags of rotten food reeked and were white with maggots, but something hard glittered in there.

Could it be glass? Could God's glass grow in that garbage? Ned turned his head away and looked into the crowd. He had to speak now.

"Well, come on," said a guildsman with leather cuffs on his blouse. He spoke for the rest of his clique. The guilds tried to stand together and smile condescendingly at everyone else.

"I thank all of the electors," Ned said, "and all of you who elected the electors who elected me to this office. I don't really understand why I was picked for this. . . ."

His attention wandered. He was looking into the alley. Something sparkled. Something moved. But Ned could not make out what it was; he forced himself to look into the crowd.

". . . but for whatever I do, I shall do my best. I may be mistaken, but I believe that this office confers sacramental powers and responsibilities upon the holder, even if that be the upholding of a tradition most of us have forgotten the meaning of. I imagine this office to represent all the world through God. . . ."

The crowd was laughing, guffawing, booing, trying to drown him out with a song. A few holy women shouted psalms to counter guildsmen's songs, but the crowd was with Fat Cravett, who led with the first verse:

> Back and side, go bare, go bare
> Both hand and foot go cold,
> But belly, God send you good ale enough
> Whether it be new or old.

The tattooed girl, her eyes closed and mouth open, tried to unbutton her blouse and let her tits wag, but the older women quickly covered her and slapped her face with the backs of their hands.

"Another verse for tattoos and tits," Mama Fishbine shouted. She started it and was happily drowned out by the crowd.

> Let fearful souls refuse their bowls,
> And tremble for to tipple:
> Let moon-men fear to *domineere*,
> And halt before a Cripple.

"That's right," shouted a beggar. He waved his crutch in the air and sang for alms—on President's Day no beggar could be given short shrift.

Ned tried to leave the platform, but someone hit him in the eye, another kicked him sharply in the shin. He fell back; he could not defend himself against a thousand fists and feet. Children scampered around him, screaming and poking with sticky fingers. They stole their first feels from Hilda, who shouted and giggled and stood her ground. Ferris Angleton held a rock in his upraised hand; his daughter Flora smiled, showing off rotten teeth. Old women waved at Ned, but they were ready to pull or gouge, should he lean over too far or take a wrong step.

"Speech, speech," the crowd chanted. "Finish your speech."

"Some think that the presidents used to rule the world, even the outside, even Hell." Ned listened to his words flow, amazed that it was really his voice speaking. "Even the most thoughtless of us—me, for instance—live under the shadow of eternity. All around us lies Hell. We know its geography, its climate, its monsters, almost as well as we know our own land. . . ."

"You may know its monsters," someone from the crowd shouted, "but we don't."

Another voice: "We don't look upon Hell."

"Denounce him."

"Faubougher."

"It's bad luck," yelled an old man holding a mug, his face scrunched up and wrinkled as if he were forever peering at the sun. "And you've certainly got it." His friends laughed and the younger men patted him on the shoulder.

"You are right," Reverend Surface shouted to Ned. "That office does confer responsibilities upon you. That's why we taunt you and laugh at you. That's why we will love you and respect you for a year, even though we may blacken your face now and bloody your skin."

Someone threw a stone at Ned; he ducked, but a flying shard of metal cut his face. Hilda was screaming under a hail of sharp stones.

I must get away from here, Ned thought. But it wasn't the crowd that frightened him.

"Enough of that," shouted the Reverend. "Perhaps you will rule over Junction and Hell for us. But those are words from other books, books to which we cannot give complete credence. But we'll take no chances. We'll laugh at the books and obey them—if that's our wont, mock them for being apocryphal, love them because they might be God's."

"Your lips honor holy rule, but your teeth chatter," shouted Reverend Blues, a fat man with a smooth face, large nose, and black curly hair. He stood beside Reverend Surface, who remained grim and tight-lipped. All the priests stood together, an unusual holiday sight. They were a black knot in the colorful quilt of peasants, serfies, freemen, guildsmen, wives, whores, children, and Fauboughers.

The crowd cheered, now given an excuse to throw mud and dung at the foolspresident. But no more rocks were hurled.

"April fools," shouted a whore.

The old woman with a wicker basket shouted, "Scapegoat the faggot," and threw a rotten tomato at Ned.

Ned ducked. Beside him, Hilda was teasing a potential customer, a young guildsman. Another guildsman, wearing a red cap befitting his rank, beat his chest in mock solemnity. Ned was reminded of his father. Would he be proud or ashamed?

When will they let me down? he asked himself, ducking a clump of dung and grass that passed over his head. Ned could not see his father in the crowd. As he looked, a clump of mud caught him squarely in the face, followed by a dungball and a piece of rotting meat. "You sonofabitch," he shouted and wiped his mouth with his sleeve.

"Good shot," Miss Jenkens shouted.

"Look at the kingpriest, the foolspresident, the ruler of Hell."

"He's full of shit."

Even Reverend Surface was laughing. He accepted a flagon of belch beer from a burly peasant standing behind him.

Ned shielded his face as best he could and thought about tomorrow. Tomorrow (he hoped) Junction would return to its normal state. It would be quiet and respectable and dull. The whores would not shout or dangle their breasts from window-holes. The Fauboughers would not be out, and the Reverend would not laugh. Ned would be in the Stone House; Hilda would be back at work. The farmers and peasants would be working in the fields, careful not to glance into Hell. The shopkeepers could make money, and the guildsmen could protect their own.

Let them throw their garbage, he thought. Next year I'll throw stones at one of them. He looked at the church and then into the alleyway behind it.

A figure with a plastic face and a yellow beak stood in the alley, ankle-deep in muck, and leaned against the church. Its mottled yellow body was covered with eyes, some closed, some blinking, each a different color of Heaven: henna, milori blue, topaz, fluorite, viridian, stammel, umber. One iris looked as if it were made of black glass, pure and untainted by the grays of Junction reality. The angel from Hell wore a halo around its head that killed any insect that chanced to be near it.

"Forget stones and next year," said the voice inside Ned's head. *"Next year is already over."* Ned pressed his palms against his ears, but the voice was gone. He screamed and pointed at the creature, but it stepped back into the darkness before anyone could turn around.

The crowd was not interested in Ned's screams and visions. They were watching the ragged, drab procession of Fauboughers coming toward them.

Forester and his son led the parade. With scourge in each hand, Forester beat himself and his blood flowed as if he'd been cupped. And to further prove his faith in God and immolation, some of the spikes were bent into hooks so they could rend the flesh more effectively. He flogged himself mechanically as he marched, two lashes for every four steps—that was the cadence the Fauboughers followed. They sang and whipped themselves with scourges and netting filled with sharp stones.

The catcalls died as the Fauboughers pushed into the crowd which reluctantly parted to let them through. The Fauboughers became a great phalanx driven by Forester, gall, and a sense of purpose.

"Buggers," shouted Miss Jenkins, but it was a frail noise soaked up and buried in the stoical face of the crowd. Everyone watched the marchers, listened to the scrunch of heels and the slap of whip against flesh. The crowd seemed to shiver in anticipation, as if this ragged band of beggars held something holy, could offer a blessing. There was sudden movement, shifting position, murmurs. Could these ragged Fauboughers be the mouth of God?

The priests looked nervous. They were in a double bind: if they recognized the excommunicated feather-waker, they would break holy law; if they did not, they might lose their flock.

The marchers circled the stocks platform and then stopped, but they still beat themselves in time to an imagined step. An old man in tattered caryclothes struck his face with such force that he broke his scourge in half.

"All is well," said a woman with bloodied, bare breasts. Her voice was strong and had the familiar nasal twang of the Faubougher.

"All is ours," said Forester. "That's right," he said in a shrill voice. "The Last Days have come. We'll over-run and overturn. As God will level the world, so will he tear out Junction and feed it to Hell. Punish your-selves for forgiveness. Pray to God that he put away his rod and make judgment. Punish these foolspriests"

—he waved a scourge at the priests—"and take them down. In these last times the poor must become the priests."

The crowd strained to hear more. They were predisposed toward belief, even from excommunicants and filthy, backwater heathens. The marcher's sincerity, blood, and promise of God were proof enough. The Fauboughers would use the tools of the church to proclaim themselves "hatchets of God." They had practiced the jingoes and memorized the prayers; now, they would try to change form and substance. They were an undertone, a counterpoint to Forester's rantings. When he paused, they could be heard singing about blood and vengeance and the holy heart.

"But you can't see me, can you?" said Forester. His voice cracked and he coughed nervously, then continued on in a shrill voice. "I've eaten stones and died and seen God's angels—that I'll surely tell you about, but first you must see.

"Ned Wheeler," he said, wiping his bloody hands on his tattered chasuble, "can you see me?"

Ned looked at him as if there was no one else on the green. Forester's carycoat was in tatters and soaked through with his blood. What had once been a red, freckled face had become a pulpy mass of blue flesh. But now, bathing in his own blood, he had power. His new presence overcame his squeaky voice and shaking hands; and, in retrospect, his affectation of clerical vestments made sense—it was a shadow of today's mockery. Wearing the flags of the church and baptised in his own blood, he could speak to the people. They'd listen to a nothing man, a blue-faced frog who promised God and angels and tomorrow forever.

Ned maintained the church by ignoring him.

"Of course not, young whoremaster," said Forester. "But let me open your eyes. You're not looking through Forester the featherwaker. You're now looking at Jacob Bottomley. Forester died when he saw Heaven's Dragon, the perfect, immediate, and high enjoyment of God in the Spirit."

Liar, Ned thought, but he would not speak.

"Changing your name won't change anything," shouted a young guildsman with a flagon in each hand.

"Shut up," shouted someone else.

"But *you* recognize me," Forester said to the guildsman. "So will the rest of you. You'll all soon see with proper eyes. What does the church have to say about that? Surely now you must speak to your flock, tell them what course to take, lest they stray from your field." Forester smiled at the churchmen, and the marchers raised their voices, hoping to gain God's blessings and the crowd's confidence.

The priests, after arguing among themselves, now stood silent, looking this way and that, waiting for a decision, an agreement, or divine intervention. How could they allow the excommunicated featherwaker to escape the church's decree by proclaiming himself someone else? If the letter of the law might be twisted to allow it, the substance of the law would not. If the priests defended themselves against the attacks of the excommunicated martyr, they would be fools and hypocrites. But if they did nothing, they would certainly lose their flock to Forester/Bottomley.

Reverend Surface and Forester locked eyes, but it was an empty challenge, for the priest would not speak. The double-edged sword of the church had been turned against its makers.

"Tell us about the angel," shouted a Goodman's maid dressed in a stiff uniform and apron.

"It's true," said Forester. "I was blessed by seeing an angel with wings and as many eyes as there are people here. It was the red dragon we've been promised. And without a voice it cried, 'These are the Last Days. . . .'"

Can Forester hear the birdbeast inside his head as I do? Ned thought, unnerved, again unsure of the church. Perhaps the Last Days have come, and they've been given to Forester and his Fauboughers. And the church will be left behind to be swallowed by Hell. No, he told himself. Stay with the church.

"I saw something too," shouted Ferris Angleton, holding his daughter so she could see above the crowd. "But I saw a monster from Hell, not a heavenly angel." Although Ferris drank heavily and spoke with a bad mouth, he was considered a good father and householder. Drunk as he was, he handled Flora tenderly.

"Make no mistake," Forester said, "you saw God's angel. It's written in the Book that the Dragon of the Last Days will part the waters of Hell and choose a new prophet to warn the righteous dwelling upon the land. And I am that prophet."

"Blasphemy," shouted Reverend Blues. "That's not in the Book—it's in your filthy mind."

So it's done, Ned thought. This is the time to speak up and save the church. But he could not utter a word. Hell was crashing over Junction like a tidal wave, and he was rooted to the ground, trapped, as if in one of his recurring nightmares. He watched Reverend Surface who remained unperturbed. Reverend Blues, flushed and shaking, looked to the other priests for support.

"No, ignorant priest," shouted Forester. "It is in the Book, in the true Book, the Book the holy angel inscribed to me and those who follow. It's God's last words on Earth, his last promise. He's already punished you by slapping the earth and flooding all but this place with Hell. This is your last chance. I'm your last chance."

The crowd was shifting, growing tightly around Ned, Forester, and the marchers. The excited whispers and lowtalk of hundreds of conversations became a dull hum punctuated by an occasional yowl or tittle.

The show had begun. The marchers formed a circle and walked slowly, stepping to the beat of two sticks clicked together by a naked old man. One by one they fell down, arms and legs spread as if staked to the ground. The others walked over them, shouted "hallelujah," and beat the prostrate mimers with scourges. Forester walked among them, striking the transgressors with his scourge and repeating his prayer of resurrection. When he said, "Arise, by the honor of pure martyrdom," and touched them, they would promptly stand up, only to rend their garments and beat themselves until justified to fall down again.

A few ecstatic peasants joined the marchers, allowed themselves to be whipped and humiliated, and then fell to the ground. They were soon followed by others. The excitement hung in the air, thick, palpable, sucking everyone into itself. Several whores joined the marchers, followed by guildsmen, children, and Miss Jenkens, who had ripped off her dress.

Ned resolved to say something now, but his father's strong voice boomed from the crowd, shouting Ned's words, taking them from his hesitant son. He sat on the shoulders of Reverend Cohen, who was over six feet tall and sported a full beard that looked orange in the bright morning sun.

"The featherwaker is right," shouted Ned's father, ". . . and he's wrong. Indeed, he might have seen God's dragon, and for that I envy him. But he spoils his truth with blasphemy. He was not chosen by the angel. He is not your last chance. And he was not the first to see the holy monster." Pointing his finger at Ned, he said, "My son Ned saw it first!"

Every face turned toward Ned, who exhaled sharply, as if he had been jabbed in the stomach.

"I saw the monster stumble out of Hell," Ned said.

"It still talks inside my head." His voice was strong and full, but he had lost his chance to take the crowd himself—his father had given it to him. He looked down at the populace, felt the cold pressure of their stares, but could only find empty faces and stone eyes. Everything seemed to stop for Ned. He had all the subjective time he needed. His next few words would determine the day—he could direct the crowd's energy away from Forester and into the church, or he could blather and squeak until they turned their heads back to Forester and the marchers. In that long instant the marchers held still for Ned's tableau, their arms and scourges poised, blood-drippings slowly snaking to the ground like molasses. Forester glared. Baldanger and Seawall stood below Ned and stared grimly upward. Dirty children and older scallywags with missing teeth hovered beside Ned, all stopped in mid-movement. And the crowd was still as stone, not a breath could break the spell.

Ned was not sure whether the monster was from Heaven or Hell, but he would stand with his father for the church. And with a blink, the crowd was alive, buzzing, shoving, shaking its great filthy face, looking forward to devour anything that stood before its eyes.

"What does this angel say to you?" someone shouted sarcastically.

"It says stay with the church. Everything else is false." Inside Ned's head the voice was laughing. "If the Last Days are coming," Ned said, looking at Forester, "then we must stand together." A stone grazed Ned's neck, breaking the skin.

"Only blood will earn your judgment," shouted a marcher.

"God is with the church."

Ned and his father harangued and exhorted the crowd, but the marchers were swelling with converts, all doggedly beating themselves and their neighbors, trying for a quick ecstasy, mimicking the others. Children swooned, rolled about the ground, waited for a beating, and arose with flushed faces and beatific grins.

Fighting broke out around Ned when the marchers tried to climb onto the platform. But the marchers wouldn't fight back—so red-faced men aching for a fight fought among themselves, took sides for or against the marchers, and beat the marchers soundly when they got in the way. The fighting spread through the crowd, reaching each successive line of spectators, who became embroiled in the melee.

Ned tried to push his way down the platform stairs. The crowd gave way a bit and descended a few steps.

"Wait for me," Hilda said.

Baldanger waved his hands to attract Ned's attention. "Wait," he said. "They'll carry you to the Stone House." He pointed to Reverend Surface who was shouting, "Take Ned home."

A few peasants standing around the priests took it up and chanted, "Take him home, take him home." The word spread quickly, for tradition was strong and, even here, the church could still promise refuge and guidance. The crowd was looking for a way back. It was tired of groping and fighting itself.

But too many stood with Forester.

Ned pushed at the crowd, trying to bury himself in the mass of sweating flesh and become just another peasant.

No, he thought. Stand up. Let them rally around me.

"Stand with the church," Ned shouted. Hands grabbed his arms and legs, hoisted him atop the crowd that was shouting, "Take up the church, take Ned home." The church had recouped its losses. There were enough peasants and guildsmen to save its face. Tomorrow the church would quietly make its move.

About a thousand people made up the homecoming procession. Others were hanging out window-holes of adjacent buildings to see Ned. The crowd held Ned face up to the sky, his legs splayed as far as they would stretch. Regaining their sadistic playfulness, the freemen carried Hilda behind him, passed her back and forth, bit and squeezed her extra portions of breast and thigh.

Ned listened to her screams and watched the sky. He examined the strange angles and lines of the buildings that pointed to the sun and tried not to look at the people hanging out the window-holes. They smiled and leered and shouted at him. An old woman spat at him. He had won the day for the church.

He felt his face being pulled to the right.

The angel from Hell sat atop the rusting metal frame of an old razed building, all eyes open, halo attracting and killing insects.

Or perhaps anything that came near it, he thought.

He closed his eyes, unable to pray.

4

Most of the old buildings had been razed long ago, although rusting skeletons, rubble heaps, foundations, and standing walls remained to remind Junction citizens that they weren't living in an infinite present and that God's wrath had and could be unleashed once again against his progeny. Scripture had it that when God raised Hell all around Junction, he also leveled the buildings and let rivers of rock bubble and steam through the land to cleanse it from sin and make it poor and natural and humble once again. Of the few buildings that remained after the shaking and drowning, the most famous were the Desert Midland Bank and the Stone House—both buildings stood beside natural avenues of cracked stone, old lava flows which were blocked by natural fingers of fused silica glass, obsidian, and pitchstone. The bank had been converted into a church, and the Stone House became the president's palace.

Originally the modest home of a mayor, the Stone House still resembled a Mexican hacienda, which was the architectural vogue when the house had been built. Cement and stone concealed old stucco, and with each decade more stones were added until the soft, easy lines were squared off and the house became thick and gray, a monolithic hutch. The house was situated in the middle of Main Street east of the shops. Its neatly tended lawns and garden served as a boundary line between Portus Park and the elegant

Southside, although both districts claimed the landmark as their own. Behind the house, just southwest of Main Street, stood three barns, and stalls and huts for the horses, chickens, and half-dead bull. The church had declared the barnhouses as prebends for the priests, and the, young priests who lived in the musky, dark rectories kept them in repair and tended the animals and gardens. In the corner of the barnyard farthest away from the Stone House was the dung heap. When the wind was right the wealthy guildsmen's wives could be seen pressing tiny rags to their powdered faces as they passed the contaminated area on their way home.

The large front doors of the Stone House opened into an empty anteroom that led up three steps into a hallway. To the left and right were once luxurious sitting rooms and a library without books. A wide staircase with a broken iron bannister led upstairs to the bedrooms. To the rear of the house a small kitchen was connected to a pantry and a sunken dining room. A kitchen stairway led into a cellar where food and wine were kept.

Ned paced back and forth in the library; he was waiting for his father and Reverend Surface. The room was bare except for a settee and a few simple wooden chairs. The black and gold parquetry on the floor had faded from use, and the stairs leading up to the hallway were due for repairs. A vase of daffodils rested on one of the empty bookshelves that ran the length of the room. A Bible, the only book displayed in the house, lay open on the desk. Ned remembered the fight he had had with his father last night over the church; the old man had only one passion, and that was for the *idea* of the church—that idea was more important than life or his son, more important than conversion, the Last Days, or even God's angel.

Looking out the window-hole at the end of the long room, he watched a few people running across the yard. It was late afternoon; they're probably on their way to church, he thought. Compared with yesterday, President's Day, and the long night of shouting, marching, fighting, and praying that followed, this mild dusky afternoon was a quiet relief. Enough people had been hurt last night, and several killed, but that was expected, for even on a normal President's Day there were always a few broken jaws and ribs. The Fauboughers had returned to their hovels, and the last of the proselyte marchers were sleeping on the streets. Ned had been kept awake all night by the screams of Faubougher children, angry peasants, and vigilant marchers who stood before the Stone House. But yesterday's burst of holy vehemence had turned to quiet fear. Last night's bruises were nursed by obedient wives who had visions of heavenly ascension for their children, if not for their husbands. Everyone was ready; every thick-tongued, hung-over citizen believed in the miracles that surely would come. By now the church would be full of supplicants praying for the Last Days and an end to the Fauboughers.

Ned stared into the yard, but saw nothing in particular. Sunlight poured into the room and seemed to gather around him. Dust motes turned and danced in the air. Everything is too bright, he thought, sensing something ominous even in God's sunlight. There was something of a nightmare quality about the afternoon. He turned around as the library doors opened and Reverend Surface walked into the room, followed by Ned's father. The Reverend sat down on the settee and motioned Ned over to the chair beside him. Ned's father nodded, but he didn't speak; he preferred to stand an uncomfortable distance away from his son.

So nothing has changed, Ned thought. He still expects me to fight for the church, to follow the bird-beast into Hell if need be for *his* idea of holy duty. Instead of strengthening Ned's faith, yesterday's events and miracles had shaken it. Ned was wary of his father and the priest, unsure of the church, afraid of the birdbeast.

"Come on, sit down," Reverend Surface said. When Ned sat down beside him, he patted Ned's leg with his long fingers, fingers that looked much too fine and narrow for such a squat man. Ned ignored the Reverend's sour smell; it was **not** the priest's fault, for the clergy were supposed to smell like the people— and Reverend Surface was known to hang around the dung pits and keep time with the peasants. He wore a black and gray carycoat, and his overhood was so full of holes that his hair stuck out of it. His toes peered out of his worn shoes with their thick soles, and his stockings hung about his ankles on all sides. Although the church and its vassals held wealth and power, the clergy had always donned the vestments of the poor.

And the poor usually accepted it and pretended to believe that only God held the riches death would bring. But now that they were sure of the birdbeast and quick miracles, they were less sure of the church.

"You, no doubt, know that the creature from Hell is still in Junction," said Reverend Surface. "It's been seen by peasants and priests alike; Reverends Briar and Blues both claimed to have encountered it in the morning mists near Sticksveiller Bogs. . . ."

They're all liars, all hopping on the haywagon, Ned thought. What were they doing on the bogs at that hour, if not trying to cobble a miracle?

". . . And the townspeople are calling last night's dream a miracle."

"What dream?" Ned asked.

"Surely you know. We all had the same dream; in those few precious moments of sleep the creature held court and decided the Last Days in a church made of glass and transparent gems."

"*I* had no such dream," Ned said. His fears were growing; events were overtaking him, trapping him.

"Well, everyone else did," Ned's father said impatiently. He was dressed in a simple, loose overshirt with faded brown pants and leather sandals.

"Everyone's afraid that the Last Days have come and the birdbeast is God's messenger," said the Reverend, ignoring Ned's remark. "And if the dream was a true manifestation, it just might be. . . ."

"The dream is true," Ned's father said, standing stiff for effect. "I'm sure it's true, and it's up to you to meet God's monster," he said to Ned. "You saw it first. You must see it again."

"I don't want to see it ever again," Ned said.

"You told the crowd yesterday that you saw the beast cross from Hell into Junction," said the Reverend. You told them that it speaks inside your head. You stood for the church, redeemed it in the eye of the unsure, and threw dirt in Forester's face. Since you were the first to see the beast, it is felt you should see it again. For the people and the church. The townspeople believe that it is looking for you; you're our Jonah. But if it finds the falsepriest instead, and already too many believe his blasphemies, then the Last Days may sweep us all into Hell."

"You told me yourself that the beast warned you there'd be no future," Ned's father said. "It told you that it's waiting. Waiting for you."

"I told you that I heard noises in my head, gobbledygook words, things that didn't make sense." They want to push me into Hell, Ned thought.

"Then did you lie to the people?" his father asked. "Did you try to fool them back into the church? Can't you even believe your own words? Your own eyes?"

No, Ned thought. I can't. "Do you really believe that this beast brings the Last Days?" he asked. "Are you so sure of that?"

"The beast, the dream last night, the holy sounds in your head, they all point to Heaven and last things."

"But there's no mention of such things in the Book," Ned said loudly.

"The Book says that God will come to take the church," said Reverend Surface. "That can be taken to mean God's messenger."

"Do you expect us to disbelieve our own eyes and discount the dream?" Ned's father asked.

"Then you agree with Forester and *his* book. Why not let him find the beast for you?" Ned could feel his father's anger; it was like a black bird flapping about the room, winging closer to Ned with each frenzied flight. Yet his father stood still and calm.

"Because Forester stands against the church, and the church is God's vessel," said the Reverend. "He saw God's angel and then befriended Satan. Forester claims that the beast brings Heaven, but he claims himself as God's prophet. And a true prophet can only come out of the church."

"What if the beast is from Hell and belongs there?" Ned asked, already feeling himself being dragged into Satan's sump. Every conversation, every dream or thought, every decision brought him closer to Hell's shores. It was as if Ned had no free will, only its illusion.

"Then you will fight it," Ned's father said. "God will be with you."

He's so certain, Ned thought. "Others saw the monster, too. A priest's word would be better than mine."

"Right now," Ned's father said, "you speak for the church. You're the President; you represent us. And by your own admission, you're the one the beast is looking for. Unless, of course, you believe that Forester is the true prophet."

"Send a priest with me," Ned said.

"This is one thing *you* have to follow through," his father said with disgust, "for without you the church will fall." Ned wished he had not confided in his father the night before. It was a mistake to talk to anyone about the beast buzzing in his head, least of all his father who would use him as a foil for the church.

But Ned had to try. It didn't make any difference, he told himself, for the sticks had been thrown and he would have to meet the monster. The thought of wrestling the birdbeast at the edge of the world chilled him like cold sweat.

"Anyway," Reverend Surface said, "everyone is waiting to find out what will happen. It's between you and Forester, and the monster. Rumor has it that Forester is also going to look for the birdbeast tonight."

"It's significant that you saw it first," Ned's father said. "And then you were elected President. Can't you see God's plan? You must follow his orders. You have been chosen."

"Just like that," Ned said. He felt as if he was being pursued by all the hounds of Heaven and Hell in the guises of Junction's townsfolk, Fauboughers, priests, and his father. Now he was the puppet dangling on the gallows. He wanted to hide, curl up in a loft and breathe the sweet smells of dung and straw. He wanted to screw Hilda and sleep with Sandra. He wanted this to be just another warm afternoon.

His father leaned against the bookshelf; he rested his arm on the old dark board, ran his fingers along the surface of the vase, and solemnly nodded. "Just like that."

It makes no difference which side I'm on, Ned thought. He still shows me the same face. "And if I remain here?"

"Many people are afraid to be out now," Reverend Surface said. "The hours are short until dark. The townspeople will wait; but if nothing has happened by morning, they'll gather together and force you out of Junction, push you into Hell. You'll be their sacrifice. No matter what Forester does, you'll be tormented if you fail them. Now you have their faith; tomorrow, if you have failed, they'll try to destroy you in desperation and fear of the coming days, and frustration with their dying church."

"You must leave now," Ned's father said. "This time stand it through. There's more at stake than your whores up the street."

Ned knew he would have to confront the birdbeast, but that was his private affair. He stood up and turned away from his father; it was an empty gesture.

After a pause his father said, "Find out what it wants with us. Meanwhile we'll light the church and pray for you. Leave us now, if you've the spine to turn around. We'll wait in the church."

"There is one thing," said the Reverend. "The beast has been seen in several places at the same time. It is possible that there are more than one, so be forewarned."

"We saw only one beast in our dream," Ned's father said, "although it might have been one of the four beasts that Ezekiel saw in his holy vision of fire. Tonight you'll probably meet the same spirit. I would that I were going instead of you."

"Then come with me." Ned turned around, waited a bit, and walked to the door. His father might as well be made of stone, he told himself. If this is my last look at him, so be it. "What if this beast of your dreams has nothing whatsoever to do with God or Satan? What if it's just another animal, an animal that lives out there like a cow in the fallows?"

"Get out," his father said.

"And what do you want to call 'out there?'" asked the Reverend; he smiled as if he had already won an imagined philosophical argument. "Is God here and not there, even in the midst of Hell? Explain all you want; look for natural causes if you're too afraid to find God. But without God you have no premises, only slippery words."

Ned had already spoiled the moment, but he continued. "What if I choose to wait here?" He looked at his father.

"You cannot be sure that the angel from Hell will come for you," said the Reverend. "It has stayed outside, never once entering a house, except in the holy dream that God granted us last night. And if it were coming here, wouldn't it have already arrived?"

"You must find it," Ned's father said. His hand was shaking and his face was still drawn into a tight mask; he did not speak in gutturals, but with the soft soughs of love and family-talk. It was an uncharacteristic gesture. "That's what it wants," he said. "You must seek out the Lord."

Ned left quickly. He slipped on the smooth parquetry and did not close the doors behind him.

Outside, the streets were almost empty. There was a musty smell in the air; it would be a damp night, full of rot and sweat and the heavy smells that midnight breezes carried from the bogs. Brushing tears and invisible spiderwebs from his face, Ned walked up Main Street. There could be no going back now. He listened for the voice inside his head, but it was quiet. The wind was still light and cool. In the first shadows of dusk the village seemed to fuse with the leaden sky. Houses and shops became part of the great edifice of sky and street. As Ned walked through this dusk palace, he forgot about his father and the children screaming above; only the solid block of street and sky seemed important.

Children shouted, "Ned, Ned, wrestle the monster." They peered down at him from window-holes and greeted him with cheers and jeers. It was as if they were all trapped in a ship that was drifting past Ned, a gray ship of stone that somehow would not sink. The window-holes were warm yellow blobs that kept out the cold ghostfingers of dusk.

"Are you scared?" shouted a little girl leaning out a third-story window-hole. The dormer roof above her head suggested a doll's house, its open front filled with a bobbing, freckled face. But Ned already felt like an alien in this familiar place—people were talking at him, not to him; he was a wraith walking the streets, pushed toward his destiny by all the dead faces he had known since childhood.

"It will kill you."

Children threw flowers and garbage at Ned, and freemen and their wives watched him silently, oblivious to their noisy children.

He marched up Main Street through Portus Park. He daydreamed that he was present at his own funeral.

The smells and shouts were strong and familiar, reminding Ned of hard work and sweat and ale and after-hour whores. But all that was far removed from him now. Everything was gray and heavy, warm without life, and chilling like summer sweat. As he passed ramshackle huts built like pueblos under the steel framework of an ancient building, ragged peasants with greased hair and large smiles praised him and blessed him and made up new songs in his honor. But few would step on the street, and some had closed their window-holes in preparation for the miasma of evening.

Ned followed the street to the Congress Bar, which was to his left. To his right was the church; it was probably full by now, full of holy dreamers like his father, old men with strong lungs and a right to God.

He paused and listened to the singsong chant of the Standing Prayers. The machinery of God had been set in motion; he was anxious to get out of Junction and find his fate, whatever it might be. He had the pounding heart of someone about to go into mortal combat—he wanted to get it over with, wrestle the demon, either win Heaven or be thrown into Hell to rot, or dissolve, or break like windowglass. There could be no escape: he could run and hide, but that would be another kind of death—and surely the birdbeast would flush him out.

"Hey, Ned," shouted Baldanger, leaning out the second-story window-hole of Ned's old room in the Congress Bar. "We're all waiting." Sam Sense, Free-glass, Tom McCall, John Seawall, and Old Herman stuck their heads out of the window-hole.

"We'll be here until you come back," said John Seawall. His dark wrinkled face puckered into a toothless smile.

"If he comes back," shouted one of the whores.

"Good luck."

Hilda pushed the men out of the way and said, "Go find me some glass, Ned." Her cheeks were flushed from lovemaking and mead. "I miss you already. Be careful."

They don't care if I come back, Ned thought. "Where's Sandra?" he asked.

"I don't know," Hilda said. "Nobody's seen her since Election Night when she was screwing with us."

Ned heard a chuckle inside his head, but couldn't find the voice; he continued walking. Whores waved good-bye from their window-holes and across the street candles were being lit in Ned's honor. Faces peered out from church windows; Ned thought about his father who would probably spend the night in church with his cronies, praying and crying and hoping that Ned would find the monster. There, in the soft candlelight, he could safely dream of a wrestling match that would shake everything up again and bring down Heaven to stop the tumult.

I hate him, Ned thought, afraid that he would never see his father again.

As Ned turned onto Junction Road, the human sounds became muffled, soon to be replaced by crickets and birds and the scratching of wind in bush. His heels clicking on the cobblestone path, he walked on through woods and wastes, commons, meadows, and lammas lands. And with each step the unfamiliar noises became louder. Ned had never been out of Junction-proper this late—every shadow was a demon-spirit, every noise was ominous. He shivered and walked faster.

Dusk had turned into evening, revealing a preternaturally bright full moon surrounded by a pale white halo. As the evening deepened, the moon turned from gray to silver and drifted through purple-black clouds, creating a false twilight. Ned wished for the security of complete darkness. In the dark he would be able to feel the unspoken presence of life around him. He would feel safe, cloaked in the same eyeless garment that protected all nightcreatures. But the moon set everything aglow, exposed all the secret, light-shy beings. The moonlight was an intrusion into the crackling, cackling dark world, and it exposed Ned as an intruder, a daycreature separated from his dark surroundings.

Fighting his fears and an urge to run and hide, Ned stopped to get his bearings. In the distance, Hell's sky looked pitch dark, unaffected by the moonlight. The black sun seemed to be pouring its own night over Hell. As Ned stared northward, he thought he saw a ring of light, but his eyes ached from strain, and when he looked again everything was dark. He was near Bild Bridge; it stood out from the flat wastelands and tundra ahead like pylons from dark water. Beside it steel beams sparkled, relics from an ancient bridge that had not survived God's shaking. Sticksveiller River purled under Bild Bridge. Now it was a small stream that ran down the center of the Susquehanna riverbed, but Ned could remember times when it had regained its former strength and flooded over the dry, cracked banks. It would spray over water-smoothed rocks and pursue its course through the boglands and around Junction, carrying small clumps of yellow moss and strange objects from Hell.

Ned saw something on the bridge, a pale wraith in the moonlight. His heart quickened and seemed to climb into his throat. So here it begins, he thought as he remembered his dream. First the bridge, then indistinct figures, and soon the mountains and tunnels. He wondered if the mountain in Hell was still growing, or had it been transformed into something else?

He was afraid and wanted to turn and run, lie flat on the ground and pray, huddle in some safe corner.

He drew closer. Two figures, a man and woman, stood close together in front of the bridge. They were both naked; their skin looked pasty white in the moonlight. As he approached the bridge, he could see them more clearly, and hear the water gurgling below, a dim wash of sound—noise that was soothing and cool in the daytime had turned into unnerving sighs and groans.

"Who are you?" asked Ned.

"They've already gone, Mister President," the man said in a thick Faubougher accent. He was tall and thin with well-muscled arms and a small, sharply defined chest. His arms and torso were covered with old welts and new slashes ribboned with pus. He squinted at Ned, his face hollowed and lengthened by shadows.

"Then I'm too late. . . ."

"Forester, Lord bless, has met the holy monster and gone into Hell with him," the man continued. "All the others are waiting their turn to meet the monster."

"Except us," said the woman sarcastically. Even in the moonlight Ned could see that her long straight hair was thinning. She would soon be bald.

"You can find Simon, Forester's son, and the others by walking in a straight line that way," said the Faubougher, pointing his finger toward Hell. There was an iridescent smudge on the northern horizon where tundra gave way to Hell; it was the halo he had glimpsed before. Ned tried to stare at it, but his eyes began to ache again. Hell kept shifting in and out of focus.

"What's that glow?" Ned asked.

"It fools you, doesn't it," said the woman. "You'll have to approach Hell to see anything, and even then your eyes will deceive you. The light is from the mountains of Hell."

"They've gone to meet the Lord," the man said, speaking to no one in particular. "They're stepping into the Last Days together."

"And we're here," the woman said to her companion, "because you're afraid." She scratched her crotch and turned toward Hell.

"Did you see the monster?" Ned asked.

"I saw something in Hell," the man said. "So did everybody else. It had to be the monster."

"But you weren't sure?"

He paused. "I'm not sure. . . ."

"Well, I'm sure," the woman said, turning around. "I saw it. It had too many eyes and a yellow beak, but unless you really looked—and not just with your eyes— it was just a ghost, barely there in the air." She turned to her companion and said, "God's monster is only visible to those who seek him out. He can be found only by those with enough courage to walk through Hell to find Heaven."

"Then why don't you go by yourself?" he asked.

Ned walked away; he could feel the Faubougher and his woman staring at him. He felt cold filaments of fear touching his neck, felt the coils of Hell pulling him. . . . There was no noise inside his head, no rasping voice, only the echoes of his thoughts and the transparent images that were his memories. But he had to try to find the beast, even if Forester had found it first.

Stepping on trampled grass, Ned followed a trail strewn with torn clothes, jewelry, wooden ornaments, leather straps, pennons, rings, and broken scourges. The embers of discarded marching-torches still glowed in the grass like the unblinking red eyes of stalking animals.

Ned clung to whatever security he could find—warm memories, the crunch of grass and twigs underfoot, the whisper of wind in grass; he listened for the familiar sounds of the river, but instead heard only a vague hiss. He wished for boredom; that was safe and secure. If the next moment mirrored the last, and the tedious seconds stretched into hours, Ned could live an eternity just picking his nose. But he was afraid and vulnerable. He was getting drunk on fatigue, fear, and exhilaration.

The grass gave way to scrub and lower ground, then to sandy tundra which was gray and rocky and stretched much farther than Ned had remembered. Hell was an ocean; its tides pulled it away from the tundraland, revealing a flatland of dead shore, and then in the early hours Hell would slip back to swallow this gray expanse. But Satan's hand was capricious; in a minute Ned might be swallowed up, drowned under a giant wave of black nothingness.

He felt as if he were pushing through layers of gray gauze, scrims which obscured and concealed Hell. Several times the grayness dissolved and he glimpsed Hell's lights. He would rush forward, only to find himself still trapped in the same gray land.

Hell gently lured him on, and then opened up before him.

Luminescent mountains banded the horizon. Smooth ice shapes and gem faces were slowly melting as they pushed higher into a black starless sky; but Ned could not be sure of what he saw, for Hell was a specious solidity, a palimpsest of shifting illusions. Ned could not keep anything in focus for more than a few seconds. It seemed that the mountains were subtly degrading; yet when Ned blinked his eyes, or shifted his attention, everything would be built up and solid once again—for a few seconds. It was as if Hell was remaking itself, remaining pliable until by trial and error or divine wish it could find a proper reality. Then it would surely solidify. Perhaps, Ned thought, Junction would fade as Hell became solid. Then he could never go back.

He wondered if his mother had passed through those mountains, and realized that under his breath he had been chanting her name. He wanted to run, but he continued on, lifting one foot, then the other, as if he were piloting some infernal machine that would stop dead without his constant attention.

As he walked through the tundra, Hell seemed to recede before him. The mountains grew as he watched them. Diamond peaks sparkled and cut into an empty sky while crests of tourmaline and chrysoprase rose beside crystal alps. Mountains of topaz and spinel sported opal towers and moonstone ridges; ivory lowlands sprouted amber flowers. And Ned could see, if he looked out of the corner of his eye, small fluorescing gem-spurs growing out of the ground nearby. The floor of Hell was bursting with inorganic life.

He forced himself to take another step, and then another.

Finally, Ned found the edge of Hell. Only shadows separated reality from illusion; firm tundra gave way to the phantasmagoria of Hell. But perhaps the shadow line was an illusion. Perhaps his next step would carry him into Hell. Then he found Simon and a small crowd of marchers facing Hell's mountains. It was as if they were standing upon a narrow proscenium and staring into an immense stage. Under the vault of Hell the sky could be made of sailcloth and the mountains might be painted props.

"Hello," Ned shouted at the crowd to break the silence. The marchers ignored him; but they milled around Simon like dervishes, small things scurrying about in aimless motion against the quiet backdrop of Hell. Hell seemed to dampen and suck up every sound. It tugged gently at Ned and Simon and his marchers, slowly leaching light and life into its maw of nothingness.

"Hurry," Simon said to his flock, "or you'll lose the way. Be blessed, punish yourselves for forgiveness. You're the martyrs for the Lord." He intoned the blessings and then shouted for attention. He'd scold his martyrs into Hell.

And they stepped into Hell. Children cried and tried to wrest themselves from thick-armed mothers; families covered their faces and ran towards the mountains; respected citizens whipped and beat themselves and their wives before charging into Hell while remaining Fauboughers and freemen and serfies stood anxiously together, watching and waiting.

Ned drew closer, but it was as if he were a ghost. Children and emaciated Fauboughers looked right through him, and his attempts at communication were left hanging in the air, harsh words to be soaked up by the darkness.

"There goes another soul risking the punishment of Hell for God's sake," Simon said as he waved a Faubougher into Hell. "And another." A ragged family ran past Simon, their arms outstretched in the marcher's gesture of contrition. A little girl stopped and turned around, but Simon raised his arms and chased her away.

"Go on now," Simon said. "Find the Lord."

Ned watched the frightened little girl run into Hell. She was naked except for a gagne; her spindly arms and legs reminded Ned of a stiff and skinny old woman who was unsure of every step. But an old woman could not run that fast without breaking apart like a runaway cart.

Although it strained his eyes, Ned kept her in sight.

It was like watching a fish flit just below the surface of a muddy pond. The little girl was well into Hell now; she was an indefinite figure which disappeared like a flatfish diving deeper into stagnant water. He thought of his mother again.

Simon turned to Ned, smiled, and said, "Welcome. But you're too late. Father has already met the monster and found Heaven. But, then, you were warned."

"How do you know the monster is out there?" Ned asked.

"We can see."

"Can *you* see it?" Ned asked a heavy-set freeman standing apart from the others. "Do you see it there, or over there?"

"He sees God's monster with his faith," Simon said. "His eyes are clear because he has something to see."

"You mistake blindness for sight," Ned said. "And you'll destroy yourselves."

"Don't listen to him," Simon said. "He's fallen—the grace is ours. So now let's all leave together." The crowd turned away from Ned and pressed around Simon. But everyone was quiet; they would not even give up a whisper to echo in Hell.

"You're afraid of me, yet you'll walk out there?" Ned's voice was sharp in the dead air, but he was a ghost once again. Simon and his marchers ignored him and triumphantly walked into Hell like Sunday bathers, wary of getting wet but determined to take a swim.

"Come back. . . ." Don't leave me alone, he thought.

The marchers had disappeared and Ned shouted just to hear himself. Maybe there are more monsters, Ned thought. If I can't find them, then perhaps they'll find me. But he could not return emptyhanded; better to walk into Hell than be torn apart by angry, frightened townfolk. He would head for Sticksveiller Bogs and then turntail back to the bridge. As Ned gazed into Hell, he wondered if Simon and his marchers had found anything but their own destruction. Everything was quiet and muffled. Fighting an urge to tiptoe and slide through the darkness without a presence, Ned walked southeast. But he soon stopped humming and making up nonsense noises to quell his fear; he followed Hell's shadowline like a trapper following a river.

Ned moved away from Hell—he still followed Hell's shadowline, but he kept a good distance away from its deadening dominion. The black sun poured out darkness, the stuff of dreams, the vapors of Hell. Clouds covered the sky above him like dark islands; the sky filled up and pressed out all the light.

But Ned did not feel like a nightcreature, safe in the darkness of a familiar world. He was lost, prey to every twitter and scratch in the bush, and afraid of his own footfalls. The nightcreatures followed him, their eyes burning stones that watched and waited for the daycreature to stumble.

When Ned reached Sticksveiller Bogs, moonlight penetrated the veil of clouds. The heavy storm clouds had been pushed into Hell where they might scatter or form pools of glass in the sky.

Ned walked on, his feet sinking into the wet spongy ground. His head and shoulders just cleared the ceiling of fog that clung to the bogs. He gagged on the effluvium and his eyes burned. So here's where Reverends Briar and Blues saw the holy monster, Ned thought. A fit place. Shadow-specters roiled out of the fog and Ned felt the brush of an easterly wind. The wind would blow into every house in Junction, bequeathing night fevers and chills.

Ned grew impatient to leave the stink and find the bridge. If monsters lurked in the bogs, they were beyond sight. And fogfingers could not hide monsters. There's nothing here, Ned told himself. Only wind and rot and night fevers. He sneezed and an old familiar voice chuckled inside his head. It gurgled and brayed and tootled and gleefully poked around in his memories like a child grasping toys.

Ned ran, but he could not outrun the voice. As it spoke nonsense words, he remembered odd moments of his life; but strewn about the forest of his memory were senseless pieces that glinted like the struts of the steel bridge—they were the scattered remembrances of his future. The voice shouted and screaked; it skreeghed like a trapped bird pecking and gouging with sharp beak and talons. Hell and its surrounds became an unimportant overlay upon his sharpened senses and clear memories. He remembered towers of glass that poked into the sky, steel tunnels, a stone church, the rush and clackclack of new language, and Sandra dressed in white and shifting from dream to dream. And his father screaming from a mirror—all the senseless memories of things that had not happened and places he had not yet seen. They were incomplete visions, undreamt dreams.

The voice hacked at him until he found Bild Bridge and its steel companion. Ned was out of breath; he gagged and doubled over to vomit, but he could only retch dryly. He could not vomit a spirit, a demon raking and tearing at his insides.

"Hello," said the angel from Hell. It stood in front of the bridge; its beak glinted yellow, and all of its eyes were closed except those that made up its face.

"I've been waiting for you," it said.

Ned stood his ground, although he was trembling. Face it, he thought. Stand now and face it.

"Don't be afraid, I won't hurt you."

"What do you want?" Ned asked as he breathed in the stuff of dreams, became part of Hell's crystal night. He began to feel calm, barely conscious that a distant part of himself was trying to break out of the dreams.

"I want you to come with me."

"Where?"

"It begins in Hell."

Ned could not hear the river. Looking down, he saw that it was not flowing. It had crystalized into diamond spurs that created glacé patterns and broke up the wan moonlight into sparkles and points.

"Hell is all around us," said the birdbeast. "You've pulled it along with you."

Ned turned away from the bridge to see the mountains growing in the moonlight. They were much closer than before.

"Yes," the birdbeast said. "They're still growing. Those mountains proved to be quite an obstacle."

Ned noticed that the creature's beak did not move when it spoke, and he wasn't even sure if he was hearing a true voice. "Are you the voice inside my head?"

The birdbeast spoke, but Ned could not understand what it said. Words and thoughts were jumbled together as in a dream.

"Why do you want me?" Ned asked. His voice sounded hollow and seemed to echo.

"Because of those mountains. You created them, you know. They've been growing since you imagined them that day."

"I don't believe that."

"Then look behind you," the birdbeast said. "You've pulled those mountains here. They'll be on top of us soon."

Ned could not make up his mind whether he heard the birdbeast with his ears or his imagination. The voice seemed to be inside and outside his head. "Are you a creature of God or of Hell?" Ned asked. He could almost see dreams roiling about him like translucent streamers. He was caught by the hole in the sky.

"I'm neither from Heaven nor Hell."

"Then what are you?" Ned asked.

"A lure, I think. The dream stops here. Now we're on our own."

Ned watched the mountains silently pounding their way towards him. The mountains are alive, he thought. They're bears with glass claws and icicle teeth. He felt like a swimmer trying to break surface. The dreams were suffocating him.

And the birdbeast began to change into a man. All but two watery eyes disappeared, and its beak turned into a chin that could be construed to be weak. The beast became a short, stocky man with an overlarge mouth and short cropped black hair.

Ned watched the transformation and screamed. He broke out of the dream.

"You don't have to be afraid," the man said.

"You're Satan," Ned said. "You change at will. Why do you want me? You're bringing the Last Days, I know that." He was shouting.

"No, I'm not Satan. My name is Kaar Deacon, and I'm just a messenger from another town. A town like Junction, only a thousandfold larger. And that's where I want to take you."

Ned looked around in all directions, his head jerking as if it were being tugged this way and that by some invisible puppeteer. "What if I don't want to come?"

"Then where will you go?" asked Deacon. "Look, even now the mountains grow closer. If you return to Junction, soon there will be no Junction."

For an instant he imagined that he was a wild animal trapped in the brush, about to be skewered on a hunter's lance. "And if I go with you?"

"We don't have much time," Deacon said. "This is a dream that will begin and end again. You don't have to understand that now. Just come with me. Quickly."

If I'm going to be swallowed by Hell, better now, Ned thought. Better to get it over with quickly. A panic raged inside him, but did not reach the surface. He pondered his oblivion, resolved to die on his own hook.

When Ned and Deacon hurried toward the Helltundra, spurs had already begun to grow out of the grass. The mountains were only a few hundred paces from the tundra line. Spurs grew together to make grotesque towers and tangles and behind them were crystal hillocks that gave way to mountain cliffs. Hell was no longer a flat plain; it was a mountain wall.

Pausing at the tundra's edge, Deacon said, "I don't know how we can get past the mountains. I came through over there." He pointed toward a narrow gap in the mountain wall, but gem-spurs were already maturing into steeples and sparkling curclicues which threatened to fill the empty space. "We can't get through there now. It will soon be solid mountain." Deacon's eyes darted back and forth, looking for a break in the mountain wall.

Ned watched the mountains grow. Their crystal faces magnified the moonlight into false morning. Soon everything would be crystal and gem—no more grass and rock and hard-packed dirt. The sky would be blotted out by the sheer bulk of this growing fancy.

"The mountains will swallow us," Ned screamed as he turned to run. But new mountains had grown up behind him. The Sticksveiller River sparkled inside a dark mountain and Bild Bridge had toppled. A gem-spur pushed out of the grass and touched Ned's hand. It was the seed of a new mountain. "It's growing beneath us," he said.

"We'll never outrun them," Deacon said calmly, as if he were far away, removed from this shrinking stone world. The mountains had gained another hundred paces. They would soon merge together, fuse into a single block. "They're real. But you've let them get out of hand. You're afraid of them. Look for a way through; I can't find it."

"I haven't done anything," Ned shouted. He faced Junction and watched the tiny gem-spurs bursting out of the ground in even rows, swelling and merging together to form new mountains. What will become of Junction? he asked himself. How could I have done this?

"You won't find it back there," Deacon said. "We haven't been having that dream over and over for you to just return to Junction—if, indeed, there still is a Junction. The way out must be over there somewhere." He pointed to the cliffs before them. The mountains had gained another hundred paces.

"I must go back," Ned said.

"*There can be no turning back to Junction, for it lies in the future, and you've been caught by the past.*"

Although Deacon had changed into a man, a demon still lived inside Ned's head.

"What did you say?" Ned asked Deacon.

"Think up an opening. It's our only chance."

The ground began to vibrate as the mountains grew closer.

"There," Ned shouted and ran toward an opening in the rock face. It was a wild guess. He hoped it wasn't just a superficial crack in the mountain wall.

Stepping over growing gem-spurs that blocked their way, they reached the opening, broke through a latticework of crystal climbers, and crawled into a damp tunnel. Before Ned could determine the dimensions of the tunnel, the opening closed behind them as the mountains silently fused together.

And Ned discovered that the echoing screams were his own. It was completely dark and slightly damp in the tunnel. Ned didn't mind the dampness—he was used to sleeping in cellars, but the darkness frightened him. It was dark as death, he thought.

*   *   *

Ned could not tell how long they had been walking; the loss of sight expanded time. Although he was tired and his arms and legs ached, he followed Deacon's droning voice. He could not understand very much of what Deacon was talking about, but he would remember and think about it later.

Surely I'm dying, Ned thought; his memories spun through his mind, and he remembered that dying men see their lives pass before them.

He remembered Sandra and Hilda and began to count his steps. He lost himself in numbers; nothing else mattered.

Then Deacon suddenly stopped talking.

And Ned was alone in the dark.

Part Two

NEW YORK

5

Ned had finished shouting. He pressed his back against the cold rock wall and listened to his voice tumble away, echoing before him. His throat was raw; his eyes ached as if the darkness was a substance pressing against them. He was exhausted and blind.

"Deacon, come back." It was almost a whisper. Ned waited for the words to die, but in the blackness shouts and whispers became visual echoes, dim retinal lights exploding in the high halls of a labyrinthine cavern.

Ned knew that Deacon was not in the tunnel.

Perhaps I had stopped and fallen asleep, he thought. No, he said to himself, as he rubbed his eyes and relished the purple splotches darting across his retinal field. Deacon would not have let him lag behind. Ned had been awake, walking and listening to Deacon speak about Hell and New York City and time and minds dreaming.

"*What you call Hell,*" he had said, "*is a place where physical laws have become indeterminate. Hell is a substance, a quality that can be affected by mind. It is the unformed potential, the substratum of reality..*

"*Your town Junction exists out of sheer will..*

"*But there are other things contained in that substance, past realities that remain outside of your vision and mind. . . .*"

Ned remembered Deacon's words; they were gobbledygook run-ons that smacked of coughs and sneezes and the buzzing of flies, words that could only make sense in a dream, yet he could understand them because they came from the voice inside his head. But Ned remembered two voices—one he heard with his ears, but the other was inside his head, a new addition to the world of his thoughts. It was as if Deacon could speak with two mouths.

Ned thought about what Deacon had said and fought another spasm of fear. But he was spent, as if his glands had dried up. He sat on the cold tunnel floor and talked to himself. His thoughts were coherent, then muddled, foiled by dreams. He muttered to his mother, scolded his father, whispered to Sandra.

I'm alone, he thought. He mouthed the words over and over. But it had been his own unbridled fear, frustration, and hatred that had formed the mountains. But his aggressions, drives, and fears were buried deep inside him; they mingled in the subterranean streams of his thoughts, habits, and primeval instincts. If I can make mountains and tunnels, Ned thought, then I can dream myself back to Junction and will the mountains to melt and think up all the books that the church said could not exist and fondle Hilda and Sandra and turn Hell into fields and cities like New York.

But New York was only a vague memory. And try as he might, Ned could not dream himself back to Junction.

"Since the world is indeterminate," Deacon had said, *"the arbitrary distinctions of time are of no use. Clock time has become dream time, a state in which past, present, and future exist at the same time as possibilities. Time can no longer be thought of as a straight line or a continuous and connected series of events. It is a loop. All experience consists of loops. There is a loop for every memory pattern. A recurring dream is a loop, as is remembering the future; but you might not remember the same future as others. Over-*

laps are haphazard. They can only be consistent if one mind is providing continuity. . . ."

Ned tried again to whisk himself back to Junction; he tried to break down the material ideas of walls and tunnels and mountains and erect dreams of Sandra and Main Street. But tunnel walls could not be replaced by Ned's dreams.

He still fought the presence in his mind, the monster that spoke hurriedly of impossible things, that resurrected or created or projected Deacon and bird-beasts and pushed Ned into mountain walls. If Ned had any control over what sprouted in Hell, it was within definite bounds.

". . . if one mind is providing continuity. . . ."

Even after Deacon had explained Jung and time and determinism, Ned could not understand why Deacon could not see the obvious: tomorrow comes after today, dreams are made of sleep, and sleep is made of darkness. But perhaps dreams are real, Ned thought with a cold shiver, cobbled out of the same stuff as stone, and time is a dream that has not yet hardened. Perhaps nothing is as it seems. . . .

Pressing his palms against his eyes, he waited for the familiar purple splotches to appear on his retinal walls—the total darkness of the tunnel still frightened him. This time the flourite spots were richer and more intense. He waited until they filled his entire field of vision and then opened his eyes. Before him, the tunnel was aglow with phosphorescent light which provided security and humid warmth. Ned noticed that the walls were smooth, without seams or cracks; they were the stuff of dreams and prisons.

Then I do have *some* control, Ned thought. He tried to think up something else—food, his mother's jewel box, the Book—but nothing appeared. Disappointed, yet exhilarated by the supervention of flourite light, he took a few steps, both arms stretched before him for safety. He felt less afraid in the sham sunshine.

But as he walked, he began to feel a chill wind on his back, pushing him on with icicle feelers. Behind him it was dark.

He fought an urge to turn around and run into the darkness.

"Telepathy and psi phenomena," Deacon had said, *"did not seem to be ruled by any known physical laws. But now that physical laws in the past are gradually becoming more indeterminate, psi has become more consistent.*

"Every night eleven million, five hundred and seventeen thousand people in New York City are dreaming about Junction. And you. Every night they remember the future. Everyone, every child and adult. That's why I've come for you. Perhaps that will stop the dreams. All the dreams are centered on you. What will we dream when you are in our present?"

Why me? Ned asked himself; the thought was like a whisper.

He could not understand how so many people could live in one place. He imagined that New York City was a huge monster of flesh and steel and glass waiting for him at the end of the tunnel. Its metal jaws were ready to swallow him and make him join the screaming crowds that lived in its pores.

Ned walked on and counted his steps until it seemed that his heart and pulse and breath and thoughts were regulated by a metronome of numbers that couldn't be stopped. He was tired and hungry and had no idea of real time—the minutes or hours or days spent in the tunnel were only footfalls, subjective tickings, subvocalized countings, nightmares and memories. The damp breeze behind him ruffled his clothes and tousled his hair; the phosphorescent warmth of the tunnel was giving way to the cold, prodding fingers of wind.

Through the haze, Ned could see the end of the tunnel. It was a black dot that grew larger with every step. Could that be the doorway to Hell's chambers? he asked himself. A tiny light flickered in the distance. It turned red, then green, then blinked out. And the phosphorescent haze was becoming dim. It was being sucked into the darkness ahead—as Ned soon would be.

He fought another self-destructive urge to turn around and face the blackness. Its presence was so near that he thought he could touch it and grasp it if he outstretched his arm. He imagined it would be cold and wet. It was a tail looped behind him, pushing him forward into its wet mouth.

But Ned's only chance to return to Junction lay somewhere in the growing darkness ahead.

Trapped, he thought grimly, between the darkness and Hell.

He ran to the end of the tunnel, hoping for death and purgation and the blond face of God.

Instead, he found himself inside a huge cavern. It was a monochromatic kaleidoscope of reflections and soot and blaring noise. A subway train screamed to a halt beside him. Ned thought it was alive—a shrieking, hissing steel snake, a metal construction of his fears. It was the nightmare snake that had pushed Ned out of the tunnel.

Ned looked this way and that; there was nothing familiar to his eye, everything seemed to be clamoring for his attention. He pressed his palms against his eyes for an instant, as if to bring back the flourite light of the tunnel, and remembered that he had dreamed about this place.

People were milling about him, clawing each other, pushing for a better position, trying to reach the glass and metal doors that would soon slide shut. Men in suits, holding briefcases close to their chests, burst out of the cars first, pushing entrants out of the way. The men were followed by women in business suits and girls wearing sweaters and dungarees, ladies in shorts and torn stockings, some holding babies with gray faces and screaming obscenities, others quiet and shy. But they all had to fight the onrushing mob pushing and squeezing through the rubber-trimmed doors.

Ned was wet with perspiration; his coarse overshirt clung to his skin. It was in the high nineties in the subway station. He looked around for an exit. He had to get away from the monster and its outlandish, frightened people, from their pushing arms and fetid breath and sweat-clogged clothes.

He spied an escalator ahead, its metal steps climbing forever. Perhaps the moving stairs were a stairway to Heaven, Ned thought, and then screamed as the train noisily left the station. He could not stand the chalk and blackboard sound of steel grinding steel. And another train screamed to a halt in its place, a shining painted warrior hungering to fill up the empty space.

Ned pushed toward the moving stairs, his hands clasped to his chest and elbows raised like fins to swim through a new rush of people. It was truly a monster, he thought. All of these people, breathing through a thousand mouths, sweating in a million places, might as well be one. Ned wondered if he would be forced to remain in caves and caverns, pushing and grasping with the rest of the gray faces.

Everything seemed to be converging upon him.

He needed room to breathe; he had to escape.

"Hey, it's Ned," an overweight schoolgirl said to her companion. They were both dressed in identical blue sailor outfits.

"Hey, look, it's Ned," they shouted at the crowd as they ran after him. But the crowd was still dumb, perplexed, concerned with its own things. It was a great greasy animal looking for its fingers.

Ned ran for a door made of iron bars. Beyond the door was a stairway in a metal cage filled with people hurrying up and down. Some turned to look at Ned.

"It's the one in the dreams," shouted a man in a faded blue suit, acne sores and collar rash visible on his neck. His face was round and splotched and puffy, his chin a small knot piercing rolls of flesh—he bore a slight resemblance to Reverend Shorter.

"Well, get him," shouted a young woman with short hair who was carrying an armload of books.

Ned ran past the turnstiles, pushed his way through the door, and was pulled into the waiting crowd. Poking and pushing, bristling and gnashing, it reached out for him.

Have to get away from here, he thought. Have to get out of their dreams.

He turned to run the other way, but people were all around him, showing him one face, the face of an awakened beast.

A boy in a torn black leather jacket crawled through the crowd forming around Ned. He stood up and grabbed Ned's arm—Ned tried to wrench it free, but the boy had a strong grip. He had a smooth unshaven face, and his greasy black hair was combed into a pony-tail.

Ned punched the boy in the face, breaking his nose. The crowd howled. Other boys wearing black leather jackets appeared, and they grabbed Ned by the arms and neck. They pushed him through the crowd.

"Fuckers," Ned shouted.

Arms reached out toward his face. Ned tried to disengage himself from the youths and someone hit him in the face. It was the smooth-faced boy; his nose was bleeding heavily.

Ned felt a sudden numbness; he spat out a tooth and swallowed salty blood. He made another effort to wrench himself free, but the crowd pummeled him. Punches became dull thuds booming and beating somewhere else. Scratches and gouges were not part of the white static in his head. They were shop noises, the tearing and stitching of clothes, the jabber and fast-talk of seamstresses measuring with outstretched arms and open hands. Noise and heat and sensation were far away in a synchronistic land where cause had no bond with effect. Ned had time to think and open his eyes to watch the contorted faces. He matched them up with faces he knew and remembered pleasant thoughts.

He remembered how time seemed to stretch out when he was in a fight—especially if he was losing.

"Come on, man," said an olive-skinned boy with high cheekbones and sunken cheeks. "We can't drag you up the stairs." His mouth opened and closed. Ned could hear words and smell rancid sweat, but all the noise and sights were echoes of another world.

"Up the stairs we go, Ned. Shit, we got Ned."

"Get out of the way," shouted the smooth-faced boy at anyone who might try to stop them. There was blood on his face, hands, and shirt. He waved his switchblade and the crowd opened to let him pass. "Chicken bastards, we got Ned. And we're all going to Junction."

Ned's face was beginning to throb; soon he would feel the first brushstrokes of pain and then the burning agony of a broken face. The boys were all around him. Ned smelled their pomade and wondered if it was a strange blend of black honey. Ned found it difficult to breathe. He coughed and swallowed blood.

The crowd followed the gang that held Ned. They seemed to be waiting for the right moment. They shouted, and gaining confidence, began punching the youths. One of the boys fired a pistol into the crowd. That drove everyone into a frenzy. Ned saw a group of young girls pull the smooth-faced boy down the stairs. They scratched out his eyes and kicked him with small, deft strokes.

As the gang toughs were swallowed by the crowd, Ned tried to propel himself forward to the top of the stairs. But ready arms were waiting to seize him and pass him through the crowd. Together all the selfish entities made up a synergetic, unselfish whole. They were content to handle Ned for a few seconds, perhaps punch or caress him, and then pass him on.

Behind him, Ned could hear the crowd chanting, "Get the Dreamer, Ned. Ned. Ned's ahead. Ned's ahead. Get the Dreamer before he's dead."

And someone started singing a familiar song:

> Back and side, go bare, go bare
> Both hand and foot go cold,
> But belly, God send you good ale enough
> Whether it be new or old!

"Let him alone," cried a nun dressed in white with a black cowl that framed her pink face.

> All lie down, as in a swoon,
> To have a pleasing vision.
> And then rise with bared thighs,
> Who'd fear such sweet incision?

The words were inside Ned's head. They were sung in a familiar voice with different words and, for the moment, Ned understood them. Others took up the song, and it spread through the crowd. "Don't hurt him, don't hurt him. He's the President, bim, bim, bim."

"He's the President?" shrieked the nun, and then she fainted.

Fifteen meters from the stairway, on the second level, which looked like the first, they dropped him to the floor. A fat woman wearing bright orange lipstick sat on his chest and gently touched his face. Ned gagged from her sudden weight and tried to push her away. Someone kicked him; he felt a sharp pain and closed his eyes. But this huge room on the main floor was etched under his eyelids; for a few seconds it would remain intact, a fading image soon to be relegated to memory. His memory could reconstruct it again, even give it solidity. But only sometimes. Only when it would not interfere with the plans of the howling voice inside his head.

The ceiling was high and crusted with carbon. Cement slabs and temporary, makeshift rooms broke up the parallel attraction of perspective lines. A hamburger stand with tiny stools and smeared plexiglass containers on the counter faced metal doors and compartments and turnstiles. Numbered luggage lockers lined the walls, jutted out to provide corners and alleys. Overhead signs and arrows pointed to the IRT and D and N and RR. Sharp contrasts of black and white, shadow and light, turned the station into a natural cavern lit by bare lightbulbs.

Ned felt removed from everything around him; it was as if he was not Ned, but only a spectator in the crowd. He moved his arms close to his body to protect his hands from clumsy feet. They'll kill me, anyway, he thought. But he was in shock, numbed and comfortable. The scum on the floor bunched up under his fingers. There was an acrid taste of urine in the warm, damp air. Ned knew if he opened his eyes, he would see sticky dust falling slowly, settling into scum on the cold floor. He thought about metal. It fascinated him. It reflected faces and lights and sparkled, yet would not break like glass.

This must be Hell . . . he thought.

Music blared out of nowhere.

Thoughts jammed into his mind. Everyone shouted different thoughts and experiences. And Ned learned about roller coasters and tea and China and migraines and cancer and movies. Other emotions and sense impressions blinded him, made him vomit, gave him an erection.

"It's a phonograph. That's what makes the music."
"Can't you hear him? He's shouting."
"His mouth isn't moving."
"Neither is yours."
"Let him alone."

Silence. General agreement. Group telepathy. Ned sucked air through his mouth and the grays behind his eyelids turned black. For an instant, he thought he was back in the tunnel. Alone. But he could feel the weight of the people above him, pushing down on him with their pulpy hands and scouring minds. Now trying to revive him. Hundreds of faces turned inside out. Mass Penance.

They became a huge toeless foot about to step on him. And he was an insect waiting for two-dimensional death.

6

Washed and bandaged, hair neatly combed and smelling of soap, Ned stared out the window at the street below. Although the sun was high in the sky, it was a gray day, as if the gray of the cement and skyscrapers had been stamped into the air itself. In the distance the sky turned blue—a drab ceiling vaulting over a colorless land. Ned pressed his nose against the cold windowglass, felt the cool rush of air escaping from the air conditioner vent beneath the window. He looked down at the blank theater billboards and the crowds in the street. The street had been cordoned off by police and no cars were permitted in the area.

Yes, he thought, the Book told of this place. . . .

Like moths banging against a lightbulb, trying to burn themselves up in a white-hot nirvana, the crowds pushed, jostled, and fought to break through the police lines. Ned could hear an occasional *poppop* of riflefire, greatly muted by walls and glass.

As Ned watched the crowds below, he remembered the faces he had seen in the subway. They passed before his mind's eye, portraits locked in the cellar of his memory. He examined their scars and birthmarks and wrinkles and expressions. And his mind wandered into new rooms of recent memory. He remembered being carried from the subway station by uniformed men who wheezed and snorted in the blue heat. He could still hear the screeching of subway machines and taste the rubber of the gas mask that was pushed into his face as tear gas bombs bloomed over the scum floor.

Ned could feel the crowds below tugging at him with their dreams and emotions. I don't want to hear them, he thought. But they would not let him alone. They wanted him, needed him. But why me? Ned asked himself. What do I have that they want? Events seemed to be whirling past him. He felt vertigo, as if he was falling through his life. He dreamed of crashing through God's windowglass and falling into the outstretched arms of the crowd. That would relieve him of his sins and propel him to Heaven.

But I'll be safe here in the hotel, he told himself, trying to force himself to believe it.

The crowds tried to pull his face against the windowpane with their thoughts. Draggle-tailed youths, tanned ladies, and business men carrying leather briefcases waved to him. Even the blue-uniformed policemen standing in cordon were waving and winking and smiling.

Ned tried to feel secure within the large hotel room with its smooth white walls, twin leather couches that faced each other across an expanse of rich brown carpet, dining table surrounded by high-backed chairs, bookcases filled with musty smelling books and bric-a-brac of Hummel china, butler's tables and end-tables covered with green-edged glass, and well stocked bar, small refrigerator, and early model television. This room reminded him a little of the library in the Stone House, perhaps only because both rooms contained floor-to-ceiling bookshelves. It was a haven from the harsh realities below. But it was a precarious, transparent nest.

Ned's warm breath fogged the windowpane.

"Everything's gradually changing, soon the whole world will sink into the past," said Renny Weissman, the plainclothes detective assigned to stay with Ned.

He wore a blue serge suit and a brown striped tie, was almost two meters tall, and combed his thick wiry black hair into a pompadour.

Ned didn't turn around, although he could feel the pressure of Weissman's gaze on the back of his neck. He felt the pressure increase as Weissman stepped closer to the window. "Please don't come any nearer," he said, watching his warm breath explode on the cold window.

"It's stable for a while, and then there's another change," Weissman said, standing beside Ned and gazing distractedly out the window. "Take this hotel. It used to be the Astor Plaza, a fairly new office building. I was in there a few times, but I didn't like it—it was too big and too sterile, reminded me of a hospital, and I've been in enough hospitals.

"Before the Astor Plaza, there was the Astor Hotel. This hotel. It had been here for years, a grand tourist's hotel—this is the center of the theater district, or used to be. The Astor was a landmark. And then they tore it down to build the Plaza building.

"Well, after the change—we seem to be getting them more often now, every few days it seems—the old Astor Hotel had replaced the office building. Just like that. In the blink of an eye. It was almost the same as the old Astor, except for those gargoyles on the ledges."

Ned looked at the ledge that passed under the window. It was discolored by pigeon droppings and the slow burn of pollution. By pressing his face against the window, he could see the gargoyle's outstretched arm. But he remembered what the gargoyle looked like: a mottled marble body covered with eyes, some closed, some open; eyes staring blankly in all directions. He had seen similar gargoyles in the hospital lobby. They stood under a stained-glass window that depicted the baptism of Christ by Saint John.

Ned tried to ignore the crowd whispering inside his

head; he was afraid of being overwhelmed by its dreamers. He was vulnerable to every slack-jawed citizen on the streets below. He turned his thoughts to Junction and was comforted by Weissman's gravelly voice.

"I don't mind the change at all," Weissman continued. "I always liked the Astor. Used to stop at the coffee shop on Sunday mornings in the old days.

"Strange thing, though, is that when the office building blinked out and the hotel took its place, all the hotel people were at their old jobs. And the office workers—anyone who had been in the building when it blinked out—were all missing. But it happened around one o'clock, and all the executives and company presidents were out to lunch." He chuckled and said, "We lost about four hundred secretaries and office people.

"Anyway, the city government proclaimed the hotel to be government property—the mayor and mayor's mansion had disappeared, too, that day—and fired all the workers. Some scientist came to the conclusion that the hotel workers couldn't be real, anyway. Well, they are. I tracked them down on the welfare books."

"Can you hear the whispers of the crowd inside your head?" Ned asked. But Weissman didn't reply; he stared out the window as if he was a stone gargoyle. Ned felt something change; it was as if familiar reality was coming apart again. This was another dreamtime; and, as if in a dream, he was calmly watching the world dissolve. There was an electricity in the heavy air, and Ned felt he was submerged in Hell. Objects degraded into older forms; the world was in flux. . . .

Ned watched the people below. The crowd was a great beast, moving and shifting as if it was the floor of Hell itself. Youths were carrying placards and silently shouting at him. They pushed against police cordons to no avail. Mace and gas fouled the air. Ned listened to the hum of the air-conditioner and heard their thoughts.

"We believe in God and Ned."

"Were dreaming each other in God's sight."

A young girl, dressed in dungarees and a paint-stained pullover sweater, held up a pane of glass as if to reflect the sun into Ned's eyes. But the sun passed behind a gray cloud which threatened to cover the entire sky, gray on gray.

"Glass is holy. God protect us from encroaching Hell."

"We are penitent. We await purgatory, knowing that God's in sight."

"Give us another dream, Ned. Tell us what to do."

"Another dream. Another dream. Tell us. Tell us."

I can't give them dreams, Ned thought as he drew his finger across the steamed window. He tried to manipulate the dreamstuff, but he was caught; he dreamed that everything was changing, growing more indeterminate for a few seconds, or moments, or hours. He waited for the glue of the newly created reality to harden.

"I believe we're all dreaming each other," Weissman said, as if he could hold reality together with words alone. "Our dreams create the changes, and we wake up to find they're real. And I believe God is dreaming us all, dreaming the changes. So all the dreams fit."

"How did you come to believe that?" Ned asked.

"It's common knowledge."

Ned listened to Weissman's theories, fears, and thoughts, and then reached out into the city, as if his spirit, afloat in holy joy, could travel the streets. Beyond New York were other cities and towns and farmlands and mountains; but Ned sensed that they were changing faster than New York City, that they would soon be swallowed up by Hell.

He let his mind wander down Broadway, then west into Washington Square, into the heart of Greenwich

Village. He smelled the marigolds, peonies, petunias, geraniums, tulips, and laughed, for God was transmuting cement into soil and life. There was something boisterous and ludicrous about creation.

The narrow, old streets had been transformed into gardens; flowers bloomed everywhere. Flowers of every description grew on lush lawns that had once been cement. Bluebonnets, red clover, goldenrod, black-eyed Susan, pink and white lady slippers, iris, dogwood, red roses, Indian paintbrush, bitterroot scented the air, choked the allergic with pollen. It was a watercolor world. Cars and shops became hothouses for tropical plants. The sun was hot on the buildings, the air was muggy. Old men sat upon cracked stone steps in front of dirty brick buildings and looked at passersby walking lazily through natural gardens. Old women with their middle-aged sons and daughters wiped their faces with perfumed handkerchiefs and drank beer out of brown glass bottles. This was a place for lovers and children to play in and hide among flowers.

Everything was quiet, as if the heavy air and wild growth had choked off all sound. But Ned's thoughts filled the brick and cobble streets like holy laughter.

Ned investigated Wall Street, the small roads and high buildings of the business section, the old mixed with the new. Towers built out of dark glass rose like unnatural trees from a cement earth. And everywhere stone gargoyles stood, sentinels blindly watching. . . .

He grew impatient and left. His mind lingered in the Brooklyn Battery Tunnel—a cool, secure haven, then floated uptown, past himself and midtown, through Harlem and the Bronx, up the Henry Hudson Parkway, to settle on the cold steel of the George Washington Bridge. Soon, he knew, that, too, would be destroyed. But here was beauty and calm, he thought. His spirit was a bird perched on a high cable. He could almost believe that he had dreamed

New York, that he had been high on good grass from Bridgehead and would now follow Junction Road to the Congress Bar. But even this great silvery bridge could not span the oceans of Hell.

Ignoring Weissman (who was babbling on) and the crowd below, Ned investigated Westchester and its environs through the minds of those who lived there.

But the crowd was hungry for him; it stabbed him, tore through his defenses, thrust unsure fingers into him, burned him with its agonies.

"Help us. We believe in God. We believe in you."

"We believe in you. We believe in you. Webelievein-you."

Webelieveinyou Webelieveinyou Webelieveinyou We-believeinyou."

"Ned. Ned. Ned. Ned. NedNed. NedNedNednedned nedned."

People in Westchester heard the chorus, reached out to Ned and augmented the drone of thoughts. Ned tried to talk, but could only broadcast fear—he was afraid of the crowd, afraid of New York, its dreams and ghosts, afraid of himself. He pressed his face against the window and screamed.

Weissman came out of his own private dreams. His large hands locked over Ned's arms, pulling him away from the window. But it was too late. Ned felt the crowd reaching into his mind, pulling, tearing, taking, searching for a dream of redemption, a dream that would put the world back together and deny time.

"Leave me alone, I want to stay," Ned said, trying to break loose from Weissman. But he thought, Please help me, get me away from them, everyone leave me alone, give me the tunnel, I can't stand flesh. But Weissman was flesh. He was part of the crowd, caught in the same dreams. Ned felt Weissman's thoughts as snakes crawling through dimly lit corridors, as gray moths fluttering in closets. But he could not break away.

Then it was over, the world became familiar once again, reality became a steady thing, whereas seconds before it was the shifting, roiling stuff of Hell. Weissman crossed the room to the bar and mixed himself a drink. Ned returned to the window. He pressed his face against the cold glass. He felt trapped. No way out, he thought. Trapped. And they were still in the street below, still shouting, raising their placards, praying and beating their chests.

But Ned couldn't hear them; he was shut inside his room.

Ned and Weissman were alone in the hotel. The maids and other necessary personnel were permitted inside at certain hours, but other than that the hotel was empty. Nevertheless, it was well guarded. Policemen manned the roof and ledges and formed a human wall around the hotel. Double panes of bulletproof glass had been substituted for the old imperfect window-glass. Ned had not allowed the windows to be covered. Although he yearned for home and the solitude of the tunnel, he had to be able to see into the city, its glass and steel and people. Ned could not understand this ambivalence. But he would add it to his list of sins.

Although Ned felt comfortable for the time being, he did not like policemen walking on the roof. He could tolerate them during the stable periods; but during the dream-times when reality was loosened, they would bear down on him with their thoughts. And he would feel the weight of every cell in their bodies.

He thought it was curious that the position of a body could so affect his mind. Perhaps its cause could be traced to the Mount Sinai Hospital after he was taken from the subway. White-capped nurses with small breasts had constantly watched him and doctors in white smocks came in and out without warning.

They had tested him for everything, given him upper and lower GI's, and spinals, pricked his fingers, tied hoses around his arms, measured his brain waves, tested his eyes, drugged him with this and that, x-rayed him, probed, asked questions, and would not permit him a whore. Pretty nurses ordered him about, collected his urine, gave him morning enemas, and slapped down his erections. Although spots were detected on his lung, the other tests had all proven to be negative. A dentist who specialized in implants replaced the incisor that had been knocked out in the subways, so he would not lisp like a Faubougher. Psychological tests had been in order. A doctor named Kheal who wore his dirty gray-white hair long and dressed in baggy green trousers and blue smock came to visit every day (and night) and ask questions. And there were visits by other scientists and more doctors and a philosopher and a few members of the trade press. They all asked questions, wrote in note pads or clicked on recording devices which made Ned feel self-conscious when he spoke.

Ned had screamed to be left alone, so he was given sedatives and re-examined. He had taken to sleeping for long periods of time in the hospital as if he could sleep away this bad dream and awaken in Junction. Pads were placed on his eyelids when he slept. Electroencephalograph electrodes were placed on his neck, face, and head. Subliminal movements of tongue and lips, psychogalvanic reflexes, heart rate, variations in blood pressure, fluctuations in blood glucose were all monitered.

Doctor Kheal's voice would awaken Ned several times each night.

"Ned, wake up," Kheal would say. "Tell me about your dream. Then you can go back to sleep."

"I can't remember," Ned would say, feeling that there was something just out of reach—a thought, a dream, perhaps it was only a color or smell. He would become angry, tear off the electrodes, try to break out of the room, and he would wish as hard as he could to be back in a familiar place—he was nothing but an animal in a cage here, an animal to be fed and tested, and trained. With tears and knuckles bloodied from pounding and punching the walls, he tried to retain holy honor.

"Ned, our instruments indicate that you've just had a dream. Now try to remember. . . ."

Sometimes he would try to find the dream, but it would be bunched up in a secret room in his mind. He just couldn't remember. The harder he tried, the more his head would ache. It was as if a demon-spirit dwelled inside him and was punishing him for trying to mouth sacred thoughts and prayers.

Every night Ned would have the same conversation with Kheal. It had become quiet ritual—Ned had stopped screaming and fighting, for he was tired of being gagged and wrapped in strait jackets. Ned began to feel more and more claustrophobic. He could almost feel the weight of cement walls and ceilings and floors, the weight of the sick, the dying, the dead souls. Slowly, inexorably, the outside was pushing its way inside. He began to hear sirens, traffic noises, the whoosh and whistle and whirr and hum of the city. But Doctor Kheal assured him that his room was soundproof. He was, most assuredly, alone.

But Ned sensed a change coming, a numinous dream that would twist time and reality—he had begun to trust his intuition.

The doctors indulged him. They waited. They wanted to know why he couldn't (or wouldn't) remember his dreams, and why everyone else had stopped dreaming about him. They told him he was repressing his fears. And they had seemed to know that everyone would soon dream of him again.

Ned told them that he could not dream correctly in the hospital. He said that the ghosts of the soon-to-be-dead were crowding into his sleep and taking his dreams. Traffic noises were becoming louder. He could hear conversations in the streets.

The world began to change as Ned had sensed it would. Ghosts swam through hospital halls, hung in the rooms like cobwebs, and crowded into everyone's sleep. The present degraded into the past. And the world changed subtly: objects could not be found, people were lost, long-dead relatives reappeared, Long Island returned to its former swampy state, complete with the tweeting of birds, the susurrus of reed and wet leaf, and the perfumes of decay. The Astor Hotel appeared, although for a time the ghostly lines of the office building that had disappeared could be seen in the strong light of afternoon. A few flowers began to grow out of cracks in the cement in the West Village, a precursor of the next dream change.

When the change was over, the doctors and psychologists persuaded themselves that it was time to move Ned to a "dream conducive atmosphere." Ned asked for a hotel because he had tried to read a book by that name one Sunday afternoon in Junction.

Although it was easier in the hotel, Ned still could not remember his dreams (even though he was awakened after every one), nor could he affect the dreams of others. And the indeterminate times were becoming worse: too many minds clawed and raked him, gleefully sucked out his energy. When it became intolerable, Ned would fortify himself with Demerol and dream of home.

Ned stared out the window at the crowds below.

The crowds had thinned until there were more white-helmeted policemen than spectators. The spectators were losing faith and drifting away, leaving the policemen with no one to watch but themselves.

These city people were so greedy for something more, that when they found it they tried to tear it apart, Ned thought. Although they wanted to merge together—a primeval urge, tradition and morals and blocks of cement and steel and gray skies choked with dust and ennui assured separation. In desperation, or just for fun, they built and then destroyed, one a rationale for the other.

But Junction-folk were no different, he told himself. He had once thought that New Yorkers were demons that looked like folk, basilisks disguised in human form. Now, as Ned remembered Miss Jenkens, Old Herman, Mister Brownlaw, Stan, Freeglass, Reverend Surface, Sam Sense, his father, Hilda, Sandra, he realized that he belonged to no one nor any particular place, for every day removed him from habit and the past, and his old friends had turned into ghosts. They would be as alien to him now as New Yorkers. I'm truly lost in Hell, he thought.

Weissman stepped out of the bedroom and, pulling his narrow brown necktie under his collar, said, "Come on, Ned. Get away from the Goddamn window and get dressed. These people will be here in a few minutes."

Ned ignored him and thought about Hilda. In the indeterminate periods he dreamed about her jellyfat body and auburn hair and tried to make her real. But something was wrong—he could not give her substance. He tried Sandra. She remained a pleasant memory: a pale chiseled face, a pouting mouth, short-cropped hair, and black fuzz around her large brown nipples.

"Come on, Ned, dammit." Weissman finished tying his necktie and smoothed it against his starched white shirt.

"Alright, alright." Ned turned away from the window and sat down in a tan leather chair. Although he was sweaty and needed a change of clothes, he didn't feel like washing and dressing for company. Since he left the hospital, Ned had taken to wearing flamboyant silk shirts—notably those with colorful Hawaiian patterns—and dungarees. The dungarees reminded him of the coarse trousers he used to wear in Junction. In the last few days everything—smells, sounds, the play of light on a skyscraper—reminded him of Junction. Memory was beginning to color the past and replace it with its own reality. He felt as if people he had once known were reappearing. Everyone he saw seemed to have another aspect, as if they were shadows of people he had known in Junction. Even Weissman reminded Ned of someone: a dog-faced Faubougher he had seen walking the streets of Junction on an election day.

"I'm not going to change," Ned said. "I like this shirt, anyway."

"Well, you'll have to, there's some important people coming up. So take a bath. You smell."

"Screw them," Ned said, guarding himself against a disquieting sensation that something was about to happen. He imagined that he could hear echoes of Weissman's thoughts—Weissman was orderly and lonely; his thoughts were cold slivers cloaked in sadness, an overwhelming sadness.

"What do they want?" Ned asked.

Weissman stretched out on the couch beside the bedroom door, patting his kinky hair in place before he rested his head on the sideboard. "It's something important," he mumbled.

"What's so important?"

But Weissman closed his eyes and his left leg slipped from the couch. He buried his toes in the shag rug. "Something that will happen, like a dream, can't quite. . . ."

"What the Hell's wrong with you?" Ned asked, shaking the policeman's shoulder. If this was the beginning of another dream-change, it wasn't like any of the others, Ned thought. Weissman grunted and smiled as if he had just sighted Heaven. His face softened. By clenching his teeth and sucking in his cheeks, Weissman could tighten his face and give the illusion of alertness and strength. But sleep restored it to its true form. It was as if loose layers of skin were draped over his skull, ready to be pressed into a desired mask at will.

Weissman had always waited until Ned was asleep before he would catnap. And he would never sleep for more than two hours consecutively. At least now Ned could daydream without feeling the pressure of Weissman's gaze on the back of his neck. He could walk freely around the well-provided suite without being spoken to or followed. Or he could try to dream up Sandra or Hilda or even Reverend Surface or Deacon—he wondered if he would ever see Deacon again. And what about the birdbeast? he asked himself. Was it only a dream dreamt in Junction?

Everything around Ned seemed hard and cold, impervious to his thoughts.

Trying to rationalize a sin he was about to commit, Ned started for the bathroom, which was adjacent to the bedroom. And he remembered his father's words: "Onanists will forever fall through the mirrors of Hell."

Ned's father had once told him that Hell could not claim any glass. That's why Satan invented mirrors, which are made out of darkness and can only show up the evil nature of people. There were no mirrors in Junction. It was said that they had all been thrown into Hell where they reflect and magnify sorrow and pain.

But there was a mirror over the black porcelain sink in the bathroom. And all the monsters of Hell were on the other side watching and laughing. The bedroom was even worse: it sported full-length door mirrors and a vanity. Ned could lie on the bed without being seen by monsters on the other side. In the bathroom, at least, he could duck out of sight of the Hellglass.

Yet he had not asked Weissman to have them removed. If he was going to stay here, he would live with mirrors and Hell as God had prescribed. He might even become used to them in time, as one does a nasty relative. He would watch himself sin and grow ugly. He would learn his evil nature. He would tolerate Weissman and the men on the roof. And he would give the monsters behind the mirror an eyeful before Weissman woke up.

Ned looked into the bathroom mirror and saw his father's face. He started backward, felt the vertiginous touch of a dream, tried to escape into the living room; but he was caught. He leaned against the sink for support.

"How do you like it here in the midst of Hell?" Ned's father asked.

"How did you get here?"

"Go to sleep and I'll tell you."

Ned noticed that his father's hairline had receded several inches since he had last seen him. And his aging face seemed weaker, less defined. Perhaps this was not his father, but a creature from Hell, a misdirection.

"Are you my father?"

"Does it matter, son? Go to sleep and I'll explain."

"I'm not tired," Ned said, "and I don't wish to sleep;" but a great lethargy overcame him and, like a sleepwalker, he stepped into the bedroom, sat down on the double bed, and watched his father in the vanity mirror. He struggled against sleep.

"Well," his father said, "lay down and go to sleep."

Ned hesitated, felt he was about to swoon. He prayed it was his father—but if it wasn't, then it was

God's fate—and lay down and held his breath for luck. As he exhaled, he heard his father speak.

"You dreamed that scene in the bathroom, you know. Although events might appear to be causally connected, time can be cut up any way you like. . . ."

"What's *causally*?" Ned asked.

"Just listen," his father replied. "As I was saying, time can be shuffled. Substitute the middle for the end, the end for the middle. It doesn't matter. Your notions of time and space are psychologically conditioned. Time and space have no independent existence; they are, like numbers, concepts born of the human mind. The bathroom scene was hung in the middle of the dream. I reshuffled it so that it would make sense to you. And make you go to sleep."

"But I thought I *was* asleep."

"In a manner of speaking, you were. Different states of consciousness equate to different levels of sleep. At any rate, I simply turned things around. For example, you could easily conceive a child before you were born. And, in fact, you did. Remember Donatello Toth? No, you wouldn't; he died from Parkinson's disease when you were very young."

"Are you my father?" Ned asked.

"No," said the voice, after a pause. "If you like, you can be with him. But eventually you've got to face this, me, if you like. It is a piece that cannot be ignored if all the reasonable alternatives are going to be—or are, or were—experienced."

Ned tried to open his eyes, but he couldn't. A light flickered before him and he dreamed that he was back in the tunnel.

"Who are you?" Ned asked.

"A piece of your future," was the reply. "Would you like to see Donatello Toth?"

"That's crazy," Ned said, mumbling in his fitful sleep, dreaming of desert, stone churches, and souls shedding their flesh—dreaming the future.

"No, it's not. Cause and effect are only pieces that happen to fit together. Consecutive time is a mnemonic device, that's all."

What's a mnemonic device? Ned thought. The voice had lost all its affectations and pomposity. It did not sound like his father and was developing a Brooklyn accent. It rose in register until it sounded like Weissman.

"You know what that is," the voice said. "Push yourself forward, or backward, to wherever the answer lies."

And Ned remembered what a mnemonic device was, although he had never heard of one before.

"You really know everything that has been accomplished through evolution. And, of course, everything that has been lost. So, in a way, you know everything. But you must learn how to look, use your intuition, think laterally, or you will remain amnesic."

"Then what's the end?" Ned asked, feeling lost in his own thoughts.

"What we're doing now. And what we'll do later."

"I don't understand. . . ."

"Just open your eyes." But Ned was afraid he would find himself looking into his own eyes, afraid he would see his own death.

Spread out before Ned was New York City, shimmering in a mantle of smog and mist. It was a dead-gray world of glass and cement, yet Ned could see through, around, and beneath the buildings and streets. An opaque world of walls had suddenly become transparent.

Ned stood upright. "Am I walking in my sleep?"

"Don't worry," the voice said. "Everyone is watching you. You won't fall."

But the city was caught in its own time. Cars and trains and people were caught in mid-movement. Wings outspread, a pigeon hovered between buildings. Ned glanced at an old woman standing with one foot off the ground and a gnarled hand lifted to touch her face. A little boy who had jumped into the air during a temper tantrum was stuck, as if pinned to the background of buildings and wide avenues. The world was sealed in amber; only Ned seemed to be able to move about.

Ned stepped through the crowds, as if making his way around so many natural obstacles. He imagined that the thoughts and emotions of these motionless people were on display like candies at a counter. He was overwhelmed by their tiny sadnesses.

"What do you see?" asked the voice.

"A city of churches," Ned replied. "Everything's transparent. I can see all of God's glass." But it was a melancholy Heaven.

"Look toward the East River."

"It's turned to glass," Ned said.

"What do you see beyond the river?"

"I can't tell," Ned said as he walked through the crystal-clear city. He passed Rockefeller Center, Saint Patrick's Cathedral, and meandered around Saint Bartholomew's Church which had turned into yellow chrysoberyl. The streets were still gray, but Ned could stare through them, see the tracks and trains and subway stations below. The commuters looked like tiny glass figurines placed under a glass topped table. Ned felt that he would fall right through the streets; but he was bolstered by the dream.

"Cross the river," said the voice impatiently.

The distance across Manhattan had been reduced to a thought.

Spread out before Ned was a field scattered with boulders, moss clinging to the interface between rock and soil.

"Keep going."

Ned exhaled through pursed lips, as if he had been struck in the chest. He found himself on the outskirts of Junction. But the town was surrounded by desert, mile upon mile of cracked, parched land and soap-white sand. He could see huts and hovels and the glass church, the highest building in Junction. The ground and stones and sand seemed to be whispering, holding conversation, a dialect he could not yet understand. The wind was a barely audible voice, a melancholy lowing, then an excited whistling.

But Ned fought for control, for a graspable succession of events. He did not allow himself to move randomly. By choosing cause and effect, he forced one event to lead into another and ignored the *psi* handholds that would make him dizzy.

"It doesn't work that way," said the voice. "Let yourself go, think laterally, you can't see with blinders on."

"I can't do it," Ned said, "I don't know how."

"Yes you do," said the voice. "You've done it before. But you're thinking vertically now, using old patterns as your code for thinking and perceiving the world around you. You're digging yourself in deeper into the same narrow hole. Break down the old patterns of thought, combine them into new ones, and those into even newer patterns. Let the process happen to you, overwhelm you. Let loose your intuition."

Ned followed the voice as if it were a path leading through the countries of his mind and out into the world.

As he watched, Junction was buried under new growth.

Large split-level houses sported tiers of windows that overlooked rolling hills and pine forests. Swimming pools filled with blue water and bikinied girls with dark tans (and wealthy men with bald pates and pinky rings) became the private oases of this summer green desert. Sleek cars moved slowly along the picturesque winding roads.

"Call it Goshen," the voice said. "It's the far suburbs. We'll meet here."

"Why?" Ned asked. "Why do you want to meet with me?"

"Not only with you."

"With whom, then?"

"They're on their way. Wake up."

7

"Come on, Ned," Weissman said. "Get away from the Goddamn window and get dressed. Those people will be here in a few minutes."

Ned ignored him and thought about Sandra. In the indeterminate periods he dreamed about her pouting mouth and the black fuzz around her large nipples and tried to make her real. He dreamed that they were in love, shared secrets, talked about eternal things, contemplated children. If anyone had been his friend, it was Sandra—the scatgirl who knew more curses than Portus Park beggars and more philosophy and prayers than the priests in the church. She had let him read all the mildew-stinking books that she kept hidden in the Faubougher Woods.

But something was wrong—he could not give her substance. He tried Hilda. She remained a pleasant memory: a freckled face, jellyfat body that smelled of potatoes, and thick auburn hair. Then he thought of his father and his dream in the mirror. Although he had lost purchase on the dream, he felt that something had awakened within him, and he could see with as many eyes as the birdbeast.

"Come on, Ned, dammit." Weissman finished tying his necktie and smoothed it against his starched white shirt. Although Weissman wore his suits as uniforms, there was always something undone about him, always a loose button, or tucked-in pocket flap, or a patch of bristle on his otherwise smoothly shaven face. They were his own private semaphores, the tiniest signs of discontent.

"Alright, alright." Ned turned from the window. A bath was in order: he was sweaty and his hair smelled sour. But what was wrong with the smell of sweat? he asked himself. It was a good strong stink.

Ned was not in the violet-scented lukewarm tubwater for five minutes before Weissman insisted that he get out and dress. While Ned glued his light brown hair to his scalp with orange pomade, Weissman laid out a conservative blue suit and white shirt on the bed for him. But Ned wore a red and blue flowered shirt with a long white collar and tartan plaid trousers.

There was a knock on the door. Weissman, who had been in telephone and radio communication with the guards and police, placed the receiver on the cradle and walked to the door. Ned stared out the window into the darkness—he was nervous about meeting new people and being in close propinquity with them for any length of time. But the darkness turned the window into a mirror and Ned watched Weissman pat down his cowlick before opening the door. He shivered and remembered his dream of his father. "One should always look *through* a window, not *at* a window," Ned's father had often said. As Ned watched the door open, he added another sin to his list.

He took a long look at the lights of the city and then turned away from the window to greet the guests that entered the room.

"Good evening, Ned," Doctor Kheal said in his usual mumble—his words seemed to roll out without accent or pause. "I hope you've had a pleasant day." Doctor Kheal, a tall, skinny man in his early forties, had light brown hair that was beginning to turn gray and a smooth relaxed face. His green corduroy jacket with brown elbow-patches (the same one Ned remembered seeing at the hospital every day) was frayed at the cuffs and his black trousers had lost their crease long ago. Ned noticed that he needed a shave.

"I'd like you to meet Doctor Ingrid Oolan, who has been waiting quite some time to meet you," Kheal continued. "She's a parapsychologist from Saint John's University." She had long coarse black hair and pale, almost translucent skin. The delicate network of veins was clearly visible on her throat.

"Sandra?" Ned asked, taken aback. "Is it you?"

"My name is Ingrid," she said, smiling.

Is it just chance that she looks like Sandra? Ned asked himself, remembering stuffy, sweaty nights in the Congress Bar and long afternoon conversations. And he remembered the voice inside his head that had said: *You'll see Sandra again. . . .*

But the woman standing before him and smiling had slightly different features than Sandra. Her lips were thin and colorless and her eyes were set a bit too close together, giving her the appearance of always staring. This woman had a feral intensity about her; she radiated purpose and fear. Ned didn't like her—she's doublehanded, he thought—but he felt drawn by her nervous sexuality. He wondered if she, like Sandra, had black fuzz around her nipples. She wasn't wearing a bra, and Ned could see the outline of her nipples on her open collared shirt. Her black hair and dark skirt contrasted with her pale face and white shirt. She was a pen and ink drawing on white paper.

"And this is Doctor Taharahnugi," said Kheal, gesturing with his arm. Taharahnugi, an albino black of medium build, stood beside Ingrid, his pale hand almost touching hers. His pink eyes were buried deeply into his square face, and he wore his kinky white hair long—it framed his face in a bleached halo. Ned guessed he was a sociologist, then reminded himself to stop thinking sideways, "lest cause should be sundered from effect," as his father would probably say.

"And you remember Doctor Ladislas from the hospital"—but Ned had never seen this man. Nicholas Ladislas had a lined, sour face and a shock of white hair that was thinning in the back. He had what was known as "lazy eye," and his heavy lidded eyes never seemed to move. Ned knew that he sometimes wore an eye patch, but that was an affectation. Ned didn't like him, sensed he had an inflated fragile ego, and told himself to stop thinking sideways.

There were too many people in the room, each one filling up space with thoughts and smells. Ned hoped they would leave soon—he was beginning to feel the familiar effects of claustrophobia.

"And here's someone you haven't seen in some time," Kheal said. "Doctor Deacon is a colleague of Miss Oolan."

Ned had not recognized him. He was much thinner than Ned remembered, and his face was drawn, giving him an older appearance. He looks like a cadaver, Ned thought. His large, dark eyes seemed to be sinking into his face. Although his movements were shaky, he handled his cigarette with aplomb and brushed off the ash with his pinky finger. Ned was surprised and happy to see Deacon; it was like meeting an old acquaintance, even if this man had been born of a creature from Hell.

But then he remembered being alone in the tunnel. . . .

"I hope you have found New York interesting, Ned," Deacon said, using one cigarette to light another and then looking around for an ashtray. "It's quite a bit different from Junction." He laughed and choked it off—"I suppose you could consider me a friend from home."

"You left me alone in the tunnel."

"My dream was finished," Deacon said, "and so I must have disappeared from yours."

Am I dreaming now? Ned asked himself, desperately wishing to be back in Junction. But this room was solid in stone.

"You didn't even seem to be afraid," Ned said to Deacon.

"It was a recurrent dream. I'd become used to it—as if I were an actor in a play that had run for a while."

"You look different," Ned said, feeling embarrassed and exposed; he tried to ignore the presence of the others.

"Do I? I don't feel any different."

No doubt he's ill, Ned thought, remembering when Deacon was in Junction and had changed from a bird-beast into a man. Perhaps he has a tumor of the gastrointestinal tract, Ned thought. Or Hodgkin's disease. It was probably Lymphosarcoma. Ned remembered a few of his father's homilies and forced himself to think along previously earmarked paths. He told himself again that he had to stop wandering and side-stepping and thinking laterally.

And he remembered what the voice inside his head had said: "*You really know everything that has been accomplished through evolution. And, of course, every-thing that has been lost . . . But you must learn how to look. . . .*" Ned wanted to close his eyes, did not want to see the ghosts skiffing through the room, or know the thoughts and memories of the people standing around him.

"Well, it all worked out, didn't it?" Deacon said after a pause. "You're finally providing New York with its dreams."

"Everyone's been dreaming each other's dreams for a week," Kheal said. "The dreams ran in a sequence and we've just come to the end of it. I think we have enough information now. We've come to talk to you about your dreams."

"But it's not a week," Ned said. "I only started dreaming today. I can't remember dreaming be-fore. . . ."

"Well, that's news to me," Weissman said, standing awkwardly beside Ned and Ingrid Oolan.

In one vertiginous instant all the threads of familiar conditioned reality were torn apart, and this was not a dream-time. Ned imagined that experienced time was made up of loose chains of interchangeable, self-contained instants. He had fashioned one chain of time; they claimed another. And he was living simultaneously in all the real and alternate pasts, presents, and futures; caught in an infinity of prisons.

"Let's sit down," Kheal said, taking the initiative and motioning Ingrid to the couch near the bedroom door. The others followed. Ned sat down between Ingrid and Kheal, tried to forget everything but the present, closed off his mind to the frightening abyss of information and possibility. Ladislas sat down on a soft chair beside Taharahnugi, who had claimed the antique rocker and was drumming his long fingers on the small end-table, while Deacon pulled one of the high-backed chairs away from the dining table across the room. They were mapping out a tight, defensible niche in the overlarge suite.

Ned let his hand slip from his lap until it touched Ingrid's leg. She tensed for a second, then moved toward Kheal and crossed her legs, showing off blue climbing veins that reached for her knees.

She looks so much like Sandra, Ned thought. You can't escape the moment or break the chain by touching her leg, he told himself, and then frowned as he caught himself thinking of Junction and whorehouses and his mother's delicate face buried in the mountains of Hell. He felt the onset of another dream-time; everything in the room seemed slightly blue and wavery. Weissman brought out drinks for everyone: a sherry for Ingrid and cognac for Kheal, bock beer in tall frosted glasses for Deacon and Ladislas, and soda water for Taharahnugi. Before retiring to the couch at the other end of the room, Weissman served Ned the last bottle of a particular Mexican beer that had a green tinge when held to the light. Ned loved it. Weissman had once tried it and suffered the next few hours with diarrhea.

"Tell us about your dream," Ladislas said, rubbing his eyes as if he would soon go to sleep.

Ingrid stretched her legs out and Kheal nodded to Ned. So Ned told them about the apparition in the mirrors and Donatello Toth (who could not be) and Junction and Goshen, where they all would meet. But memory had changed the landscape of his past, colored it, changed its shapes; images were sized like so many photographs to form a more personal, comprehensible collage.

The visitors listened (although Ingrid seemed to be daydreaming and Ladislas in a trance), then asked Ned questions and argued amongst themselves. The dream-time was upon them; now dreams and visions would pull apart the natural laws of the world. Ned tried to remain alert, but his head kept lolling forward, dipping into sleep. In his dreams the words would take on a life of their own. They became animated film characters running through their own pathos of life and death. As he dreamed, he fashioned new experiences, new chains. . . .

And he would awaken with a start, feeling fuzzy and warm, seeing after-images of Junction and familiar faces and desert places, slightly shocked to find himself in this room of things and people, only to dream again. . . .

"Although our dreams were different than the boy's," Ladislas was saying as he scratched at the corner of his eye, "we all received the same directive to go to Goshen, just as we dreamed that we would meet together here. . . ."

Although Ned fought to stay awake, he fell asleep again and dreamed of Ingrid's blue-veined legs. Words and letters acquired form and personality and passed before him. It was strange, he thought, that the others did not recognize this as another indeterminate period. Yet the presence of other people did not bother him as much as it had in the past, although he could still feel the weight of the guards pacing on the roof.

He took a deep breath and allowed himself to drift freely through the unformed potential, dimly realizing that he was holding the stuff of the room together. He glimpsed other possibilities, alternate worlds just a gesture away, worlds where he was Kheal or Taharahnugi, where he had never left Junction, never met the birdbeast nor heard voices inside his head, never dreamed for anyone but himself, never had children before he was born.

And he discovered that walls and doors and ceilings could just as easily become trees and snow and gray skies. The world was not yet solid; objects could be easily shaped, or created out of wild thought.

So trees and snow could easily be transformed into sand and stone. It only required the alchemy of thought.

Ned tried to dream of Junction, but felt himself caught—as if in another's dream.

Perhaps someone was dreaming them all. . . .

He dreamed he was lying in desert sand. His crotch itched. A scorpion was making its way towards his extended arm, its feelers touching the ground, sensing and feeling movement that was miles away. Ned noticed that it was carrying five young scorpions on its back; they would soon be mature enough to drop from their mother's back and forage on their own. The scorpion would crawl a few inches, curl up and wiggle its pincers, clean them with its lobster legs.

Ned could hear the creature whispering to him, but its comments were too simple to be understood. Ned found that his arm was pointed toward a church carved out of the soft, porous tuff of a stone cliff. He knew that he was seeing through the stone into its holy insides. He glimpsed the faded, stylized portrait of the Emperor Genetos in the narthex entrance hall and the chapels to the east and the frescoed ceiling domes. He remembered that around the Ninth Century in Cappadocia, a province in central Turkey monks had whittled God's stone into this church, cutting into the rock from above to reveal a church they would create inside.

From the outside, the towers, cones, hills, and walls of rock were overpowering in their monochromatic contrast of light and dark. They hid hundreds of God's monasteries and churches. Jutting into a pale, cloudless sky, they stood as a true synthesis of man's way and nature's display. Although Ned felt life all around him, he was certain that it wasn't of a human form.

"Do you want another beer, Ned?" Weissman asked. "You'll have to take bock, we're out of the Mexican stuff."

Ned shook his head and tried to retrace the conversation. The dream-change was over, the world solid once again: Ned felt alert and restless, confused about his dream. Ingrid was still sitting beside him, her legs crossed, right hand just touching Ned's leg. Ned listened.

". . . But I can't believe that an alien presence is responsible for the breakdown of our known continuum and laws, as Ladislas suggests," Taharahnugi said. When he wasn't talking, he would drum his fingers on the end-table.

"I think the answers might as easily lie within ourselves," Kheal said. "Everyone will agree, I think, that this is, at least in part, a *psi* phenomenon."

"Yes, I agree," Ingrid said. "The fact that we all dreamed of that desert church is indicative of *psi* phenomena. But synchronous dreams are not unknown in psychoanalysis. It is not uncommon for a patient to have precognitive dreams that penetrate into the analyst's private life. Emilio Servadio, an Italian psychoanalyst, conjectured that telepathy was a secondary line of communication. When a patient is so frustrated that he cannot communicate in the traditional ways, he might resort to more primitive means such as dreams."

"But we are not dealing with the situation of a patient dreaming about his doctor," Kheal said. "Everyone in New York is dreaming about Ned, or dreaming his dreams."

"And we don't even know what the rest of the world is doing," said Taharahnugi. "It's as if *we* are the world, trapped within the city, able to go on as if nothing was wrong, and yet unable to communicate with the outside."

"That's not entirely true," Deacon said, as he snuffed out a cigarette and lit another. "In a very real sense nothing has changed. We must have communication with the rest of the world or commerce would fail, we would have no food, no electricity, no medicine, and so on. No, there's a real world out there and we interact with it constantly. We just don't remember, as we don't remember the dreams we live through the night."

"As I was saying"—Ingrid looked at Deacon and Kheal—"about the telepathic relationship between patient and analyst. In the late forties, when the excitement of *psi* phenomena was at its height among psychoanalysts, there occurred an interweaving of patients' dreams. In fact, it was known as 'telepathic contagion,' a situation not unlike our own."

"Then," said Ladislas with a smile that was more a frown, "you would have us all be the patients and Ned the doctor."

Ingrid blushed and continued. "And the religious symbolism of our dreams corresponds with Ned's beliefs. In fact, the paintings on the walls of the church we dreamed about looked very much like the sketches Ned had done for Doctor Court several days after he arrived at the hotel. Ned is quite talented; they could easily be dream paintings." She pressed her hand against Ned's leg as if she was familiar with his body, had touched him many times and, in turn, had been touched. This was a new Ingrid, a softer woman, an old lover. She was more at ease, Ned thought. More like Sandra. Perhaps she was turning into Sandra. He wondered what far-reaching changes had been wrought by this last indeterminate period.

"And all the figures Ned imagined in the Rorschach tests had white haloes," Kheal said.

"I made them up," Ned said. "I didn't really see them in the ink splotch; I drew them in myself."

"Well, that's what you do with that kind of test," Ingrid said, patting his hand.

"No, it's different," Ned said, consciously resting his knee against her leg. "All the other stuff I really saw"—but I've dreamed myself through time again, he thought; turned it inside out, changed lies into truth like a politician. And they imagined that they can test for reality. Another dream. He felt as if he was thinking with other minds and told himself to stop looking into the abyss; but words were turning in his mind like dustmotes in clear light.

"But how could Ned know anything about the place we've been dreaming about?" Ladislas asked, resting his head on the back of his chair and staring at the wall from under half-closed eyelids as if sleep was almost upon him. "Goreme is in Turkey."

"I just dream it," Ned said.

"Well, why couldn't he dream about Goreme?" asked Kheal.

"Because Junction is isolated, as we are," Ladislas said. "Deacon's seen it, or dreamed he did. It's surrounded by chaos, their conception of Hell. And who knows. . . ."

"Goreme would have been in a library book," Ingrid said. "And Ned read everything he could find."

"Yes," Ladislas said, sitting up, "and he remembers all the titles he read, which is a considerable amount. That much we know. He's very suggestible, a perfect subject for hypnosis. He has a photographic memory, yet he did not remember anything that could even remotely tie in with Goreme. It seems that Junction's holy estate had everything relating to geography and world history destroyed, except for a few fractured biblical accounts. Ned could not dream an exact duplicate of Goreme, detail by detail, by chance."

"Not chance," Ingrid said. "Synchronicity."

"Ach," Taharahnugi said disgustedly; he tapped his fingers on the table loudly, as if to distract everyone.

"Yes, he certainly could dream Goreme, just as I dreamed Junction," Deacon said. He sounded as if he was out of breath. "As the world becomes more indeterminate, our arbitrary distinctions of time must break down. They seem to work here only part of the time. We have also experienced the breakdown of certain spatial relationships. But what we simultaneously experience as space does not necessarily have to correspond with real space. We can overlay our experienced space onto its equivalent geometer's space and then merge any overlaps. Just as in aerial photography, the overlaps insure reliable mapping. But in aerial photography, when we have blank spaces, we have to use our imagination to fill in the gaps. That is our only available means of connection. Mankind is, and has always been split in time and space. It is through Ned that we have established contact with another community beyond our time. . . ."

"Aren't you forgetting about yourself?" Kheal asked. "You initiated the contact, remember that."

"And that contact was possible because time is not a straight line. It is made up of loops, or may be a loop itself. The only way I could reach Ned was by imagining the necessary overlap into the future, that's how I stepped into a possible future. The same holds true for the past, as witnessed by Ned's journey here."

"What, then, do you think will happen when all the overlaps merge, if they ever do?" asked Ladislas.

"I don't know," said Deacon, "but I think we will soon find out."

"Bullshit," Taharahnugi said. He stopped drumming on the table.

Ingrid's hand was actively pressing Ned's leg. Could I have dreamed this to happen before? Ned asked himself as he put his arm around Ingrid, resting his hand on her shoulder. He felt as if he was sitting with Sandra, and his thoughts wandered. *He imagined two trains racing down parallel tracks, two great clocks synchronously ticking, dreams inside dreams, and felt himself caught in a loop, reliving an alternate present that was a distorted reflection of his remembered past. As Ned breathed, imaginary clocks ticked, trains raced, dreams unraveled like twine; he was completely lost in the mirrors of time.*

"No, I don't think it's bullshit," Kheal said. "Deacon did not exactly imagine his way to Junction. He dreamed it. And the way things are now, that's just as real."

"Oh," Ladislas said. "Then you're dreaming me and everything else, and I'm dreaming you and everything else so cleverly that our dreams match. I think Shrödinger said something like that, didn't he?"

"I didn't mean that, but it's possible. An interesting solution."

"Then," Ladislas continued, "there might be an integrating force drawing us to Junction, dreaming us all."

"Your alien?" Kheal asked.

"Hooray," said Ned, annoyed that everyone had either patronized him or ignored him, as if he were a child. He glanced at Taharahnugi and smiled. "Dreaming works as good as anything else. I'm dreaming that there's a hole in Heaven, how's that?" he said, thinking of Hell's black sun. "How do you think I manage to ogle Ingrid, if not by fooling around with this stuff of chance and change?" With that, he tweaked Ingrid's breast—and was immediately embarrassed. For an instant he had dreamed he was with Sandra, and he had lapsed into a former self, a past guise. It was as if the past had sucked away his thoughts, leaving only a wraith that used to stare into the abyss of Hell and live in a ghostland of whorehouses. Ned had changed; he was ashamed of what he was, and afraid of what he might become.

"That's all been set up," Ingrid said, ignoring Ned's gaucherie. "We've all been dreaming about it for a week. All those moves—and everything you've said and thought—have already been plotted. The stuff of chance and change you talk about has already been determined . . . and dreamed."

"That's not true," Ned said.

It can't be true, he told himself.

"And we've been dreaming of going on a trip to Goshen—Goreme," Deacon said. "Perhaps we'll find some answers there."

"I'm sure we will," Ingrid said, giving Ned a curiously knowing look.

"Can we all be ready by tomorrow morning?" asked Kheal.

Ned saw the end of the dream; but they had dreamed different endings, so Ned played along. He was becoming impatient for them to leave. He felt the first temple-stabbings of a migraine. Soon, imaginary hands would apply themselves to the task of crushing his skull.

"All right," Kheal said, "then I guess that's about it."

Ingrid acted as hostess and escorted the others to the door, laughing and promising to be ready in the morning.

"Well, are you coming?" she asked Ned as she

stepped into the bedroom which was catercorner to the door leading into the hallway.

Ned followed out of curiosity, leaving Weissman in the living room to happily read his *New York Times* (last week's) and smoke hand-rolled Cuban cigars, a commodity that had suddenly appeared on the market after the last change.

Rationalizing his uncountable sins, Ned watched Ingrid in the full-length mirror. Beautiful Ingrid, this lovely alternate Sandra. He imagined all the hollows in her body where he could rest his face, all the wet spots, all the fleshy handholds he could squeeze as he came. For a few moments he could end his isolation. But he could also turn around and walk out, thus confounding their dreams.

"All we have to do is do it," she said as she combed her long black hair, not a hint of warmth in her voice. "It's all been set up, we just follow along."

"Well," Ned said, "you do have a choice. You don't have to be a slave to your dreams. Are you so sure of them?"

"I've made my choice. I agreed to it." She stared at herself in the mirror, cocked her head to the side as if she were watching a stranger, and unbuttoned her blouse.

"Why are you doing this?"

"Because there's no other way to get to the end; if this sequence falls apart, another will begin."

"If you break the dream, you can make your own time," Ned said.

"It's already been fixed."

"Well, it's not fixed for me," Ned said as he took a step toward the door—it was an easy thing to do, for he would rather commit the sin of Onan than love this cold fish.

As she took off her blouse, exposing her breasts fed by visible arteries, she said, "Wait a moment, Ned. Yes, they do have hair around the nipples. If I am

Sandra, we cement past to present, make a bridge to the future."

"You're not Sandra," Ned said.

"But I can be," she said.

And Ned remembered living through this dream, remembered Sandra just as she was now, the same woman standing before him.

Ned felt himself caught in a loop.

And a smile of even white teeth drew him back into the room.

8

The crowds filled the street and backed up against the windows of the plush Fifth Avenue shops. Fleeing from their dreams, they chanted and shouted and sang songs. They co-opted policemen, gray ladies with hidden clubs and scissors, and pompadoured boys to help them break through the many weak points of the police lines. Secretaries in colored scarfs and office boys sporting sideburns and Hawaiian shirts threw handfuls of confetti from skyscraper windows. Sparkles and streamers spun and danced their way to the glass-strewn streets below. They would soon be swallowed up by sweeping machines intent on restoring the world to a sober gray. But just now the world belonged to the crowds, to thousands of nameless individuals drowning themselves in an orgy of dreams. Time had been choreographed. Dreams and people whirled like dervishes.

The crowds sighed like a great fantastical beast drawing breath, readying itself for some glorious battle. It was certainly a monster made of eyes, moving in the direction of its constantly changing face.

Ned waved to the crowds from the back seat of an armored black Cadillac limousine. He was seeing through the haze of a migraine. So many people, he thought; they were in control right now, but for how long?

He sat between Weissman and Bunker, a young detective with a pockmarked face and a swollen lower lip. Bunker's aloof style and quiet manners reminded Ned of the "cool fifties." Lately, Ned found it easier to remember details of a past he had never experienced. Past and future seemed to be contained in present memory.

The car moved east in a cavalcade of cars, tanks, and trucks along Forty-fourth Street, past banks (*Banker's Trust* to his right, *Chase Manhattan* to his left) that reminded Ned of the holy church of Junction and the Congress Bar, past restaurants such as *The Golden Lion, The Blue Ribbon, Sa Crepe, La Gargouille,* past brightly colored awnings and lettered windows, past the rumdum bars, the pubs, the movie-houses playing *Angel's Last Tango* and *Body Fever,* the liquor stores, photo shops, billboards, and hotels. Ned thought that *The Biltmore* must be a church with vaulting windows and metal-cage balconies. Even with the *crackcrack* of rifles and the explosions of tear-gas bombs, Ned remembered Junction on prayer days when the church and Congress Bar were filled. He remembered deserted cobble streets, Sandra leaning out her window-hole, and the yellow glow of holy candles in the church windows.

"Sit back in the seat," Weissman said. His voice was gravelly, as if he had awakened from a sound sleep to find himself in the midst of a mob.

Ned settled back into the cushioned seat, but he felt a rage building, a hatred toward Weissman, although he regretted it. Whenever he was given an order, he could feel his glands open up; all his life it had been building inside him, pain atop pain, until he felt he would burst with anger, murder a man for a penny theft. But Ned liked Weissman, knew his moods, guises, fears, and small hopes.

"How far do we have to go?" Ned asked.

"Just till the end of this street, to the Pan Am Building."

Ned had to have a fix on what was happening; he

began to feel the combined weight of the crowds in the street, and experienced vertigo. I'm not ready for a change-time, he thought as he sat up to watch a girl climb onto the hood of the car. Facing the windshield, she straddled the silver hood ornament. Long blond hair covered her shoulders and part of her thin face. She wore a loose dress, and Ned could see her tiny breasts jiggle with each movement of her arms. What does she want? Ned thought, and he was frightened again.

The driver motioned to her, then turned around to take a quick look through the rear window. His face was smooth and his brown hair was clipped short, giving his head a squared-off appearance.

"How the Hell did she get up there?" Weissman asked. Bunker, of course, would not answer. He pleated the fabric of his trousers and sucked in his cheeks.

"Ned. Ned. Get out of bed," she screamed as she pounded on the windshield with red fists. Two policemen with red armbands pulled her off the hood and were swallowed by the crowd.

Ned thought he heard her scream, "Ned. Ned. I want to love you before you're dead." He looked around at the crowds he passed. Faces focused for an instant, each one, somehow familiar. It was as if he was staring at Junction folk, at friends, cousins, and Fauboughers. Everyone was shouting with the girl's voice, singing her songs.

"Ned. Ned. Ned. We want to love you."

"Before you're dead."

"Dead Ned."

Boys with painted faces sang contralto. Children waved handkerchiefs. Mothers held up babies. Someone thudded against the car and rolled under the tires, giving himself for his faith. Ned watched his proselytes disrobe as he passed. A wave of his hand and new faces appeared out of a pastel fog of confetti.

"Christ is here and Ned is his prophet," shouted a boy in a white robe who bore a marked resemblance to Simon, the featherwaker's son. He prostrated himself in the road. Ned felt the car lurch as it crushed the boy's chest.

"Why didn't the police stop him?" Ned shouted. Could Junction be growing in New York City? he thought wildly. Am I dreaming people out of Junction?

The crowd was singing. A policeman with his cap cocked over his left eye gave Ned the finger. A blond girl cupped her breasts for him. Onanists lined the street.

> Thou shalt not have leave,
> Thou shalt not fly to the wood.
> Thou shalt not escape me,
> Nor go away from me.
> Sit very still,
> Wait God's will!

And the dream-time began. Ned could not stop it, nor see the end; all he could do was hope to ride it through.

Once again the world seemed to shift slightly into the blue.

Ned prayed. He felt a familiar claustrophobia. His head throbbed. Thousands of people watching him. Threatening to crush him inside the soft interior of the car. The pressure of eyes. Sharp knives of thought. And as the world was destroyed and reborn a thousand times in an instant, Ned imagined all the splittings of the world, the alternate pasts, the might-have-beens, distant presents all the equally real worlds of the future. He sensed that time was a tree constantly growing new branches, new presents, pasts, and futures.

He fled from one dream, only to be caught in another.

He felt tied to something greater than himself, a neutral thing without voice, a being that placed ideas and thoughts and memories in his head as if they were objects.

"I can't stand it any longer," he said to Weissman as he pressed against his temples with the palms of his hands: his headache was becoming unbearable.

A rock bounced off the unbreakable windshield. A pistol was fired twice. Screams, laughter, and more confetti snow fell for the hero. Ned sat up straight in the car, braced himself, played his role in the hope that he might retain some control over the moment, and waved with an open hand, fingers aflutter. A perfumed silk handkerchief would complete the tableau, he thought as words and ideas lit his mind.

He felt something unseen pushing—or pulling—him.

He was thinking laterally, seeing as if with all the eyes of the birdbeast. He felt that trouble was imminent; but he could not find the end of this dream.

"Alright, Ned," Weissman said. "That's enough. Stop waving. I'm tried of your hand fluttering in front of my face."

"But that's what they want," Ned said.

"I don't care."

Ned stopped waving and the crowds pushed past the police lines to converge on the car. They beat their fists against the windows, slashed the tires, crawled over the hood, and some were crushed as the car slowed to a halt. Screaming for Ned and God and a new order, they rocked the car, picked it up and dropped it, then picked it up again. Ned was thrown against Weissman, who was swearing with his best Brooklyn accent. Regaining his balance, Ned readied himself for the next shock.

And he screamed as he saw through the dream.

"This wasn't in the dreams," Weissman shouted, speaking to no one in particular, shouting at the window. "The streets were cleared. Where's the police line? This is the wrong dream."

The crowd paused, like a weightlifter slowly inhaling and curling stiff fingers around a steel bar, and flexed its muscles by throwing the car on its side.

"Sonofabitch," Weissman screamed, as Ned and Bunker squeezed him against the door. Ned banged his knee on the floorboard trying to move out of Bunker's way. In that instant Ned realized that *he* had changed the dream. The observer affected the outcome. Everything was either/or. Life or death. Reality decided by the onlooker. Every thought split the world; every movement carried the mover into another present—another world. But Ned was still trapped, for he sensed a force pulling and pushing him, a being that was spread across all of Ned's possible pasts, presents, and futures.

"*. . . if one mind is providing continuity. . . .*"

"No," Ned shouted. "I would not change it like this." He tried to reach whatever it was in the future that was directing his dreams and his destiny.

The window burst. Shards of green-tinged glass were followed by long fingers and fists. Bunker fired several shots, and a skinny girl fell, or was pushed, through the window. She smelled of strong perfume, urine, and sweat.

"Stop it," Ned shouted. "Don't fire."

As Bunker pushed the girl out of his way, a man in a green suit crawled through the window and grabbed his arm. "Be with us, Ned," said the man, slurring his words as if he were drunk or dreaming. "We're all thinking together, dream with *us.*"

"Get out of the way, Ned," Weissman said, pointing his pistol at the man in the suit.

"Don't fire," Ned said. Sensing another change, he

thought of the dream-time as an ocean that could only be felt, and another wave was breaking over the world.

The girl beside him moaned and whispered, "Dream with us." Her arm flopped behind her head which was resting against Ned's knee.

"Mother of God," Bunker screamed as he was pulled out of the car by his hair.

Weissman fired into the window opening, but there were more people than bullets. He shot an old man and two young girls; they thudded against the car and were replaced by a middle-aged woman and several boys fighting for space. Arms reached into the car as if searching for something lost in a dark cubby.

Ned screamed, feeling the pain of those near-by; he was buried, and every atom of every body seemed to be pressing against him. He tried to push through the dream-time, alter the stuff of change and chance, but he was a participant and could not see the outcome. If the indeterminate period was not soon over, he would strangle on the crowd's thoughts—or it would strangle him with strong hands and love.

"God is the mother of Ned," whispered the girl lying beside him. Her left eye fell open.

"Get Ned," screamed the crowd.

Weissman pulled Ned under him, straddled his head with meaty legs, protected him with his muscular body. Another wall of flesh, Ned thought, repelled by the proximity of so much steaming life. Let me alone. He thought he could still hear Bunker's screams. In his mind's eye he watched an old lady pinch Bunker's cheeks. Then, with a howl, she stuck her fingers into his eyes, and he was swallowed by the crowd, the thousand-headed dreaming beast.

"We love you, Ned. We love you, we love you, weloveyou," the crowd screamed with one voice.

The beast has found its tongue, Ned thought, searching his mind for a place to hide.

Weissman screamed as his ear was torn off. He was pommeled, strangled. . . .

Ned fought, but to no avail; he could not fight an ocean, he could not control the dream.

"Save the world for Ned."

"God is the mother of Ned."

"NedNedNednednednednednednedned."

And a dissenting voice: "Fuck you."

Ned prayed for the world to freeze into a familiar reality, but everything was in flux. There could be no place to hide. His world had become luminous and as soft as a dripping candle; even the hard shiny tufted upholstery seemed to give way to the touch. He was aware of the exploding CS and CN tear-gas grenades; but it took such a long time for a second to pass, long enough for him to glance out the window at the buildings that were haloed, as if charged with the very air. A fog machine belched HC smoke. Cannisters of Nausea gas and Blister gas exploded into the crowd. But the crowds were, for a long instant, unaffected; cause was once removed from effect.

Ned felt the slowtime as a peaceful reprieve. The shouting and bullets and acrid smells and heat were unreal, made less effective by slow-motion.

Then a propellant cannister of mace was shot into the car by a giggling policeman.

The policeman was quickly replaced, thrown underfoot by jeering street-boys and a very fat, red-faced girl; but not before the cannister exploded, filling the car with smoke. Ned choked, still remembering the pungent odor of Weissman's crotch. Reality had been loosened like knots on a string. He could gag on the smoke or dream himself into another present, another world, another crowd.

But he was trapped; his dreams were as fixed as the stars.

Ned coughed and arms reached into the car to pull him out. Don't fight it, he thought. He was passed among the crowd, as he had been when he was crowned president in Junction. He was worshipped and beaten, carried along like a gnat atop a great stalking beast.

He smelled the rubber of a gas mask being fitted over his face. He gagged and remembered the subway station, its noises and people with their pushing arms and sweat-clogged clothes.

He remembered Weissman, lying dead on the car-seat, his arm around the dead girl as if they were hiding together, locked in love.

"Don't kill Ned," shouted the crowd. "Love him. God is his mother. Mother of God."

The police were a wall around Ned.

Ned felt the dream-time suddenly over, but imperceptibly another began. . . .

He listened to the shots being fired and dreamed that the universe was a cell undergoing mitosis, constantly splitting into new fissioning universes. He imagined that the world was being continually created; every interaction, every thought and coupling created a new world. He remembered thoughts that were not his own, dreamed other people's dreams; and a voice spoke through his dreams, the selfsame voice that whispered to him as he made his way through the dream-fashioned tunnel from Junction to New York.

He dreamed that the voice was his own.

His thoughts roiled like smoke: You remember. You just died in the car, died with your face in Weissman's crotch. And the girl lived, had a child and named him Ned. *All the possibilities exist, all the worlds are possible, even the impossible worlds where the sun is black and grass is fire, worlds where we die before we're born, where children give birth to their parents, where stones talk and ghosts gather. A quantum transition occurring on the farthest star splinters our world, smashes it into uncountable copies, splits us into as many doppelgängers—a billion Neds, all breathing*

*and thinking, unaware of their myriad reflections; and
a billion more dying by all the hands of God.*

Ned screamed as everything went white around
him.

"Leave me alone," he shouted at the police. One of
the policemen, who was about Ned's size and build,
looked at him quizzically. The streets were almost
empty, as if it were after dark in a city under curfew.
The Cadillac limousine was parked. The driver sat in
the car and watched Ned enter the Pan American
Building.

Although the policemen provided cover for Ned,
Weissman (followed by Bunker) led the way under
fluorescent lights, past modern wall-paintings of
black, white, and red stripes, through the marbled
lobby, up the escalators flanked by stairs to the elevator. A sign over the elevator read:

**COPTER CLUB 57th FLOOR
HELIPORT CLOSED**

"Well, Ned, are you coming?" Weissman asked as he
stood in the elevator.

Part Three

GOREME

9

The elevator doors opened and Ned found himself on the roof of the building. He was relieved to find himself in this topographical dream of empty streets and tall buildings and safety; but his heart was still pounding like a fist in his chest. This is real, he told himself, trying to ignore his memories of the crowds in the streets.

"The crowds were just as real . . ." whispered a voice inside his head.

But he was safe now; the world was solid, the indeterminate period over. Standing on this concrete roof, he could see the spires of the city. Southeast was the Chrysler Building, the United Nations, the East Side Airlines Terminal; southwest was the Empire State Building, Pennsylvania Station, and in the hazy distance, looming large over the city like glass tombstones, were the World Trade Towers. The sky was gray and polluted by city fumes, as if a cement lid had been erected high over the city to keep out color and contain the smog. As Ned looked at the buildings around him, he could not help thinking that the city was deserted, that every last citizen except those huddling together on this roof had disappeared through the gates of another dream—a dream in which crowds were shouting for Ned's love and opportune death. The clarity and fullness of Ned's memory overshadowed the prosaic immediate reality of wind and sky and buildings.

Ned experienced vertigo just by remembering the crowds overturning the car. He concentrated on the here-and-now, submerged himself in its sights, smells, and sounds, and escaped from the past; for an instant he was lost in the present.

The heliport was smaller than he expected. It was merely a perch for a bird, he thought, staring at the helicopter before him. The copter was turbine-powered, a commercial version of the U.S. Army YHC–1. Although it was ungainly on the ground, (How could such a pregnant fuselage be supported by those frail rotor arms?) Ned thought it was beautiful. Its six tiny portholes were like coins made of glass. And the ship was white, the color of Heaven and virtue. But would the air in Heaven hold it up? Ned asked himself, hoping that God would provide an answer. The gray sky, filled with pollutants, was surely heavy enough to hold the ship. But Heaven was clear as blown glass and evanescent as a snowflake.

But he didn't have to worry yet: he was still a safe distance from Heaven.

"Come on, Ned," Weissman said.

"Another second," Ned said.

"There is no time. Everyone else has already boarded, and they're waiting for us." Weissman firmly held Ned's arm and walked him across the landing roof.

The pilot, dressed in a brown suit with an open shirt, hurried them into the copter. Ingrid waved as Ned entered, and he sat down beside her. Weissman took a seat beside Ladislas, opposite Ned. Ladislas looked nervous. Kheal and Taharahnugi were seated together. Deacon sat alone, three seats separating him from the others. Deacon smiled and nodded to Ned, then lowered his head as if to go back to sleep. Ned thought that Deacon had seemed most alive when he was in Junction.

"How are you, Ned? Aren't you a bit frightened?"

Ingrid asked in a condescending tone. "I certainly am."

Although Ned was drag-tired and battle-shocked, he could feel a tiny coal of fear burning inside him. He nodded his head and touched her leg as a gesture of friendship; he was curious to see her reaction since they had made love last night. He remembered her breathing sharply through clenched teeth, turning her head from side to side as if she were a trapped animal trying to pull away from its pinions. She had looked beautiful then, even fragile. For a few seconds Ned had even thought he was back in his room in the Congress, screwing on the sweat-soaked floor mats. Ingrid had become Sandra; the dream sequence was completed. But she had left his bed at dawn. He had tried to talk with her as he used to do with Sandra, but she ignored him, as if she had slept alone in her own bed and was just getting up, as she did every day, to make her morning ablution and go to work.

She crossed her legs and huddled close to the window. Ned rested his hand awkwardly on her lap, deciding what to do next. Even this was contact with someone else, he thought. But her walls were up; Ned imagined that everyone else was trapped inside battlements of fear, just as he was.

"I wanted to have a chance to talk with you," Ingrid said, moving slightly closer to him, glancing at his hand which was now resting between them like a pink bug. "I've been very interested in your dreams—the ones you didn't share with the rest of us."

"What makes you think I've had any such dreams?" Ned asked, wondering how he could have dreamed that this woman was Sandra.

"I think you have."

"Why would you want to know?"

"Because I feel that they might be a key to this puzzle."

Ned searched into the future, then lapsed into the past—he had stopped worrying about sidestepping into a past he had not experienced; he wandered into possible pasts, presents, and futures for diversion or information. But he was still trapped; for although his prison seemed infinite, the very rooms he wished to enter were locked.

"My dreams are not important," Ned said. "They're only distortions of my fears and have nothing to do with this trip."

"Well, why don't you let me be the judge of that?"

Ned leaned toward her and whispered, "Why did you leave so early? I was awake, but you ignored me. Why?"

"What are you talking about?" Ingrid asked, stiffening, afraid, as if she knew what was to come next.

"You could have stayed longer, we could have talked, tried to prolong the closeness, maybe made love again. . . ."

"I beg your pardon. I don't know what you're insinuating, and I don't like the way you're talking to me, I'm not one of your Junction sluts. You've been dreaming too much."

Yes, I've been dreaming, Ned thought, and that coupling created a billion new worlds, countless pasts, presents, and futures. "You seemed to enjoy my dreams, and I didn't dream this," he said, touching her breast. He could feel the padding of her brassiere. "It's all been set up. We just follow along. Remember?"

She bit her lip and slapped him squarely on the mouth with her open hand. "You awkward, boorish, sonofabitch," she said, adjusting her bra.

Bitch, Ned thought. He felt the blood rushing to his face and wanted to strike back. But it wasn't her fault. She was blind, just as he was plagued with sight. Did she have any inkling that they had made love last night in his hotel room? That was before the dream-change when the crowds tipped over the car. That was the real world and this the shadow.

Perhaps both were shadows. . . .

A "Fasten Your Seatbelt, No Smoking" sign blinked on over the aisle and the pilot checked everyone to make sure the seatbelts were fastened tightly. As the pilot walked to the forward compartment, Ned noticed that he had a slight limp. He resembled one of the Fauboughers that had followed Simon into Hell.

Then the engines started. Ned listened to the rotors cutting the air with a whooshing sound, like a scythe cutting grass. Ned liked the rhythm and followed it as it gained momentum. As the helicopter lifted, Ned leaned his head back against the seat rest and closed his eyes. He let himself be sucked into the machinery of God, concentrated on the whirring of cogs and blades. But even with his eyes closed he could see Taharahnugi's smiling face and Kheal's close beside it. Ned dreaded another long dream-time, but it passed quickly and he awakened with a start.

"Sorry," he said to Ingrid after jarring her elbow. She nodded, gave him a wan smile, and returned her stare to the porthole.

They were flying over an urban area. Gray buildings jutted into a gray sky, reaching for, but never skewing, the wafer clouds that drifted by. The clouds insulated the city, but could provide little protection from the unformed potential that was engulfing previous reality.

In another future, Ned thought, New York would be only a part of the Bos-Wash Corridor, one of the pincers of urban drift. But that was not for this future. Soon, he expected to see Tarrytown in the distance and the first mimicries of open country. But Ned distrusted the calm open sky, distrusted the security of fleecy clouds that looked like featherpillows. He dreamed that he was falling across the sky and pushing himself through feathery clouds. The sky was paradise; the clouds were God's thoughts. And Ned felt that something was awry.

He turned his gaze from the porthole and leaned toward the aisle, away from Ingrid's tightly laid out psychological space.

"Well, then what do you believe?" Kheal asked Taharahnugi. Ladislas leaned forward in his seat and looked very interested.

"I believe in 'Dreamin,'" said Taharahnugi sarcastically. "That's the aborigines' word for the dream-time of the primordial when the Earth Mother Goddess and the Rainbow Serpent were born out of dream-stuff. After the Rainbow Serpent created The Road, the Earth Mother dreamed the world around it. Does that satisfy your need to know?" He smiled and stared at the ceiling.

Ladislas shook his head and muttered to himself, but Deacon only smiled and said, "That's very interesting. Perhaps the Rainbow Serpent symbolizes time and the Earth Mother Goddess space. Then your aborigines' dream-time might be something like a collective unconscious where past, present, and future exist at the same time as possibilities. We are not so removed, after all."

Taharahnugi chuckled and folded his large hands on his lap. "And to continue the analogy, we have been moving along The Road since the primordial dream-time when events and processes occurred in nonlinear fashion. But we're all moving at the same pace, so fathers will always remain older than their sons; and we all wear blinders, or did, so we see nothing but The Road. We're blind to the background of time and space. And, of course, we all walk backwards; that's why we remember the past and are dumb to the future."

"Perhaps we've left The Road," Kheal said.

"Of that I'm sure," replied Taharahnugi.

Although Taharahnugi had told the story as a joke, Ned was certain that he believed it. The substance of the analogy rang true, and Ned imagined that Taharahnugi drew his strength from a hidden past, a dream-time that boiled into the present. He was wary of this man who contained the Rainbow Serpent's dreams of time.

"Are you still interested in my private dreams?" Ned asked Ingrid who was still staring out the window, seemingly oblivious to the banter. Everyone was nervous, trying to fill the empty spaces with words, any words, just so the heavy silence of Heaven could be swept away. The sky seemed to be reaching into the copter, swallowing words and thoughts, a baby-blue manifestation of entropy—and Ned remembered the silence of Hell.

"Yes, I'm interested," Ingrid said, turning toward him with a smile, the professional woman in a blue suede suit.

"All right," Ned said. "I had a dream that when I left the hotel the streets were mobbed. Police lines couldn't contain the crowds. It seemed that the crowds had become one person with a thousand voices shouting for blood. I dreamed they stormed the car and killed Weissman. Then I remember being pulled out of the car." As Ned spoke, he could feel the closeness of that world, that dream. He filled in the details for Ingrid: screams, faces, bombs, smoke, his own thoughts, Weissman lying dead on the carseat with his arm around a dead girl, everything turning white, a slow fall into unconsciousness, finding himself on an empty street, the car behind him, policemen around him, Weissman stepping ahead.

"What do you make of your dream?" asked Ingrid.

"I don't think it was a dream; and if it was, then it was real, as real as what we're doing now."

"Why do you think it's real?"

Ned told her about the voice inside his head and his dreams of what it had said: "*All the possibilities exist, all the worlds are possible. . . .*"

"And only you can remember those other 'possibilities,'" Ingrid said. She was mocking him, scolding him for dreaming as if he were a child. Ned felt a surge of anger, frustration, and revulsion; a sudden spout of anger, as if his glands had opened up inside him, washing his insides with venom. He was angry at himself for telling them anything, angry at Ingrid for her mocking face, angry at Deacon for playing birdbeast and tricking him into New York; but most of all he hated the demon presence that gave him unwanted sight—but not true sight.

Weissman forced a smile and said, "So I died with a girl in my arms . . . Could be worse."

The heavy silence rolled back in and Ned found himself counting his breaths, then listening to the other's breathing, as if he could examine their character and tell their fortunes by the way they pulled and pushed at the air. Kheal and Taharahnugi watched Ned intently, as if they expected him to attack Ingrid, roll about on the floor, rush forward, kicking and screaming, to get at the pilot and crash the copter. Deacon seemed removed; he stared at Ned, but it was as if he was seeing into Heaven. His time is past, Ned thought. He's just another shadow now—or perhaps the effects of his dream have not yet been felt. But there was something about Taharahnugi. Although he tried, Ned could not look beyond him into the future. Perhaps that was where Taharahnugi's power was hidden.

"You said something about a hole in the sky when we talked with you yesterday in your hotel room," Ladislas said. "Just what did you mean by that?"

"I meant just that," Ned said. "I was talking about dreaming, and I said I *dreamed* that there's a hole in Heaven." Ned felt his mouth move and he marveled at his words, his speech patterns, as if they were not his own; indeed, he felt they were not. He listened to the demon inside his head, repeated its babble; he was trapped, lost in nonlinear spaces, hating his words and the ease with which he spoke. It had become too easy to slip out of the world, to drift through the possibility on the hand of God, to pretend he had angel's vision and was different from Kheal and Ingrid who had only their own thoughts and memories. But Ned was caught, as were the others.

Another dream-time began. He dreamed, and the copter and sky and clouds became no more than thoughts. Or perhaps he was caught in Deacon's dream. Or Taharahnugi's.

". . . And all manner of demons and ghosts and strange things come from the hole in the sky," Ned said. "It's like a black sun shining on the world, creating new thoughts and mixing up time and space. But it has no reason except God's."

"That's nonsense," said Taharahnugi.

"He's talking in riddles," Ladislas said, adjusting a black eye patch over his right eye which was almost closed, "yet one would almost think that he was aware of the phenomenon of black holes. Except he'd have no way of knowing. . . ."

"Maybe he was 'dreamin',' " said Kheal with an ironic look at Taharahnugi who ignored it.

"A black hole is a sun, isn't it?" asked Ingrid, her knee touching Ned's.

"Well, not exactly," said Ladislas, relaxing in his seat, as if just talking could shore up his anxiety. "A black hole comes about when a massive star at least twice as large as our own sun collapses upon itself. As with any star, there comes a time when the forces of gravity overwhelm the internal nuclear pressures and the star collapses; but in a massive star the gravitational forces are so great that nothing can halt the collapse. The star's matter is compressed to a point of infinite density; the gravitational forces are so strong that not even light can escape. In that region of infinite compression, known as a singularity, geometry breaks down, as do the laws of physics and causality. Time can run backwards, anything goes."

"Do you interpret Ned as saying that a black hole is affecting us?" asked Kheal. "That it's changing the world?"

"Anything goes," said Taharahnugi. Deacon remained quiet.

"Until recently," continued Ladislas, "it had been assumed that a singularity had to be contained by its Event Horizon—a zone through which matter and energy could pass into, but never escape. However, theory now has it that in time a black hole will evaporate, exposing the singularity and its effects to the world beyond the Event Horizon. Some physicists have claimed that the singularity can not only pull in matter, but can also expel it. In fact, it could expel *anything*—and, as Ned would say, for no reason except God's. In theory, a black hole could emit doppelgängers of any of us, distort time, create Hell and angels and Junctions and all the sundry things that go bump in the night. . . ."

"Such as Ladislas's alien presence," Kheal said.

"And so goes our cozy rational universe," Deacon said, looking around. "Prediction must fail in a universe that permits such holes to exist. So causality might simply be a local phenomenon, and temporary at that."

"But the fact is," Ladislas said, "that if any such thing existed, we would have detected it. I was only chasing fancies; there is no near-by black hole, no singularity, just our familiar heavens. And it is extremely unlikely that any of the known black holes could affect us."

Ned heard himself say: "You won't find a hole in the sky today. Look tomorrow. You've got everything backwards, it's the future affecting the past, the hole's in tomorrow."

He felt as if he had been pushing through scrims of gauze, through the heavy curtains of dream, only to find himself back in another present, another "would-be." His hand brushed against Ingrid's leg—as if that touch would be enough to hold him.

"Look out the porthole," Ingrid said. "Something looks wrong out there. How long have we been traveling, anyway? This trip should only take twenty minutes, more or less."

"Well, we haven't even been in the air five minutes," Deacon said.

"What?" asked Ladislas. "We've been flying for at least a half-hour."

"No, we haven't," Ned said. "But we've been flying longer than five minutes."

"And so it starts," Taharahnugi said.

"Shut up," said Ladislas in a whisper.

There was not a cloud in the robin's-egg sky. As Ned looked past Ingrid's hardened face (so unlike Sandra's) and out the porthole, he could not discern where land began and sky ended. It was as if the sky had swallowed the ground below. Now Ned realized what had been bothering him before: the skyscrapers and four-lane highways and rivers and hills and grasslands and suburban towns had not been believable. Their reality had been so diluted that they became illusions. But it was a gradual process.

No one could have survived in the towns they had left behind—they were just palimpsests to be erased. Real flesh would have whithered and the countryside could only become a painter's wash on a blank, white canvas. And now, Ned thought, everything was erased. Yet the world went on as usual, truckers drove goods in and out of the city, railroads functioned, planes flew, people ate, slept, dreamed, died, worked, and made love. But that was another world, one of tidy dreams and everyday get-up-in-the-morning real-time life. There, freight trains rattled over track and trestle through upstate New York and Pennsylvania. Truckers drove their great rigs on imagined roads to imagined destinations. Perhaps they returned to different New York Cities. New York might be only a reflection of some kaleidoscopic beast that exists in all times at once, spread through the infinite shuffle of possibility.

All the dream worlds merging, Ned thought. Everyone trapped in dreams, all the dreams of the world roiling, providing reflected worlds for everyone. . . .

"*. . . if one mind is providing continuity. . . .*"

Natural law had fallen apart behind and below him. Chaos was, for the time being, blue, baby-blue, the blue of dreams and crayons and picture books. But blue was as good a color for the stuff of the universe as any.

As the engines sputtered and the rotors lost momentum, the plastic blue potential for a new cosmos congealed around the helicopter.

It slowed the blades to a halt.

The copter was stuck in the sky, like a fly in ice.

Ned felt suddenly faint. Fight it, he thought; this is just another indeterminate period. But it was unlike any of the others he had experienced.

"What the hell is this?" Ladislas shouted, his sleepy eyes wide open, eye patch in his hand.

"That's it," said Taharahnugi. "We're in the belly of The Mother. The snake will wrap itself around us until we can't see." He moaned, then began to scream.

"Come on now, quiet down," said Kheal, who was sitting beside him; but Taharahnugi shook his head at Kheal and ran to the forward compartment. Weissman followed. Ned started; but Ingrid seized his hand and said, "Let Weissman take care of him."

"Open the door," he shouted, banging it with his fists and trying to pull it open.

"It's all right now," Weissman whispered, restraining

Taharahnugi gently, but he broke free and Weissman pinned him against the forward bulkhead.

"Why doesn't the pilot answer?" Ladislas asked. "He can't just stay in there and do nothing. Perhaps he's hurt. The ship is dead, why doesn't he come out of his cabin?" His voice rose in register.

"Because he probably doesn't want to be attacked by a lunatic," Deacon said.

"He can't just stay in there and do nothing. I think we should find out what happened." And with that Ladislas got up and began pulling at the metal door. He kicked at the latch. "Well," he said to Weissman, "let go of Taharahnugi and help me."

As Weissman released Taharahnugi the latch gave way and Ladislas pulled the door open.

Taharahnugi shouted and tried to dive forward, but Weissman pinned his arms back. Ladislas held onto the door as if he was paralyzed.

There was no pilot nor forward compartment. Only blue sky pushing into the doorway. The sky seemed to be thick as glue, as light as spun candy. It would fill up every space like foam sprayed into a closet.

It began to roil into the passenger compartment.

Ned felt its pull. Ignoring Ingrid's screams, he stood up; he wanted to run and jump out of the copter into the soft blue.

"You stay there," Weissman shouted at Ned.

Taharahnugi screamed again. Weissman pushed him into the aisle, pulled Ladislas out of the way, and then disappeared into the blue Hellstuff that was as thick as smoke pouring from a chimney. Ned remembered a little girl in a gagne running and disappearing into Hell. He stood still.

There was not a sound. For an instant, Ned feared that either time had stopped or they were all dead.

But Weissman had pushed the door closed; the blue Hellstuff inside the cabin dissipated, and the world began. Ladislas ran down the aisle away from the door screaming, "Help, I'm falling." Taharahnugi lay unconscious against the raised seat platform, after running blindly into it head first. Kheal made sure that Taharahnugi was all right while Deacon tried to quiet Ladislas. Weissman and Ned stood in the aisle, as if waiting for something else to happen. Ingrid, who had for a few moments been transformed from an observer into a participant, returned to her former state and stared calmly out the porthole. There was, of course, nothing to see except blue, an expanse of blue that appeared hard and tangible as rock.

"Well, what do you think?" asked Kheal.

"I don't know," said Ingrid without turning from the window. As she spoke, the outside blue became mottled with gray; then the gray became dominant, soiling the sky, as if a washerwoman was wringing out dirty clothes into a basin of clear water. Ned could almost make out the slight definitions that could mean hills and rocks and artifacts.

"Look," Deacon said to Ladislas, who was beginning to lose control again. "Something's happening out there."

"I don't want to see it," Ladislas said.

"Are we making that happen?" Kheal asked, leaving Taharahnugi to sleep in the aisle.

"Ask Ned," Deacon said, but Ned felt the entire weight of the sky and his neighbors' thoughts, especially Taharahnugi's. After a long pause Deacon said, "Yes, I think we have something to do with the changes outside. That substance out there is the unformed potential, the substratum of reality, a quality that can be affected by mind. Soon it will set like plaster; this might just be another indeterminate period. But will we find ourselves in Goshen?"

"Who knows," Ladislas said. "Try intuition." He laughed in a high-pitched voice, an operatic mockery.

"No," Taharahnugi whispered. "This isn't Goshen.

This is The Road and that, that is the Earth Mother." He mumbled in his sleep.

The helicopter shuddered and a buzzing sound swept through the fuselage. The illusion of shaking was only a manifestation and magnification of their fears. And without being told they all seemed to realize it. Then the copter seemed to settle, and a creaking sound such as one might hear on a ship worked its way fore and aft.

Ned knew that the copter was at rest forever. It was stretched across all the possibilities, between all the times. The weather outside is made of time and the ground is the solidified smoke of Hell, Ned thought, imagining shapes in his mind that took form in the grayness beyond the helicopter.

"Just another illusion," Taharahnugi mumbled and then chuckled. He was having a fitful sleep.

"Spatially, perhaps, we may be in the vicinity of Goshen, but that's quite meaningless now," Deacon said. His hands were shaking. After a pause, he said, "I'm cold."

But Ned did not hear, for he was swallowed by another dream. . . .

The dream-desert spread out around him like a shadow, silently sucking the life out of the moist soil and warm creatures and replacing them with reddish-yellow sand and soft tuff. The spires, overhangs, and cut cones of rock were overpowering in their monochromatic contrast of light and shadow. He was dreaming a country of flat plains of sand and salt, barren tablelands encircled by red mountains of porphyritic rock. Rough-hewn cathedrals jutted into a pale, cloudless sky. A breeze pushed the sand into waves (or were these the swellings of rocks millions of years old?) and bit microscopic pieces out of stone which would soon become reddish-yellow sand again.

Although the sun was high in the sky, the colors of the land shifted as if gauzy veils were constantly obstructing clear sight. The dominant hue would change from red to yellow and then white. Shadows as dark as the eyes of demons seemed to change their shapes between rocks. This was another region of Hell, Ned thought. If the shifting Hell of Junction was made of diamond shapes, this Hell was of a softer nature. Every breath wore it away, revealed new shapes, new colors. But this was a muted world; only the shadows seemed tangible. The rockscape with its attendant shadows could almost be a city, a diorama created over millenia by the touchings of sunlight and the gougings of wind.

And while Ned dreamed, the others watched the plastic-coated walls of the helicopter melt into the sand and rock around them. Taharahnugi was still asleep and started to snore. He dreamed of verdant forest, of a thousand shades of green, of African life-forms, of the music of the heart and ghost-dances; and the powerful green world curled around him, swallowing Deacon, Ladislas, Weissman, Kheal, and Ingrid.

Only Ned was alone, trapped in his dream of sand and stone.

10

Ned was lying in the desert sand. The air was dry and irritated his throat and lungs, as if he were breathing the motes of yellow, brown, and red sand. Colors and shadows shifted around him as the midday sun was obscured and revealed by the slow moving continents of clouds. All around him was tableland, the redlands of Ürgüp, the whitelands of Nevsehir, and in the deep distance Ned could visualize the gouges and polished crags cut by the now dead river Kizilirmak and its nameless tributaries. Ned was lying in a human-sized desert. All around him was dry, dead land, a land of skeleton shapes, a desert of sand, rock, and mirage.

But all this would change. The land would be frozen in winter, glazed over with blue ice, new shapes forming on the old. And snow would blot out the sun and sky, turn the world into a flat white surface. Later, Kizilirmak would come to life for the thaw, if only as a stream.

But time was grinding on so slowly. An eon might pass before a drop of rain fell, a millennium before the soft touch of snow.

Ned waited, lost in this expanse of desolation. He was thirsty and hungry and benumbed by this desert dream. Soon, he thought, he would be touched with fever. His arms and legs felt light. His crotch itched. A scorpion was making its way towards his extended arm, its feelers touching the ground, sensing and feeling movement that was miles away. It was carrying five young scorpions on its back; they would soon be mature enough to drop from their mother's back and forage on their own. The scorpion would crawl a few inches, curl up and wiggle its pincers, clean them with its lobster legs.

Stand up, Ned told himself, but he was without strength, drained. The scorpion will kill you, he thought. Move! He felt a surge of revulsion for the segmented thing crawling toward him; but still he could not move. Perhaps this miniature monster could deliver him into Heaven. . . .

Fight it, he thought. But he was too tired to fight.

Ned could hear the scorpion whispering to him, but its comments were too simple to be understood. But as it came closer, the creature's thoughts became stronger and Ned compensated for its lack of intelligence.

"You would do better in the shade," it said. "There, in the church where your arm points."

Ned looked ahead, past the scorpion, but saw nothing but distant rockscape, the rubble and detritus of Hell. He sifted coarse sand through his fingers, then scooped out another handful. If there is a church in Hell, he thought, it must be a sham, a trap. For Ned, Hell was the utter absence of God.

"Why can you talk?" he asked the scorpion.

"Because I am conscious, as is everything hereabouts. Listen to the sand you're shifting, and the rocks beyond. They all have a whisper. But you're supplying the words and conceptions. I'm just communicating a sensation, and a simple sensation at that."

Ned watched its slow, agonized movements towards his outstretched arm. He was wary of a euphoric feeling that was beginning to come over him. It made him wish for Hilda and Sandra and, perhaps, Ingrid and great chunks of green-tinged glass.

Something green sparkled in the distance, perhaps a mirage or sunlight caught in the recesses of rock.

"Of course," the creature said, "if you don't move I will poison you."

The scorpion was only a few inches away from Ned's fingers. Ned curled them into a fist, hoping to gain time. He was sluggish and could feel the energy being sucked out of him. It was as if the land was draining him of breath and fluid. Ned watched one of the young scorpions drop from its mother's back and wriggle in the sand like a spider crusted with dirt.

And Ned thought he could hear himself snore.

He sensed an infinity of sand, porous rock, crags, and mountain folds around him. Everything whispered. His quickened breath was the chatter of washerwomen; the wind was old men and children talking. The rocks conversed with sand, and sand with sun. The sky was a blue ceramic bowl with clouds pasted inside for effect. Slowly it was flattening out, soon to crush him into glass.

The sky hummed, but Ned did not listen to what it was saying; there was no time. The vainglorious scorpion was hoping to deliver death, or at least a respectable sickness. With a supreme effort of will, Ned pulled his arm to his chest and stood up. He was dizzy, as if his head was filled with water sloshing from side to side.

His thoughts were jumbled into desert sounds. He listened to the whispering, whistling, and humming. He listened to the broken syllables and almost-words. The scorpion inched past Ned's foot, but Ned was too far above to understand its simple cursing.

I still don't see a church, Ned thought, secretly addressing the scorpion, which was burrowing its way into the sand.

"Go straight ahead, in the direction of your face," said a voice inside Ned's head. The voice was familiar. It was Deacon and the birdbeast and Weissman and Ned's father; it was the thrumming of thought, all the streetsounds and bar noises, all the whispers of imagination and memory.

"What about the others?" Ned looked around, but could not see a trace of the helicopter. Perhaps it *is* in the sky, he thought. He wondered if Taharahnugi was still unconscious. Were the others looking for Ned or were they lost in Taharahnugi's dream?

And Ned caught a glimpse of green forest on the western horizon where two dreams seemed to meet like great continents pushed together. He shuddered, realizing that he was locked in this dream, that the world was slipping back into the great primordial dream-time. He thought he could hear drums and chanting. Where are the others? he asked himself; he stood motionless, waiting for a reply.

"Forget about the others," the voice said. "You'll know what they're doing."

Was this a directive from an outside source? Ned asked himself. Or was it his own intuition? He tried to think laterally and enter Taharahnugi's verdant dream, but he had lost his sight. While Taharahnugi was dreaming back the ancient past, Ned was powerless and alone in this conscious, mocking universe of hills and rock and shadow and sand.

"Are the others caught in Taharahnugi's dream?" Ned asked. But the scorpion had disappeared and the desert was silent.

Ned walked on. The sand sucked on his feet, trying to bury them. Each step was an attack on the sand and a retreat from its grasp. It was as if he was walking on the back of some huge fleshy beast, but the beast was asleep in slowtime and had not as yet taken a breath.

Is it possible that God's church could be buried in Hell? Ned asked himself. The church was his only hope, his only chance. But would he find Heaven's holy sanctuary or the burning eye of Hell? As he quickened his pace, the desert noises began again.

The sky hummed, the sand whispered, occasionally finding its voice and drawling out a few syllables, and the air gave him enough space to walk in. Soon the smooth waves of sand would give way to rougher ground. In the distance he could see a stone crown of spires and cliffs.

"It's both," said the voice inside Ned's head.

"What?" asked Ned.

"This voice inside your head constitutes both your own intuition and an outside intelligence. One nudges the other. You know: feedback. A cozy synthesis."

"What are you?" asked Ned, once more feeling his energy being sucked away. He imagined that he was falling to his knees in the hot umber-colored sand.

"I'm more than the scorpion and the sand sucking on your feet. But I'm just a part of the whole thing."

"Shit," said Ned.

"Now you sound like Taharahnugi." The sand and rockthrusts whispered "haha," each tiny bit adding its own measure of mirth, as the wind ran its fingers toward the east.

"How do you know about Taharahnugi?"

"The same way you do," said the voice. "I know everything that you know, or could know if you knew how to see. And I know what you're in the process of learning."

"And what's that?" asked Ned. Mirages danced ahead with dust-devils. He focused his eyes on the rock formations ahead, the grotesque stone monsters shaped by volcanoes and beaten for centuries by feathers of wind.

"That everything here is conscious: the sand, rock, scrub, and crawling creatures, even the air. In this place every particle of dust and mote of sand is in perfect empathy with everything else. The sand under your feet feels joy when a spider is hatched; and the spider see, senses, and suffers when a bird falls from the sky. They suffer for you and the wormwood you kick out of your way. We are the unformed potential you first talked about with Deacon, who, incidentally, is dead now. Died of lymphosarcoma.

"But we are all the bits of an ordering principle of mind, if you like, that has created itself out of its own potential. Everything around you is made up of the stuff of mind. We think around you, and with you. We are simply taking the natural direction of matter, for entropy is only an aberration, albeit a widespread one. But soon the entire cosmos will become conscious . . ."

Determined to find the church and the end of this dream, Ned continued on, stepping over rocks, trying to keep his balance and find footholds on the rocky ground. Stone shards stuck out of the cracked earth like rough-shaped knives; it was as if the world was warning him to be careful.

The voice had become a buzz and would not answer his questions. Making his way through increasingly rough Turkish hinterland, Ned could make out the crown cliffs ahead. Before them were miles and miles of deadland, plains that stretched from east to west like asphalt. It was a demon's dream, Ned thought, remembering highways that seemed to run ahead of cars like flat snakes. But the cliffs jutted into the pale, now cloudless sky to form that white crown. Natural shapes for God's church, Ned thought. An object lesson in perfection. God's wall.

As Ned gained the top of a ridge, he saw a field of rock cones that seemed to continue forever. The mass of even shapes overwhelmed the distant mountains which might be only larger cones, fields upon fields to cover the world, a cosmos of gray stars in a stone heaven.

"These cones are called *peri bacalari*, or fairy chimneys," the voice said, leading him into deeper levels of sleep. The peasants in the region of Ürgüp believed that a thousand spirits dwelled in the conefields. According to one legend, the spirits often fall in love with young men passing through; and that is supposed to account for those unfortunate travelers who never reach their destination. There are many myths, of course. One claims that the cones are the tents of a vast ghost-army waiting to take their vengeance when the horns of God break the world into pieces."

The cones did look like tents, Ned thought. Each one cast an inky shadow on the parched ground.

"The grotesque shapes are the stuff of myths and dreams; many men imagined that they saw the dominions of the afterlife in those rocks. And the rocks were given names: there are *Uchisar*, *Ortahisar*, and *Kiliclar*, the towers of the spirits."

"Where are the peasants now?" Ned asked.

"They're all dead, but their souls make up part of the world. The universe conserves its souls, just as it does mechanical energy. Look around you. Conscious souls are rising from the earth. They're growing lighter and stretching into the sky."

Ned stared intently at the cones. They were so close together that they looked like the spines of a gigantic petrified beast. Most of the cones were small, but some were almost one hundred feet high. In the distance, the cones seemed to be more widely spaced; there were even a few isolated cones that cast long shadow-tails. Some of the cones were topped with bricks of basalt; others had been tortured by the elements for so long that only a stone pole remained with its cap of basalt.

"I see only cones and shadows," Ned said, and then he saw the ghosts cavorting from cone to cone before they rose into the blue sky and disappeared into Heaven. The ghosts were moving constantly, floating, flowing like water or curling smoke. Some were transparent specters; others were full-bodied, complete with hair, wrinkles, warts, pimples, and rouged cheeks.

"The transparent ones will rise first," the voice said. "See?"

"But the others look human," Ned said, his eyes moving back and forth to follow the dream.

"Yes, of course," said the voice. "The monsters are still inside the cones, soon to spewed out and merged with the rest. They are the local gods, still hoping to be resurrected and worshiped by surviving natives. But they confuse ghosts with flesh. So they've been dying for quite a while."

The voice guided Ned across the conefields, past the natural rows of obelisks that seemed to be whispering to him, over ghost-laden rocks and through gray scrub. This country of ghosts and spirits was desolation itself. It was as if Goreme had been on fire, and only char remained; it was an umber and ashen world. Ned imagined that if he touched the cones, they would crumble into dusty clouds.

But where are Ingrid, Weissman, and the others? he asked himself. Can they still be caught in Taharahnugi's dream, could it be that strong? He looked behind and saw the green plain of Taharahnugi's dreamforest on the horizon, as far away now as when he first glimpsed it.

Ned moved on. If the others were trapped in Taharahnugi's dream, he could not reach them. He had to find the church. But he did not know his way through this dead land of ghosts and whispers. Guided by his sleepwalker's intuition, he investigated his dream. He watched the ghosts rising into Heaven, passing through fluffs of cloud, each spirit adding its precious load of consciousness to the universe; and he waited for the gods resting inside the earth.

Ghosts with long noses and thin lips reached out to him. Lovely spirits spoke softly inside his head, invaded his private thoughts, rested in his memories. Transparent specters drifted around him like smoke carried on the wind, passed through his skin on their way to Heaven. Ned felt repelled, then excited; the ghosts were smoke and fire, as if one could be the other. And he was at once warmed and burned by their presence.

"They are pure life energy," the voice said. "Each one is forever stamped into reality."

"But you're losing them," Ned said. "They're floating away." Ned almost regretted their passing.

And a chorus of voices shouted inside Ned's head. Each voice was that of a ghost. They laughed and giggled, held conversation, and filled Ned with new languages and thoughts, new songs and sensations. They proved their reality by inhabiting him. Ned was no longer alone, no longer a stranger. The shadows had become real, or he had become a shadow. For a delicious instant he was comfortable again, among his own, a natural part of the warp and weft of this world.

"No," he shouted. "It's a trap, I'll not be part of Hell." Ned listened for the voice that had guided him here, but it was silent. If the true church is here, he thought, how will I find it alone?

"You don't need that voice anymore," said a ghost that was losing his hair.

"We'll show you around now," said a specter that could barely seen. He spoke in Kazan Tatar, a Turkish dialect, which Ned could now understand.

"We're not lost," said a ghost that had once been a peasant girl. Her face was smooth except for brown sacs of skin that hung under her deep-set black eyes. She had evidently been dead for a long time, for she spoke Old Turkish.

"We're just passing away," said another ghost that seemed to be growing out of the peasant girl's stomach. "Just as water turns into steam, so are we passing into another state. But as we pass into each new state, we become more complex and fewer in number."

"You see," said the specter that spoke Kazan Tatar, "by losing ourselves, we're becoming more conscious."

"And he's well on the way," said the ghost that was

losing his hair. "I can hardly see him. But what about you, Ned?"

"We can certainly see you," said the peasant girl. The ghost growing out of her stomach was giggling.

Ned tried to shut them out.

"You're better off than the monsters below you," said the ghost, trying to extricate himself from the peasant girl. "But Ned, Ned, you're not dead."

"Leave me alone," Ned cried, but he could not escape, could not outrun thoughts.

The chorus took it up. "Ned, Ned, you're not dead."

Ned began to climb out of the upper dungeons of sleep.

"Do you know where you're going, Ned?" they asked. "You're passing away, too. Running just ahead of the monsters trying to break out of the ground. But your skin's too tight. Loosen it, Ned. Die a little. Be dead."

Ned broke into consciousness with a howl. The ghosts ignored him and went about their business of ascending into Heaven. Ned pressed his hands against his face and listened to his fingers break. He felt for his flesh, which would soon dissolve, layer by layer.

11

The conefield with its thousands of fingers protruding from the ground was behind Ned. Ahead was rocky ground, smooth sandy ridges, grotesquely shaped rocks, salt deposits, and a broken wall of sheer mountain cliffs. Everything was quiet except for the wind which screamed as if moved toward the crown of cliffs ahead. Shadows defined the landscape, transformed isolated rocks into demon faces.

Working his way up another hill, Ned listened for voices, but could only hear the crack of his eardrums as the air pressure changed. He rested beside a ragged copse of wormwood and wild lavender scrub and thought about Junction, his friends, and the church. I've lost them all, he thought. He had promised to stand for the church, but had lived too long inside the mirrors of New York; and now he was lost. In his mind's eye he tried to visualize Reverend Surface, Sandra, Hilda, Baldanger, even Forester, but he could not remember them clearly. They were shades passing through the night-fog of memory. He closed his eyes tightly and tried to remember his father's face, but could not make out a single feature; the face was just a blur that he identified as "father." Before sleep could descend upon him, voices called from the mountains, whispered in the sand, bumbled in the breeze that chilled his perspiring face.

Ned stood up and started walking, concentrating on the whispers and the mountain in the distance. He resolved to stand for the church, and for the memory of his father and the townsfolk who had believed in him. As he stepped over rocks which protruded dangerously from the sandspills like rusted spikes, he felt a new determination. If there was a church in Hell, he would find it.

Ghosts seemed to flit from stone to stone. Shadows moved, as if massing to capture him. And all the mirages of Goreme were on display as faraway dust-devils swept sand and debris hundreds of meters into the dry air. But Ned stepped quickly, as if he were familiar with every rock and hill of this dead land.

As he neared the minarets and jagged cliffs of stone, Ned could distinguish the hermitages, monastic complexes, and churches from the natural lines of rock. To his left, nine meters up a smooth rock face, was a small opening. But the pulley ropes were rotted, and the monksbasket had long since been swallowed by the sand.

He felt himself being drawn toward a stone fist that stood eighteen meters high. A narrow staircase hewn out of the rock led into a large opening.

Is this God's church? Ned asked himself as he scanned the rock. Hot as the sun was on his face, he shivered. He could not rid himself of the fear that he would find Satan's sump instead of Heaven's door.

Ned looked up at the church which seemed to cut into the azure sky. Everything was quiet hereabouts; no dust-devils played through the stone courtyards and empty churches. Clouds drifted past, and for a vertiginous instant Ned thought that the rocks and cliffs were moving at a stately pace. He stepped up the stone stairs and paused warily in the narthex entrance. Desert light streamed through the opening and illuminated the church. Ned recognized the fresco secco portrait of the Emperor Genetos to his left; it was just as he had dreamed it.

As he looked into the church, he saw a room measuring about one thousand square meters, which had been chiseled out of the raw stone by some unknown carver-architect. But the structure had always been there, even before the carver began, somehow implied in the soft tuff. The carver was only God's tool used to coax and torture the rock into a work of art.

The plan of the church was a cross inside a square; the principal dome was situated over the crossing and the four subsidiary domes over the corners. But the structural rendering was idiosyncratic, almost pagan in its rawness and disregard for neat geometry and detail. Since the carver-architect did not have to worry about structural safety, he could create as he pleased, bring to life the impossible structures found in dreams. The cracked, tilted ceilings seemed as if they would cave in; their cupolas were stone bubbles about to burst and bury Ned in God's ruins. Painted arches didn't quite match each other, and the walls, too, were uneven. Ned had the impression of a maze, as if corners might be corridors leading to other secret rooms, ending in the sacred tabernacle of Hell. It seemed that the church would crumble with a breath; yet it could probably stand the millennia.

Slowly, cautiously, Ned walked into the church. With every step, he expected death—to be burned alive by Satan's breath, to be frozen for eternity inside his unholy eye. It was cool inside the church. He could not stop shaking. He would certainly be blinded if he looked upon the face of God. Was He here, in this stone prison? Paintings and designs covered walls and ceilings. Crude patterns of zigzags, half-circles, maltese crosses, eagles, bats, lozenges outlined the room. Crosses predominated—symbolic proof that the church had been properly consecrated. But the designs were only filler between paintings.

The Pantocrator, represented by Christ, was the largest and most detailed painting in the church. It dominated the central dome which was surrounded by the celestial hierarchy. The architect-artist had envisioned Heaven as a very busy place; the four evangelists were crudely painted in the pendentives. The eastern apse contained the Virgin Mary, her yellow ocher halo only slightly smaller than Christ's. Arches and vaults were filled with saints and holy scenes. Lesser saints, martyrs, church dignitaries, events of the earth and the flesh were left to the lower portions of the walls. And for the faithful, now dead, the Last Judgement was painted in dramatic detail on the back wall. However, most of the paintings and designs were faded or marred by fissures in the stone.

"So it all comes back to this," said a voice inside Ned's head. Ned jumped, as if the voice was a thundercrack. He turned to flee, and remembered his resolve. Trembling, he stood his ground as the memory of a crowded Hanging Saturday flashed in his mind. "Look for me. I'm here. . . ."

Feeling as if a thousand ferine eyes were watching him, Ned scanned the walls and ceiling. All the painted figures seemed to be connected by floral designs and curlicues. The artist had used a palette of only two colors: red and yellow, with red predominating. He used smears of charcoal black to outline and accentuate important aspects of the painted pantheon. Shell-white highlighted haloes and intricate designs. If Ned could not see that this was a churchroom, he would have thought it was a pagan place, painted red to represent the fires of Hell.

Perhaps it was the entrance to Hell. . . .

"The arch. Right above you."

And Ned found a faded fresco of a middle-aged man dressed in a red suit and yellow tie, holding a crumpled fedora in his hand. His face was strong, only softened by a curly red beard (the curls were stylized) and a yellow halo outlined in red, black, and white. He talked, but his lips were not synchronized with the words inside Ned's head.

"I'll speak to you this time," he said, his lips forming a stylized smile. A piece of his face fell off as he talked.

"Were there other times?" Ned asked.

"Yes. Many other times. They're all passing by right now."

"Who are you?"

"Right now I'm a plaster metaphor for Ahasuerus the Jew, who shouldn't even be here. But I think it's a nice touch. You could also visualize me like this, if it suits you. . . ."

Ned felt himself turning over in his sleep. He looked around the room, at the figures and designs that seemed to be held in fire, and discovered that the church was held together by the things growing inside. Walls and ceiling and floor were illusions, appearances held together by a more underlying form. Dieties and saints smiled at him, the very personifications of substance. But Ned felt something was wrong with them. Perhaps their smiles revealed too many teeth.

And a smooth, thin tentacle curled around his leg.

Ned jerked away, repelled by its soft touch. Another tentacle wrapped itself around his neck. Screaming, he pulled the tentacle loose and tried to escape from the church; but other tentacles curled around his arms, legs, and chest.

"Let me go," Ned shouted, straining as if against ropes. "Let me go!" This was no holy place; he was caught in Hell.

"Don't be afraid," said Ahasuerus. "That's only to secure you for a moment."

"Moment?" Ned whispered, his voice sounding to his ears like a shriek.

"As long as you like. Now follow the other tentacles outside. You can see them probing, growing, closing synapses."

Ned was shaking with fear and could not catch his breath. He felt as if the church was filled with tentacles. He opened his mouth to shout, but his screams were dreams or whispers, and very far away. He felt as if he were dreaming two dreams at once. In one dream he shouted and railed at the universe; in the other dream he was mute, or perhaps awake.

"We're taking over your psychological space," Ahasuerus said. "We now inhabit the whole continuum of psychological space. Each tentacle, as you perceive it, reaches into another reality, another dream state. All the dreams are connected. Waking and dreaming become the same."

Ned tried to pull away from his living pinions; he tried to scream, but only whispered. "Let me go!" His shouts were tiny animals that had scurried into a dark place in his mind where he could not find them. He tried to dream himself away from the church, but he was trapped. He started to gag, but his tongue was between his teeth.

"Don't worry, we're holding you tight. You've just sunk inside reality. It's much thicker than the diluted stuff you're used to."

"I'm drowning," Ned said, spitting up phlegm, clenching his fists, trying to pull away from the tentacles.

"No, you're not," said Ahasuerus. "You're dreaming for yourself and everyone else. Dreams add another layer of reality to the world, an ever-thickening atmosphere of consciousness. And every soul contributes an idea, a thought, or simply the density of its being."

Ned strained against his bonds as if they were the earth itself. He thrashed about, pulled loose from the sticky tentacles, and was caught again. New he could not move a muscle. He was bound in ooze; the mass of tentacles no longer had recognizable form.

"Let me go." He gagged and thought wildly, I'm caught in Hell forever. . . .

Ahasuerus laughed and was joined by the four evangelists. The Virgin waved from the eastern apse to the Christ in the central dome. The martyrs, church dignitaries, emperors, and holy saints were chattering amongst themselves.

Regaining some control over himself, he asked, "But why am I here?"

"Because everyone dreams your dreams," Ahasuerus said.

"Do you dream my dreams?" asked Ned.

"Not only do we dream your dreams, we dream you. It's a lovely paradox: you're a figment of our mind, yet you came into existence first. Perhaps *you're* the deity."

I'm not a figment of your mind, Ned thought angrily; the words seemed to tear his throat, yet there was no sound, only the silent turning of thought.

And then more laughter.

"You reflect us in human form," Ahasuerus said. "If you can't stand the front edge of the truth yet, then think of yourself as a lodestone around which dreams flow. When you first stood on the edge of what you call Hell, you became that lodestone. We used you as a nucleus around which to grow."

Ned felt repelled. "Where are the others?" he asked. "Where are Taharahnugi and Ingrid and Kheal and Deacon and Ladislas?"

"Your friends are dreaming you as you dream them—that's how you imagine that what you perceive is reality and not a dream. New York and Junction and Goreme are only extensions of you. And you're only an extension of them."

"Then everything is just a dream," Ned mumbled to himself, wishing he could wake up in a familiar room; wishing for friends and security.

"Dreams are made of thoughts," Ahasuerus said, "and the world is more like a thought than you'd imagine. Our thoughts, emotions, and ideas are like dustmotes in a clear light—reflecting, tumbling, constantly creating new patterns. Our thoughts are converging to create a new atmosphere. Imagine one thought filling the universe. Becoming the universe."

"Who are you?" Ned asked, trying to work himself out of this dream. He felt that the minions of humanity were choking him, crowding him, killing him.

"Just an instigator. Pushing matter into its natural direction. The alchemy of evolution turns things into thoughts. So I trace out patterns and match your dreams with those of everyone else. (Ladislas was right about that.)"

"I don't want you to select reality for me. I want to do that for myself." Ned tried to break away, but the bonds were too strong.

"I was selected by your culture, *your* reality, just as you were. Now you face unity. The only thing of value you have to bequeath to the world is your consciousness; only consciousness will survive matter and time. It is not enough to create great works and have ideas. You must give up your very self."

Ned mumbled "No" and pictured Hilda and Sandra and Ingrid, their puckered faces and loose skin, their high-pitched voices and clawing nails, their thoughts and intelligence. Each soul locked in flesh. Soft parts to push against. Single entities. Fitted tools. Ned was lost, lost again in a dream, a single dream amidst billions. He tried to shake his head, as if that might clear it. But he could not move. He prayed, prayed to a conventional God, asked forgiveness for having found the host of Hell instead of the ruler of Heaven.

"I'm thirsty," Ned said, his swollen tongue scratching against the roof of his mouth. He opened his mouth to breathe and a tentacle slid down his throat to suck his insides away. It became part of his throat, cool and wet. But he could not move, could not scream; he was locked in dreams, even as he was being violated.

"You are a mirror of the universe," Ahasuerus said, "or, if you prefer, a lens to focus its thought. Every soul in the universe mirrors all the others yet is unique. And as every soul merges with every other soul, we evolve into our destiny of total consciousness."

Ned gagged and dreamed that he was looking at himself, that he knew every word Ahasuerus would say, as if he was lifting them out of that imperceptible instant before they were spoken. He dreamed that time was still spinning, rolling like rivers, tumbling like stones, moving forward and backward like great machines digging into the earth. For all its irregularities, time was still circular, a great disk with many veins. And he was caught in its center.

". . . And it is only natural that some greater soul should evolve out of this new collective consciousness," Ahasuerus continued. "Such a soul of souls could encompass the entire world of awareness, perceive the structures and patterns reflected by every soul."

"And you're this soul of souls," Ned said, spitting the words, trying once again to break free of the tentacles which had become part of him like layers of coral on a living reef. His spark of life was being merged with others.

"Just as matter evolves into mind, so do souls converge into deity," Ahasuerus said, folding his hands and assuming the posture of a deity. "A being composed of its billions of souls can more perfectly reflect and comprehend the universe.

"Granted, the universe cheated a bit by going indeterminate here. But impatience is universal. It's only chance, of course. What difference is a few billion years?"

Ned began to sense everyone's dreams. He felt the presence of billions of souls, each a dream inside the soul of souls. He felt the weight of their thoughts, a world crushing him. All of humanity had been impossibly stuffed into this place.

"Give yourself up," Ahasuerus said. "You're part of us."

"No," Ned said.

"You were looking for deity. You've found it."

Ned howled, railed, ranted, and dreamed.

Perhaps the soul of souls is just another dream, a huge beast that is asleep and dreaming his dreams. A dream dreaming. . . .

He was sinking through the surface of things, seeing ideas and patterns instead of arches and cupolas, walls and ceilings. He traced the patterns ever downward into himself. As he followed the paths winding under his consciousness, he imagined that reality was a roof upon which the whole world of his senses had been piled. It resembled a great sparkling city; and he was a pallid animal scurrying in the sewers beneath—running, chasing down food, following living instinct. But instinct was the stuff of this world, the dark substance of these corridors of thought.

He was in Hell. All the paths led here. The universe was sliding down, burying him in the workings of its grand consciousness; and above him was that reef, glowing bits of consciousness fusing into the soul of souls.

The church was filled with the smoke of dreams, and every dreamer asserted his own presence. Ned recognized ghosts with long noses and thin lips, doctors and nurses, Baldanger, the Reverends MacDonald, Briar, Shorter, and Blues, the featherwaker, the girl who died in the car with Weissman, Miss Jenkens; and then he began to recognize the souls of people he had never known, could have never known, persons from the once dead past, the evolving future, and the pasts, presents, and futures of a thousand alternate worlds, all smoke, smoke layering the world, flushing into the universe.

He looked for Taharahnugi, Ingrid, the others.

"Give yourself up," Ahasuerus whispered, "and you'll find them. They're there."

Ned dreamed into the cosmos and drew out its patterns.

He dropped into the dark water of his soul where his instincts swam like great prehistoric fish in a realm that had not yet been differentiated into psyche or cosmos.

He passed through the layers of reality as if through the thermoclines of a lake.

His psyche was a beacon reflecting everything around him.

He was a small chip that contained and reflected the world.

Ahasuerus was right, he thought.

And he screamed as the scavengers carefully picked him apart to taste his experiences. He tried to conceal his dreams from them, tried not to remember the taste of Hilda, the whispering voice of Sandra, the gaunt face of his father. But they were now universal experience.

"I'm still here," Ahasuerus said, as the stone crumbled, leaving only his face and fedora. His mouth and nose were rapidly disappearing. His eyes were cracks in the soft tuff. "We'll disappear together."

Ned was still held by the living reefs which filled the church. "I need more space. Too much weight. They're pushing inside me." A ghost passed out of Ned's mouth and hovered above him, pinching its nose. Other ghosts appeared, smiling and scowling and scoffing at him like children. Ghosts danced on the edge of eyesight, then disappeared when looked at straight-on. Some ghosts were souls without substance; others wore flesh like old men. They were melting together, passing through each other, anchoring themselves to the walls and reefs and floor.

"Well, let them in," said Ahasuerus. "Give yourself up. The universe has taken your form."

"No," he shouted. "They're taking off my arms." As Ned screamed, he suddenly remembered something from the Book, a drawing of Satan trapped in Hell— antlers crowned Satan's head, his legs were spread and shackled, and a dead man's head protruded from his groin. Ned felt that he was similarly trapped in a false heaven, caught in an iceflow of selves.

"Let them in," said Ahasuerus.

"Give me some space."

"It's all around you, pulsing with life. Only *you* are dead; accept us and live."

"No."

Another scream as they tried to pull Ned out of his flesh.

"Let them in!"

"No," Ned shouted, and he discovered that he could move his toes, then his arm. The world was tipping again, going indeterminate. He felt time flowing around him like chill breezes. Objects blurred, yet Ned could discern their previous, ancient forms. He imagined the church as seen from God's eye—natural veins of stone, the design inhering in the tuff itself.

The arch crumbled. Ahasuerus became soft stone crumbling on the floor, dust filling the room.

Ned pulled himself out of the thick atmosphere of souls that filled the church.

He squeezed out of the church.

Ahasuerus's voice was lost amidst Ned's thoughts, a grand confusion of thought. *I'm free.* . . .

Overcome with relief and euphoria, Ned looked around and saw that this country had been touched by Taharahnugi's dreams. But there was something ominous and deadly about this verdant, suffocating place. It was a luxuriant overlay of climbers, fronds, high canopied forests, flowering plants—a concentration of African fauna and flora. Jackanapes screamed, plumed birds screaked, and hidden insects chirruped. Before him was openland, meadows and rills covered with dark flowers and flanked by evergreen forests. In the summer light the shadows appeared as purple pools. But beneath all the verdant growth was Goreme with its sharp lines and stone faces. Ned recognized this land, even in disguise.

"Are the others in this place, too?" Ned asked.

"Yes," said Ahasuerus. "Everyone is locked in your head and vice versa. They're all there. Instant communication. Just float along."

Ned remembered the crowd pressing down on him in the subway, burying him in a gray mass of flesh and thought.

He had one thought, and that was to run.

Voices chanted inside his head. Ned could hear Hilda shouting above them all. And there was Baldanger's toothless whistle. Faces flashed before him, and he kept running. He ran through specters of Ingrid, Weissman, Deacon, Ladislas, and Taharahnugi. The church was buried behind him. Mirages flashed about him like fireflies on a moonless night. But it was midday and the sun was high in a perfect sky. There were no clouds to map the heavens, only eggshell blue.

The world was stable once again, and the sky was made of ice, cold and hard, moving closer to the ground with every breath he took.

And Ned ran as if he could escape Ahasuerus, Taharahnugi's dream, the ghosts howling inside his head, the mirages of the world, the world that was becoming one thought. He felt stronger now, as if he could think sideways through the dreams and cover great distances.

"But what are you afraid of?" asked Ahasuerus who was a small hard presence inside Ned's head.

"I want to wake up. I want out of your dreams."

"You're in Taharahnugi's dream. He's a dreamer, too."

"All the dreams are yours," Ned said angrily. "You're matching them together. The stone church was a lure, just as Taharahnugi's stinking dream is a trap, your trap."

Laughter inside and outside his head. The rocks, evergreens, flowers, and yellow-veined fronds called his name. Every step was a conversation. Gaily colored birds gabbled with the breeze. Scurrying animals were laughing in the mulch. The world was made of noises, sharp and subtle. The sky shouted to him. The sun winked and radiated laughter. The ground was soft and warm, filled with moist decay; a brook murmured, wind wheezed through brush, calling him. For an instant he felt euphoric in Taharahnugi's heavy-hued dream. Everything was alive. He felt the temptation to become part of this streaming, primitive place; but he fought the ancient urge to give himself up to warm winds and animal heartbeats, to feel with the whole world.

"Why am I in Taharahnugi's dream?" he asked, resisting its effect by sheer will.

"*While you fight evolution, he gives himself up, and in so doing accumulates the world,*" Ahasuerus said. "*He dreams the past and accepts the fate of living souls.*"

"What about the others?"

"*Your friends are all dreaming. Just as they accept Taharahnugi's dream, so will they accept yours. Merge them.*"

"*You're the Rainbow Serpent made out of dreams,*" shouted Taharahnugi amidst the laughter.

"And you're Ahasuerus's tool, a weak-will," Ned replied.

"*Take us into your dream,*" shouted Sandra.

"*Accept us,*" shouted Ingrid.

"*Merge the dreams,*" shouted Deacon. "*You divide us.*"

"*You see, they're all with us, all your friends. Give up. Your thoughts and dreams are ours, as ours are yours,*" said Ahasuerus. "*Nothing is independent now.*"

"And what about you?" Ned asked.

"*I am your thoughts combined with all the others. You are connected. Give up.*"

"*Give up,*" rang a chorus of voices inside Ned's head.

"No." Ned shouted. "I am not connected. I am myself." He tried to run from the stone church and dream forests, from the stalking animals and colorful flyers. But he could never run away from the perfectly blue sky, an eggshell sky, a ceiling that Ned was afraid would crack open to reveal the props of Hell.

He ran from hillock to hillock, hoping to reach the limits of Taharahnugi's dream-country. Although he felt an urge to veer off toward the forest, which looked cool and comfortable and uniform, he continued across the meadowland toward where he imagined the conefields might be. He stepped over blue flowers that whispered to him. But he ignored the world. He wanted familiar ground, the dry country of Goreme; he had a gut-feeling that he would not have a chance in Taharahnugi's dream, and he even dared to hope that he could pass through the dreams and find the world.

A parrot screamed in the distance and Ned felt suddenly repelled by the crawling, wriggling, growing, rotting life around him. Everything was so close; not a finger's length of ground was naked, and the sickly sweet odors of life and death mingled, never quite borne away by the damp swamp breezes. Ahead, Ned could make out the rough country of Goreme, but it was fuzzy, as if seen through gauzy scrims. It was quickly replaced by the dewy pastel shades of an African afternoon, by the glint of a faraway watering place, by a line of huge, mud-encrusted beasts feeding on high grass, by the howling of predators and the preyed-upon, by the chatter and clicking of insect and burrower. Goreme was another world, and Ned could not quite reach through this dream. But he had to escape.

There could be no freedom here, he thought. Better to die in Hell and suffer the soul to whither.

The world of souls was converging upon him.

"Give up," said Ahasuerus. *"You cannot run away. You're taking the world with you."*

"I want my own space and direction, not yours," Ned said, feeling stronger with every word. He had escaped the stone church and its tentacles; perhaps he could escape from Ahasuerus and his monistical dream. "I won't be a figment of your dream."

"What matter if we dream or not, or how we shape the world? We see the same things, feel the same sen-

sations, *all this so we may grasp the structure of the world. It's being put together in a new way, that's all."*

"It's your world, put together your way. I want the old world."

"Liar. You found little happiness in that world which was built on the dreams of the dead. It was a tiny cosmos of old thoughts. But even then you were dreaming of Hell."

"And you offer more of the same."

"I offer you yourself, not the dead mythos of your past. I offer you evolution based on the workings of the soul, a new mythos."

"No," Ned whispered, only to find that he was staring into a dark field. Another trick, he thought as he opened his eyes. "Another trick," he screamed. He had lain down in high grass, unmindful of the large brown insects crawling about. He was still a somnambulant dreaming himself through someone else's dreams.

He stood up, forced himself to take a step, and then another. Every step drained his strength; Ahasuerus, Taharahnugi, and the others were trying to pull him back. He felt as if the very air had congealed and turned viscid. It was as if he was trapped in the depths of a brightly lit ocean. The forests became jade coral reefs. The high grass was swaying seaweed. He was walking on the bottom of the ocean floor in some dim prehistoric age before man. He was moving in slow-motion. The world was alive, whispering to him, laughing at him.

"Give up. Give up. Give up." The world was breathing with him, counting his steps: *"Give up, give up, giveupgiveupgiveupgiveupgiveup.*

"No," he shouted back. He ran, walked, would not even pause for breath; his heart was a bird flapping wildly in his chest, his throat was on fire, and his head felt as if it was about to burst.

"Giveupgiveupgiveupgiveupgiveupgiveupgiveupgiveupgiveup."

And minutes stretched into hours and twigs crunched beneath his feet. He skirted the edge of a rainforest. The ground was mulch veined with black tubers and rotting climbers. Leaves and twigs turned into hilly moors separated by rills ahead. It was as if someone had swept the leaves to clear the land for the coming seasons of winter death and spring birth.

Ned was nearing the edge of Taharahnugi's dream-country, and the rest of the souls were massing behind him, pulling him back. There was a certain deadness to everything, as if the world was freezing up and all the other possibilities were becoming shadows, unrealizable until reality became fluid once again.

"*We're all inside one mind and ultimately are one mind*," said Ahasuerus. "*Give up, merge the dreams.*"

If Ahasuerus can't merge the dreams, Ned thought, then perhaps there is a chance. . . .

"*You're just trading one dream for another,*" Ahasuerus said in a weakened voice.

But there must be an end to the dreams, Ned thought.

Another step before time jelled around him, freezing him in the hot African sun.

"*Give up. Give up, give up, giveupgiveupgiveup.*"

He felt the mass of souls around him like dead weight. He tore through the scrims of dream as if they were bits of brightly colored cloth. His thoughts created a din inside his head and were echoed by the thick-stemmed lianas, the high grass, the air, dead leaves, fleeing animals, ghosts, crickets and scratching insects, and burrowers and scurriers. His thoughts became transmogrified into Taharahnugi's dream. His fear and anger became large-toothed beasts stalking through grassland. And the sky was noticeably lower. It touched the trees with frost.

I cannot die here, Ned thought, shivering, as if his sweat had turned to ice. His head was bursting with noise and ideas. It was filled with souls, scavengers leaching away his will and his life.

"*You have to die to live*," whispered the sky as it settled down into the leathery leaves of the trees.

Ned caught himself snoring, winding down with the slowtime, dying pleasantly.

He was dreaming of walls and stones and caves and tunnels, dreamed them around himself.

He fashioned his own prison and awakened in his dream.

He screamed, denying the world, especially Ahasuerus, even as he shouted his name.

"I will not merge the dreams!"

"*Then go*," shouted Ahasuerus; it was a voice that cut the air with anger and frustration. "*Try to run.*"

The words were walls.

Suddenly Ned was alone, walled out of the screaming world of souls. He had been pushed into the redlands of Ürgüp, from one dream to another. Ahasuerus's voice no longer rang in his ears. Everything was dead quiet; not even the wind dared to stir and raise a dust-devil.

Before him was the red-hued, inhospitable steppelands, roughly carved out as if by God's impatient hand. Mountains were jagged against the clear sky. The earth was made of umbers and ochers. The surrounding swells and rockthrusts resembled rough buildings, a jagged city for ghosts and holymen. In the distance were conefields, white against the reddish tuff. Each cone had a basalt cap; the oldest, most weathered rocks were balanced on pole-thin bases. Not even stone could stand up to the scouring of time.

Goreme was dead as stone. It was as if time had been running backwards and the new evolving life and its soul of souls were being buried in another vitalistic dream. Goreme was just another ruse, a dream, another palimpsest.

I'm still not out of it, he thought. This place also

belonged to Ahasuerus. Ned had removed himself from one prison only to be trapped in another. He turned around to glimpse Taharahnugi's dream forest, anxious to see if it would still be there.

Like an impenetrable wall, the evergreen rain forest divided one dream from another. From Ned's vantage ground, he could see that the trees formed three distinguishable canopies. The forest glinted like chrysoprase; it was crystalizing, reflecting the sunlight and growing like the gem-spurs in Hell to connect with Heaven and close him out forever.

Ned sensed the invisible tentacles that still anchored him to Ahasuerus and Taharahnugi's dream forest. Taharahnugi was growing stronger; if he could, he would bury Ned in woodland dreams, heavy dreams that smelled of rot and time.

The deadly silence felt like pressure in Ned's ears. This dry, cracked land breathed solitude; Ned had never felt more isolated.

Perhaps this is death, he thought, bearing the dead weight of loneliness and isolation. He turned away from the forest and walked, hoping that he could pass through this empty dream into a world untouched by dreams.

Something cracked. Ned stopped, tilted his head to listen, and a thundering became louder. It sounded as if it were inside his head, the crashing noise that used to precede a bout of crying when he was a child.

But the noise was shaking the ground. It came from everywhere: from the sky, the rocks ahead, the ground beneath his feet, and from inside his head. He covered his ears with his palms, but that could not keep out the sound.

Lightning cut across the sky, bolt after bolt, as if hurled by a hundred gods; and darkness edged the sky which first turned dark blue, then viridian, and finally purple.

Ned looked around for shelter, but something

caught his eye: a jagged line that was moving toward him from the forest. The line was a crack in the earth, just as lightning appeared to be a crack in the sky, an evanescent opening into the yellow bliss of Heaven. But the crack in the earth could only be an opening into Hell.

Ned screamed for forgiveness, prayed, felt mindless terror. He could not swallow. His eyes were riveted on the growing crack in the earth. He was stone, agonized, living stone.

And he remembered a line from the Book: "And Laura turned to watch God's hand slap the earth, and was frozen for a thousand years, then melted by His grief so to become the great river that connects God's true island with Satan's sump."

Could I have rejected the one true God? Ned asked himself. No, he thought, shivering in revulsion and fear, remembering that the soul-of-souls had used him to take root in Hell.

"Take the world," he shouted to Ahasuerus, to the soul-of-souls. "Take everyone in it. I won't merge your dreams. I reject you."

A keening cut the air, and the crack ran a jagged line, throwing up dust and rock. Other cracks began to run from north to south, from different points along the edge of the dream-forest; and cracks formed at oblique angles from the original crack that seemed to be growing wider as it became closer.

The earth was shaking, rattling, groaning.

With a shout, Ned turned to run. He could feel the hot winds eddying around him, the stinking effluvium that had been pressing to be released from the bowels of the earth. But the earth was cracking apart; cracks were converging upon him from the west as well as the east.

"Help," he shouted. "God, help me." The earth shrieked as if in response.

The ground roared. Lava bubbled out of a crack

that fed into a larger one like a tributary. As the lava spilled over, filling the crack, it hardened into spurs and rills, one built atop another like crystal castles dreamed up by a mad architect. The lava was forest green; it hardened into chrysoberyl, beryl, and tourmaline.

Hell was being created once again. . . .

The earth was shaking as if unseen hands were shaking a blanket. The ground was undulating slowly, moving up and down in great stone waves. Ned no longer felt the agonizing slowtime of fear; fear was mauling him now, tearing at his insides. He felt something warm coursing down his leg. Then he was thrown to the ground.

The crack ran past him like a huge locomotive, throwing up mountains in its wake. Boulders bounced like rubber balls, and the weathered stone cones were broken as if they were exposed fingers. Lightning struck the ground nearby, fusing sand into glass.

Ned almost wished for Ahasuerus's voice to whisper inside his head, but there was only the screaming of the earth. He was thrown this way and that. He prayed that he would not be swallowed by the earth. The ground was a drumhead, and Ned could feel its every reverberation. He could see the cracks moving into the distance and guessed that they were several kilometers apart. As they reached the horizon, the ground began to groan like a wounded animal. It was almost a lowing sound.

With a shudder, the ground began to part along the crack beside him. The earth was tearing apart at the cracklines, as if it was a three-dimensional puzzle being dismantled piece by piece.

Ned was lying flat on the trembling ground, arms and legs extended as if to break a fall. Better to stay where he was; there was no place to run. He closed his eyes and prayed. . . .

And found himself on an island floating beside other islands.

The smallest worldlet was less than a kilometer across.

Lightning connected island to sky, and a mist began to form. The sky became lighter, turned from purple, to angry red, to rose, and finally faded into cerulean, the color of Sandra's eyes. A damp smell began to come off the land. Ned felt his shirt sticking to his skin; the mist made his skin shiny as if with sweat. A heavy silence reigned.

The sun appeared, burning through the clouds that now moved between the islands on feather breezes like sailships through calm water. Ned felt the heat on his face as he stared, transfixed, at an island overhead in the distance. It created a moving shadow over the arid rockfields and new mountain range of his island. The pieces of the world were wrapped in an envelope of blue-tinged atmosphere that was perhaps sixteen thousand kilometers from edge to edge.

In the distance, a storm was boiling. The islands, adrift in the pale blue atmosphere, created their own twilights and days and nights by casting shadows onto neighboring islands. A million shards of rock, clumps of turf, all the flotsam and jetsam of past age that had just ended floated among the islands; and the islands, in all their varying sizes, were too numerous to count. It was almost as if when the world was torn apart, it had become larger; as if the parts became greater than the whole. Spread out between the western islands like huge, gently rounded bobs of glass, was an ocean.

Although all was quiet again, Ned was too stunned and ill and weary to investigate his dreary island, which he guessed was about six or seven kilometers long and two kilometers wide. He was situated near its edge, and was afraid to move closer and look out into the blue nothingness.

He yearned to hear a human sound that was not his own. He could not bear this utter isolation. Loneliness was a death of sorts; it distorted his thoughts, his senses. He still waited for Ahasuerus to speak inside his head, for he had become used to these whisperings since he first sighted the birdbeast in Junction. But there was only the buzzing of his own thoughts, and yet he knew he was trapped in Ahasuerus's dream. He wondered if his dreams were affecting the soul of souls.

He could not be sure how much time had passed—if, indeed, time was passing at all. This might well be death, he thought; and he might be a ghost.

The sun remained fixed in the sky, obscured now and then by an island passing across its face. Other islands passed near-by like icebergs in a blue, calm sea. Ned could make out a near-by island covered with forest, the same dream-forest, he imagined, that he had escaped. The trees still reflected the sun like green stalagmites. It was a crystal worldlet. Taharahnugi is still dreaming, Ned thought. Is Ahasuerus dreaming there, too, he asked himself, or is every island a separate dream, a universe cobbled by the sleeping soul-of-souls? He gazed out at the other islands and wondered if there was a way out of Ahasuerus's dream.

There was a grinding sound above him as two smaller islands came together, creating billowing clouds of dust and debris as they scraped against each other. One island had the rough shape of a bird missing a wing; the other was an oval shape, and Ned was suddenly reminded of loaves of bread, hot and steaming from the oven. He was homesick for familiar folk; he could not bear the thought of being forever alone. As he watched the islands crashing together, he thought of bread and quietly cried.

The grinding continued; large chunks were torn from the groaning land-masses. The faraway islands seemed to echo the noise, drawing an edge to Ned's nerves, making him queasy, for he realized that this could happen to his small island.

He looked down into the blue which turned gray: he was too close to the island's edge. Standing up and backing away, he looked out upon the bleached rockscape beyond, at the stone hills that might have been turned and smoothed on God's lathe. He noticed only one brown, dying tree at the base of the nearest hill. Green scrub grew around it, and a thin stream purled nearby, reflecting the sun into a golden snake.

Ned made his way to the stream, washed his face, drank a bit (it tasted slightly of iodine), soaked the urine out of his pants, and then fell asleep beside the rocky bank. He dreamed that he was looking upon the surface of the ocean, which was still as a pond, but he could find no reflection of himself. When he awakened, still unrefreshed, his mouth sticky as if full of burrs, he turned his face to the stream to see his reflection.

It's the same, weak face, he thought, squinting at his face wavering in the water. But Ned looked older—his face had lost its smoothness: crows' feet lined his eyes; other wrinkles were barely visible, but they cut across his face from nose to the corners of his mouth.

A ripple washed the image away, but it returned; and as Ned stared at his face, he saw the image of his father. Ned's face had not been used enough, but it had become very like his father's: only the sternness of mouth, deep wrinkles, and receding hairline were needed to make a mature reflection of his father.

Again, he fell asleep, dreaming of his father and Donatello Toth, wondering if he might wake up in Junction to find that he had been lured by Hell, and just as quickly and easily washed ashore. He dreamed he was trapped inside his father, forced to mime his words to himself.

It was a shallow sleep, for even with eyes closed he was staring into a field of red light. He could shut it out by throwing his arm over his face, by burying his face in the crook of his arm and the hard warm ground, but his dreams would change and he would follow suit by changing position. Although he had not often welcomed darkness (even when he was sleeping with Hilda or Sandra), the sun could well become his enemy, a yellow eye always staring, trapping him in an unwanted halo.

Dreams flicked by like frames of a film. He talked and sang to himself. His skin was warmed by the sun. He dreamed of his father—his father praying, walking and praying, chatting with the old men in the "Bookwhackers" section of the church, crying without tears, and shouting the words of the Book to him across all the chasms of time, shaking the world with his hoarse voice and Godly words.

And Ned was thrown against the tree.

He awakened with a shout (his father's shout) to find that another island was crashing into his. It was a mudstone island, mottled red and gray, covered with even rows of cones which, at first glance, looked like canine teeth. The other island's surface was about a kilometer below the surface of Ned's island, which was rapidly developing hairline cracks as if it had been baked and scorched by the sun.

A crash sent a booming across the rocks. The booming became louder as the island began to break apart. Ned was on his feet at once, mindlessly running. The ground was shaking, as if in time with a slow metronome. The stone hills broke away from the island and floated beside it. Even as Ned stepped over the cracks, they were widening. He looked down into the darkness below, terrified that he would fall and be crushed between the cold walls of the fissures.

He ran toward the opposite edge of the island, but he could not make it—the land parted, creating tiny stepping-stone islands. He tried jumping across one and almost fell. Clouds wafted past him. As Ned tried to catch his breath, he dreamed that he could take hold of a passing cloud and hide inside it as he was transported back to Junction. An agoraphobic dread took hold of him.

Behind him, Taharahnugi's intruding island loomed. Crystaline trees and verdant debris hung from a forward wall of rock and soil. And the evergreen rain forest that covered the island was growing, reaching higher and higher.

The trap was closing.

And the island was drifting closer.

Ned jumped from one stepping-stone island to another, each time looking out into the blue nothingness and hoping that he would not be swallowed by it. He was still fleeing Ahasuerus, still fleeing Taharahnugi's verdant dreams and the mass of souls it contained.

Time could only be subjective here; it was dream-time, and Ahasuerus and Taharahnugi could dream as well as he, could imagine minutes into hours and seconds into days. The sun would never set; there would be endless days. Ned wondered if all these floating islands contained the soul-of-souls, or were they all just bits of his dreams?

"I won't be a figment of your dream," Ned said aloud, staring ahead, looking to see if there was an end to this dream that contained him. And he remembered what Ahasuerus had said:

"*. . . You found little happiness in that world which was built on the dreams of the dead. It was a tiny cosmos of old thoughts. But even then you were dreaming of Hell. . . .*"

I've always been trapped, he thought, especially in Junction. He didn't want that dead mythos of tradition, that wormhole in the dream of the soul-of-souls. Freedom, he thought, dreaming of a place where dreams were made of sleep and could not affect the stuff of the world. This whole world was Ahasuerus's dream. The islands were compressed universes and time was whirling on quickly in these tiny dominions.

Ned watched the terminator of a shadow moving from island to island as a larger island crossed the sun's path above. He felt a sudden chill as shadows enveloped his island. He surveyed the group of shadowed islets that had been Goreme. The islets seemed to be grouping closer together.

Looking out from the shadows, Ned saw something glitter ahead like a needle glistening in the sun. But he could not make it out, and he was afraid to island-skip in the darkness. He waited, watching faraway islands floating like clouds in blue smoke until the island passed overhead and was momentarily blinded by the sunlight.

He heard a scraping sound behind him. He turned around and squinted his eyes to see Taharahnugi's dream-forest drawing closer, pushing the outer stepping-stone islands out of the way. The dark forest island was a huge barnacled fish swimming toward him through the blue atmosphere, intent only on its prey, destroying anything in its path.

He turned to run and saw an island rising ahead, its crystal spires and buildings reflecting sunlight like huge mirrors.

Ned scrabbled from islet to islet, running from Tahar-ahnugi's green island floating behind him. The tiny islets, some no more than a few meters across, seemed to hang in the sky like gewgaws on a mobile. All the smooth and rough shapes floated and drifted together in the diffused cyanic light. Every kind of rock and stone filled the sky around Ned: sarcen, marble, quartz, tufa, dolomite, porphyry, cairngorm, adventurine, clinkstone, sandstone, limestone, smokestone, and goldstone. They all spun slowly, as if objects in a cosmic ballet.

In the grand scheme of things he was an insect crawling from rock to rock, the dream-tuff of Goreme. He scrabbled like a spider and jumped like a cricket from dream to dream. Several times he slipped, almost fell, and prayed he would not be caught in the blue emptiness where only clouds could safely float.

As he stood on the edge of a finger-shaped, stone tuff islet that had once been the site of a hermitage—an inside wall of the dug-out structure was exposed and blind saints and angels stared with fresco eyes into the blue—he calculated his chances of making the jump to the large island before him. He could barely make out its borders; rolling smog and mist muted everything on the island. But glass skyscrapers reached out of the mist, their windows reflecting the sunlight like the blinking eyes of night-animals trapped in the flashing glare of headlights.

Ned recognized Manhattan Island. Just as Junction had survived God's shaking, so had New York City survived the breakup of the world.

There was quite a distance separating Ned from the island—almost three meters, so he waited, hoping the islet would move closer to the island, or *vice versa*. It was as if the rocky islet was a satellite of the island; as if a new moon and planet had been cobbled out of this broken universe. And indeed the islet did seem to be revolving around the island, for Ned watched the opposite shoreland moving slowly by—new avenues had been made when buildings crashed and buckled, the broken teeth in the city's smile.

He heard a scraping sound behind him as another islet was pushed aside by Taharahnugi's island. Impatient to bridge the distance between Goreme and New York, he waited for a stepping-stone islet to drift by. He scanned the opposite shore, looking for a peninsula or cape that would give him access to the island. A storm was brewing overhead. There was a smell of ozone in the heavy air. Shadows danced and clouds gathered as if pulled together by a magnet. Ned watched cloud streamers rise, to be merged into the grayness above where islands drifted like purple stormclouds.

Gray turned to angry electric blue and thunder rolled across that small quadrant of sky. Ned imagined that God's metronome was marking time for the thunderdrums and lightning flashes. It was as if the smog and mist and miasma of New York were being carried by the atmosphere onto every other island near-by until the bits of the world became gritty with ash and dirt. Ned could not see very well; smog turned to darkness and storm. Heaven boomed and showered lightning sparks upon the dark islands below.

A flash of lightning lit the island, and Ned made

out a shape before him, a promontory on the opposite shore.

Now, he thought desperately, jump—and he did, hoping he would find something more tangible than darkness. But he fell, screaming, and caught a jagged outcropping protruding from what had once been the bank of the East River. He hung there, suspended in darkness, before he could find a foothold. He crawled from rock to rock, his fingers gouging, pulling at stones, digging into sod, until he reached flat land and stepped across an empty Franklin D. Roosevelt Drive.

Ned found himself on familiar ground, but he had the gnawing sensation that it was the familiar ground of a dream. He stopped and waited for the blood to stop pounding in his head.

And he remembered the dream that he had in the Astor Hotel; now he was reliving it.

Spread out before him was New York City, shimmering in a mantle of smog and mist. It was a dead-gray world of glass and cement, yet Ned could see through, around, and beneath the buildings and streets. An opaque world of walls had suddenly become transparent. But the city was caught in its own time. Cars and trains and people were caught in mid-movement. Wings outspread, a pigeon hovered between buildings. Ned passed the United Nations Building (which had been partially destroyed by the shaking; its green-tinged glass was scattered along First Avenue like so many glittering pieces of Heaven), Rockefeller Center, and Saint Bartholomew's Church which had turned into yellow chrysoberyl. Then he meandered around Saint Patrick's Cathedral. The Pan American Building sparkled as if made out of ice, and Ned could even imagine a glass helicopter readying itself to crash through the glass Heaven above.

Ned glanced at an old woman standing with one foot off the ground and a gnarled hand lifted to touch her face. A little boy who had jumped into the air during a temper tantrum was stuck, as if pinned to the background of buildings and wide avenues. Ned could stare through the streets, see the tracks and trains and subway stations below. The commuters looked like tiny glass figurines placed under a glass-topped table.

The world was sealed in amber; only Ned could move about. But the silence of dreams was being replaced by the noise of a living city, an eternal commotion of shrieks and laughter, whispers and epithets, sighs and farts, babies crying and old men croaking. As Ned stepped through the frozen crowds, as if making his way around so many natural obstacles, he realized that it was not the city and its citizens that were transparent, but that he knew every nook and cranny and idea and thought and object in this island world.

Knowledge was somehow being continuously created in his mind. It was as if he was in a room where the lights were always on, where there could be no dark corners.

The world began to whisper in his mind.

Time began winding up and people moved about. Everyone was a thought inside Ned's mind; every action and destination was known. There would be no chance here. Thoughts merged into a steady scream, all the agonies and joys merged in a rush of collective life.

But Ned was caught by his reflection in a mirror beside the entranceway to a building. He looked at his face. It changed into his father's and beamed at him, then melted into the face of Ahasuerus, a wrinkled, knowing face, not stylized like the fresco in the stone church.

All the faces are the same, Ned thought, and he was a small chip that contained and reflected the world. His face was only an instant of history. The world was crystalizing into the soul-of-souls. Ned could run, but he took the world with him. He was a spore, carrying the pattern of every other soul.

He turned away from the mirror, but saw the masks of his face on the people rushing around him. He saw himself, all his guises, as if all the moments of his life had been spliced and scattered, given various forms, and then collected here. He was a collective being seeing all his faces, confounding time, spreading new patterns.

He was shrieking, covering his ears with his palms; and he realized that he was naked in this place, that he could have no walls nor disguises, that the dreaded creatures of his psyche were visible, bathed in the white light of sight.

The voice inside Ned's head was his own, part of his dream and the billions of souls, each a dream inside the soul-of-souls. Ned searched for an underlying form. But it was not to be found in this glittering city; it was outside, or at the bottom of, his universe.

If I disappeared, would the dream remain? he asked himself. Or am I trapped in a dream, my own mirage?

He had to find the edge of this dream, even if he had to enter another dream, and another after that. He would have to find the *terra incognita* that lay outside the old mythos of the past and the new mythos generated by the soul-of-souls. He would not yield to Ahasuerus or Taharahnugi, who combined the old mythos with the new in a fusion of souls and dreams.

You are part of the mythos, Ned told himself. You'll infect the world with yourself and still be trapped in your dream.

Ned ran down Fifty-ninth Street. He could see the southwest corner of Central Park: it was overgrown with evergreen trees. Taharahnugi's dreams were already touching this island. Birds grackled in the bush and insects scratched and chirruped.

People passed Ned, ignored him, and he felt like a

ghost passing through someone else's dream. He looked into the evergreen forest that was Central Park as if the uniform trees, which were straight and slender, were transparent, as if the flowers were made of blown glass and the mulch and sod and stone below were clear gel. And in the center of the forest was a stone church.

I must get out of here, he thought. There isn't much time. Soon the entire island would become rain forest. The forest was growing like the mountains in Hell. Seeds sprouted from cracks in the pavement, grew into trees in minutes. Trees lined the streets, then covered them. But the buildings stood above the trees like glass pylons.

Ned ran toward the boat basin and the northwest edge of the island. The air pressure dropped, and Ned felt chilled as sharp, cool breezes dried the sweat from his arms, face, and chest. It was growing dark as clouds massed above.

Riverside Drive was empty as were the brownstones that stood on either side. Ned quickly passed into the park, walked down a long stone perron, and looked out over mown lawns that seemed to stretch away forever. He passed basketball courts, picnic tables, playgrounds, bicycle paths, a roofed bandstand, stone fountains surrounded by stone benches. Memories appeared in his mind like numbers—he knew everyone who had ever walked here, all the Sunday strollers who had been mugged, chased, raped, murdered, the family picnickers, the lovers, muggers, lonelyhearts, park workers, infants in swaddling clothes, and the children who had played and splashed in the fountains.

Before him, where the Hudson River had once been, was a new land-mass, another island of approximately the same size as New York. He heard the crashing of thunder and turned around. Fed by a blinding storm that roared and spat fire, the forest flourished. It covered almost all of New York, and would soon wrap the island in a green cocoon. But the west edge of the island was untouched by the storm or Taharahnugi's dream-forest, and the sky above and beyond was clear as glass. Purple-shadowed islands and islets hung in the sky overhead.

Ned looked at the opposite shore and saw the remains of the mountains of Hell which had been smashed when the earth was slapped and pulled apart. But diamond peaks still sparkled and mountains of topaz and spinel sported opal towers and moonstone ridges. In the bright noonday light the world before him was translucent. Shattered mountains had been crushed into diamond shards and lengths of emerald, opal, quartz, and shale created the illusion of tiny cities nestled in a glass country.

To his left, above the northwest coast of the island, drifted a satellite, an islet that had broken off from the larger island. It was a chunk of crystal mountain floating off the mainland and was in the shape of two tetrahedrons stuck together—it turned ever so slightly, reflecting the light like a thousand colored mirros, a sun made of gems. Ned felt himself mirrored in the crystal.

He stepped across to the other island before him, slipped on the smooth gem surface, and from a seated position surveyed this new, yet very familiar, universe. He was excited and repelled by this place. This was where Simon had led his marchers; it had been an old dreamland of flitting shapes and inorganic growth. But now it was dead. The mountains had stopped growing, and the face of Hell was bathed in sunlight.

He followed a path along the edge of what had once been Helltundra. All around him were broken gem-spurs: jasper, sapphire, jacinth, sardius, sardonyx, chalcedony, opal, shale. Now they gathered light from the sun instead of flourescing in Hell's blanket of darkness. The amber flowers, too, were smashed; they were just shards, colored pieces of glass from the Desert Midland Bank.

I'm home, he thought, feeling suddenly elated as if for an instant he had forgotten that everything had changed. He was back in Junction. But how many Junctions exist? he asked himself. He felt an old dread. Where are Sandra and Hilda and the others? He quickened his step, walked through ivory lowlands. He came upon Bild Bridge, which had not survived the shaking, but the river was a crystal belt of diamond spurs and glacé patterns. Ned crossed it, stepping carefully, but slipping nevertheless. Once on the other side of the river, he could see Junction Road winding ahead, a cobbled path bordered by crystal pinstars that had once been high grass. It was as if this country had been immersed in the stuff of another reality; and like oil and water, Junction and the stuff of Hell had separated. But Hell had settled over the tundra, high grass, meadows, woods and wastes, commons, lammas lands, and the habitations of Junction folk.

As Ned followed Junction Road, he took a look over his shoulder through a divide of smashed moonstone at the island looming behind. He could see the dark green of rainforest. The island was dark; a storm was tearing at it, throwing down a torrent of rain. A few broken buildings still stood out above the forest canopy, but soon they too would fall, he told himself.

He turned and hurried along Junction Road, running his hand along the smooth crystal bank that had been formed beside the path.

"Look, over there," shouted Flora Angleton; her strident voice echoed sharply. Miss Jenkens stood stiffly beside her.

"Flora, Miss Jenkens, over here," shouted Ned, anxious to talk with familiar folk, even if they were his old schoolmarm and the daughter of a man who had wished him into Hell.

But they didn't seem to hear him.

"Don't shout," Miss Jenkens said to Flora as she patted her shoulder like a comrade. "You must have respect for adults and angels, and we must tell the others what we've seen."

"Miss Jenkens, wait a minute. . . ."

They both disappeared over a rise of spinel before Ned could take a step. Once again the world was quiet, except for the ringing of crystal flowers and pinstars by the gentle ground breezes.

"Miss Jenkens . . . Flora. . . ."

It was as if they did not see me, Ned thought. He listened to the crystaline tinkling and the deep ringing that sounded as if someone was rubbing a champagne glass with a wet finger.

Ned followed them, and just as he could see the top of the church in the distance, he saw a crowd below him, closing off the street and standing in the crystal grass. Some of those standing in the grass Ned recognized, but he guessed that they were all Fauboughers. Their clothes were ragged and torn, as the glass flora was as sharp as knives. Hands had been bloodied when the Fauboughers had made their way through no-man's land; and the faces, arms, legs, and hands of women and children who had followed their menfolk were similarly bloodied.

The crowd parted as Ned approached them. A child with a wild brown face fell as he stepped from the path into the gemspurs; he stood up quickly, as if the cold ground would swallow him, and he bled from a slash that ran the length of his belly.

"What are you Fauboughers doing here?" Ned asked, stopping before them. "Where are the townspeople?" But the Fauboughers just bowed their heads and made holy signs. "What of the rest of your people, those who followed the featherwakers into Hell? Those who scourged themselves with the bit? Did they return?"

"No one returned," said a man in a thick Faubougher accent. He stepped out from the crowd onto the path. He was tall and thin and well-muscled; his arms and torso were covered with old slash-scars, and he wore only rough trousers belted with frayed rope. A women stepped out beside him; she was thin and although she wore her sandy hair long, she was partially bald.

"I remember you," Ned said to the man and woman. "You were both standing on Bild Bridge the night the marchers ran into Hell. Then you didn't go."

The man winced and said, "Then you can see everything." The crowd muttered, seemed to take on a different shape, as the Fauboughers crossed themselves with inturned hands forming the holy vee.

"Where are the townspeople?" Ned asked.

"Waiting for you in and around the church."

"Why?"

"To complete their dream, I suppose," said the man, his hands by his side and fingers forming the holy vee.

"What dream do they wish to complete?" Ned asked.

"Why, the dream that begins here, the dream most everyone had before Ned Wheeler left to find you—they dreamed that you would hold court and decide the Last Days in a church made of gems."

"But I'm Ned Wheeler." Ned walked toward the man he had been speaking to, but the man backed away in fear.

"Why are you afraid of me?" asked Ned. "Stand still," and the man stood before him, shaking as if he was faced with the angel of death. The crowd retreated, leaving Ned and the Faubougher alone. "I'm Ned Wheeler. Look at me."

And Ned saw two tiny images of a birdbeast reflected in the Faubougher's eyes. The beast was covered with eyes and its six piss-yellow wings were slowly beating.

Startled, Ned stepped backward. So I've returned to

complete the dream they had before I left, he thought. "Did you dream of the court of the Last Days?" he asked the Faubougher.

"No," whispered the Faubougher, as if ashamed. "Only those who dreamed of the holy court remained in Junction, the rest followed the featherwakers. Except my wife and me."

Ned passed through the crowd like a wraith and walked toward Junction-proper. The path widened into a cobbled street flanked by high crystal walls that had been part of the mountains of Hell. Flowers were frozen beneath the translucent ground which reflected the calm sky overhead. He could hear the slap-clatter of Fauboughers' footsteps behind him; they kept a safe distance.

Ned felt as if he was passing into the earth, for the street cut deeper and deeper into the clear rock; he could almost imagine that he was back in the tunnel with Deacon. The chatter of the Fauboughers echoed along the high walls—it was the coughing and guttural croakings of the Faubougher tongue, a dialect that was not pleasing to Ned's ears, perhaps because it reminded him of the street patois of New York.

As he neared the northwest edge of Junction Park, its glassy surface now smooth as an ice rink, the walls of the translucent canyon on either side of him became lower until they were even with the cobbled street. Across the park was the Congress Bar; it was layered with beryl and opal climbers that looked like sparkling ivy. The stocks platform in the center of the park was barely visible as it was encased in a block of smoky rose quartz, and the church across the street from the Congress Bar seemed to be covered with the same stuff. The church and bar looked like two great glassy creatures staring at each other. In an eternity they might draw icy breaths and continue their lives in slowtime.

A great crowd had gathered in the park and around the church. Penitents stood quietly awaiting news of the Last Days like husbands worrying out a childbirth. Ned's father and Reverend Surface stood beside the main entrance to the church with Reverends Blues, Briar, Shorter, and MacDonald beside them.

A buzzing rose from the park and its surrounds as folk lowered their heads and prayed on their fingers, waving and making holy signs—it was truly a holy day and once again Ned was in its center. Everyone was waiting for Ned to make a move. He looked around, and saw his father.

"Father, it's me, Ned," he shouted, as he ran through the crowd.

"Welcome, holy angel," said his father, echoed by the priests and the crowd that was drawing closer. "As was our vision, so is the church prepared."

"It's *me*," Ned said as he approached his father. "Look at me, look through your vision." But his father only stepped aside, opening the way for Ned to enter the roseate church.

"Don't go in there, it's a trap," Ned said, recognizing the faded, stylized portrait of the Emperor Genetos in the narthex entrance hall. Inside, the church was identical to the one in Goreme, authentic in every detail, from the designs that covered walls and ceilings to the frescoes of the celestial hierarchy. Ahasuerus mouthed a sermon from an arch to an invisible multitude of ghosts flitting and drifting in the cool air of the church.

"Get away from here," he implored. I've been led around in a circle. Is there a way out of Ahasuerus's dream?

And a smooth, thin tentacle curled around Ned's leg. He pulled away, but another caught him by the wrist. Screaming, he backed away from the church until his pinions were torn loose.

He shouted to his father, Reverend Surface, and the crowds. "It's a trap. Turn back."

The crowd parted for Ned, but Reverend Surface had already stepped into the narthex, his face awash in God's light. As the smooth tentacles wrapped around his neck, Ned's father followed.

"Pull away," Ned shouted, but his voice was lost, soaked up by the crowd. As he started after his father, the arms of the church were extruded from the narthex entrance like meat passed through a heavenly sieve—a tentacle for every citizen, every soul. The crowds swept past him.

Ned could not help his father now.

He saw Sandra (she had cut her hair and blackened her face with ashes) and shouted to her. She turned to him, and Ned thought he could detect a glimmer of recognition.

"It's me, Ned," he shouted above the din of the crowd.

But Sandra shouted, tore her hair, rended her overshirt, and screamed, "The angel sends me to God." With that she pushed her way forward until a tentacle caught her by the neck.

"No," Ned shouted, railing at Ahasuerus. "No, even now, no. I am not connected." And he thought he heard Taharahnugi in the background noise of the crowd. But it was another ruse to trap him, to divert his attention so he could be reeled into the church and kneaded into the other souls.

Tentacles snaked toward him, writhing forward soundlessly, quickly. . . .

Ned ran, the tentacles close behind him. The air was heavy with ghosts and shadowy shapes: the congregation of the soul-of-souls. Angels flicked past him, turned in the air; and the glassy residue of Hell reflected the clouds scudding past in the heavens above.

He outran the tentacles. They tangled together, be-

came vines and forest, an evergreen forest wall behind
him, a thousand trees growing glassy leaves, reflecting
the noonday sun.

When he reached the edge of the island, he stepped
onto another—another island as large as Junction: he
would leave Junction to Taharahnugi and Ahasuerus.
Let them merge their dreams, he thought.

But he found himself in another Junction; and before him, an island away, was another Junction, this
one smoothed over by Hell as if with a lathe, a city
made of glass, where shops had become jeweled pal-
aces and the streets rang with sharp music when citizens strolled along the mirror streets.

*"All the possibilities exist, all the worlds are possi-
ble. . . ."*

Memory was a cruel voice ringing in his ears; it was
the sound of wind rushing through grass. He thought
of his father and friends being pulled into Ahasuerus's
church like hungry fish. His anger flared, then sub-
sided, and he was left with an overwhelming sense of
loss.

Ned looked around, sniffed at the air, felt a sudden
stab of nostalgia, and found a catweed to chew on.
The milky weed had a familiar, bitter taste. And the
cobblestones of Junction Road turned into butterflies
that circled in the air. In the scrub below him, butterflies burst into flowers.

Here is a place where Hell holds sway, Ned thought
as he looked into the blue, searched out the floating
islands ahead, wondered; and he remembered mountains growing in Hell, children playing in Helltundra,
Simon the featherwaker lecturing him about the will
of God. The air smelled like morning, and there was
dew on the grass. This might be a new world, he
thought, a world untouched by the ruses of time and
still awaiting its Last Days. But it was also a world
left indeterminate by the tides of Hell.

Perhaps this Junction was made of the same stuff as

Hell. Maybe nothing was predictable: water could crack, the sun might be black or it might become a golden insect sucking up the world, peeing green lettuce, saturating the world in vegetable rain. But the sun was bright and yellow, and the fragments of the world floated in the sky. Shadows rolled over islets and storms broke silently over distant lands.

Ned heard someone shout in the tundra and walked through the high grass to investigate. A whore's daughter, blond and buck-toothed, hiked up her skirt for Handler, Samll Henry's youngest son, who was shouting, "Bugs, bugs, it's probably full of bugs."

Ferris Angleton's daughter, Flora, joined him immediately, shouting, "Bugs, bugs, I see the bugs."

The little girl pulled down her skirt and then started to laugh. She walked toward Handler, swinging her hips in an exaggerated fashion, and then grabbed for his crotch, screaming, "I've got the worm."

Handler blushed and Flora lifted up her dress to prance around singing, "I've got a worm and it's bigger than his, it's bigger than his, it's bigger. . . ."

"Listen to them," said Forester who stood behind Ned, his hands on his hips like a washerwoman surveying her rags hanging on the line to dry. He wore a carycoat and overhood and a blood-purple chasuble that looked to be soaked with sweat. "They'll fall off the edge of the world if they play there."

He's right, Ned thought, once he was over his surprise at seeing Forester, or his doppelgänger. The Helltundra dropped sharply into the blue; and the children were playing on the headland's edge, baiting each other and fate.

There was a curious *pop* and Small Handler and the whore's daughter disappeared.

"Get out of there," Forester shouted at the children. "I've told them not to play there," he said to Ned. "And just what are you doing here? Pissing away

God's time while your son Donatello carouses with the whores in Congress. A fine thing for an eight-year-old boy."

There was another *pop* and a large scorpion replaced Flora. It began climbing out of the tundra toward the high grass; it winked at him and composed a tune:

> Back and side, go bare, go bare
> Both hand and foot go cold,
> But belly, God sent you good ale enough
> Whether it be new or old.

There was another *pop* and the scorpion disappeared.

This might be the place to make a stand against Ahasuerus, Ned thought as he watched a blade of grass explode with a yellow spark and become a grasshopper, which then jumped, popped, and turned into a swallowtail heading for Heaven. Perhaps I could mold this stuff of change, turn it to my advantage. . . .

"Everything changes here," Ned said to Forester, but he lifted his voice as if asking a question.

"Well, of course it does," Forester said. "God changes the substance of the world so we might not become too certain of his grand design."

"That's from your Book?"

"It's not *my* book, it's God's Book."

Once again, Ned felt the eddies of time, felt time swirl about him like the chill morning breezes. Here the winds were constantly blowing, dredging up the detritus and dreams of the past, pulling in the shadows of the future. But this was a sunny eternal day, and shadows could only be gray shapes damped by God's bright light.

"Have you seen Sandra?" Ned asked. Surely this world was also a dream, a figment of the soul-of-souls; but perhaps Ned could become a colonial in this fresh country that was as capricious as Hell itself. He might be able to learn the workings of this world; if not, there would be other islands. He imagined a continuum of worlds, an infinity of islands that ranged from the determinist clockwork visions of Junction's clergy to the shores of Hell.

"I know no Sandra," Forester said. "Have you done with Hilda and Ingrid?"

"What about Ingrid?"

"Why, she followed Baldanger into Hell. At least that's what everyone dreamed." Forester sucked in his cheeks as if to taste the insides of his mouth.

The island shuddered as another island scraped against its north edge; another pushed against its east edge, and a mist seemed to be pouring from an easterly direction, bringing chill and dampness like miasmas floating off the Sticksveiller Bogs.

The island rumbled, shook (Ned imagined that everything went out of focus for an instant), and Forester fell forward. "Damn," he said, rubbing his knee. "Look there, you see, God is piecing the world together again."

Ned looked around, saw that the islands drifting near-by were all forest green. The islands were converging; islets and islands smashed against each other, hooked vines, as new forests bloomed with the passing of every second. The islands were like clouds uniting for a storm. All the islands will soon be forests, Ned thought, hating Taharahnugi. I must get away from here.

"I think I shall write another chapter of the Book," Forester said. "And I shall call it 'The Gathering.' Do you like that? And God gathered up the islands, just as he gathered his peoples and . . ." Forester's voice trailed off as he lost himself in his schemes, oblivious to the world changing around him.

The world will mend, Ned thought, become as it was before the shaking: cracks will fuse together, crystal surfaces will melt. But the world will still be a dream, and the dream a thought. He dreamed of Ahasuerus who was dreaming Taharahnugi who was dreaming forests, an infinity of narrow boles, triple canopies of dark green leaves, forests so uniform that one might think that the world was turning into a laurel garden, a tidy world without creepers, rotting vegetation, and undergrowth.

And he headed west, toward the islands and islets ahead, toward the electric blue sky filled with clouds.

Behind him, the forest islands were converging into a single land-mass as if all the possibilities were being fused into one dream.

Ned ran from islet to islet, and the islands led a path through the sky. The clouds were motionless, like ships caught on a mirror sea without a breeze.

Where is there to run? Ned asked himself. And why run, why not wait out the inevitable? Why not let Ahasuerus find me as he certainly will?

No, Ned said to himself as he stood on an islet shaped like a hand with broken fingers. He stared at a land-mass ahead, another crystal-gilded Junction, and another Junction after that. "No," he shouted at Ahasuerus. "I'm still separate." But his shouts were soaked up by the void.

There must be an end to this, he told himself; but it was not one he could find, for the world was too large, there were too many islets and islands. And he remembered his father speaking to him in a bathroom mirror, remembered that it wasn't really his father but the soul-of-souls. "*Your notion of time and space are psychologically conditioned,*" he had said. If Ned could think laterally, allow himself to move randomly, side-step cause and effect, perhaps he could confound time and space and the soul-of-souls.

He would make his way across all the broken pieces of the world. Time was behind him like a friendly breath; time could crumple space, just as it could crumble Ahasuerus's new world.

He kept moving from islet to islet to island, and it was as if time had stopped and space became narrowed. Clouds covered the sky, making his way darker; it was as if he had entered a country of twilight. Rocks, debris, islets, and islands hung motionless in the sky; and here and there sunlight played through a hole in the cloud cover. Ned had the sensation that he was inside a cylinder, a kaleidoscope that could only reflect gray forms.

But in the distance the gray shaded into a black band, a night-horizon. If Ned could get closer, he was sure that he would be able to see the stars—or would they just be sparks in Ahasuerus's dream?

He walked slowly, hopelessly, but he would not give in, would not accede to the dream of the soul-of-souls, even if he had always been a part of it and could not escape it. He was a mirage drifting through mirages.

Many of the islands were inhabited, and Ned spoke to various persons, many of whom could not understand his tongue, or ignored him, or didn't even see him. He was a wraith, a ghost flitting like all the other ghosts he had seen, except he carried his own weight, dragged it about like a bird with broken wings. He saw women who resembled Sandra and Ingrid and Hilda, but they were odd copies and did not recognize him. He felt as if he was disappearing, as if every step was bringing him closer to dissolution, as if any second he would discover that his physical self had fallen away into the void, leaving a naked being to float from island to island, a dust-devil caught in the wind.

He wondered if he was dead, a ghost that could not rest.

The dark band ahead seemed to widen. Perhaps the band is moving closer to me, he thought as he stepped onto an island that looked as if it had been slapped by God's fist and then burned. Twisted metal and glass were everywhere; not a building was left standing. It appeared that no one was alive here. Ned crossed the island as quickly as he could, but the wind whistled under the debris, creating melodies and almost-words that sounded like the tinnitus of thought. He imagined that he was hearing a familiar song.

As he neared the jagged west edge of the island, he looked behind, for he felt a pressure on the back of his neck as if someone was staring at him. And he saw a huge land-mass filling the sky. He was terrified that the continent would fall upon him, swallow him. It was Taharahnugi's dream-forest; but the world was not completely formed, the dreams not yet melded, for the islands that stretched ahead of Ned had not been taken over by the same dream.

Ned ran and shouted and railed at Ahasuerus and Taharahnugi and the universe.

He found an islet pocked with tiny craters and covered with dust; he thought that he was walking across some mysterious feature of the man-in-the-moon, and he supposed that the moon had also been smashed.

Then he came upon an island populated with people who dressed like New Yorkers but spoke in a rasping tongue characterized by glottal clicks. Ned took to cobbled streets, became lost, and finally found his way out of the dirty, smog-laden town after walking in circles. The town was built upon several steep hills, and it must have been very old as it boasted several thick city walls.

As Ned neared the island's edge, a sandy, rocky beach, he saw an old windmill. Its great blades slowly turned, as if it was a propeller driving the island on its uncharted course.

He hurried as if on a forced march—a dead man running from the hounds of Heaven, he thought, remembering the Book.

Taharahnugi's dream-forest filled the sky behind him, drawing islands and islets like a magnet. It was advancing slowly, turning the world into a single thought. But Ned was too tired to run; his terror had ebbed, and he quickened his steps and hoped for death, for he could not hope to outrun the dreams. A storm raged ahead, and the heavens looked like a madman's chiaroscuro painting of clouds boiling over a calm sea.

The band of darkness became thicker; its center was black and its edges shaded off into gray.

And Ned walked toward the dark horizon, approached what might be a crack in the dreams, a place where there was no overlap. He felt dizzy, as if he was looking downward from some great height.

Dreams confounded time and distance. Ned had no idea how far he had come, nor how long it had taken. He crossed one island to another, but the islands were spaced closely together, as if contained by the boundaries of Ahasuerus's dreams.

The air became thin and cold. Ned shivered, but continued on. Rocks floated above, casting pale irregular shadows that crawled harmlessly over the ground. Finally, through clouds and mist, Ned made out two cat's-eye stars that blinked as if some imaginary starbeast had just awakened.

The band of darkness loomed ahead; with every step Ned took, it became wider and higher.

A grinding noise cut across the surface of the island Ned was crossing as islets and islands came together. He ran, skipped, scrabbled from islet to island.

He could see the crack in the dreams.

Stars blinked above curls of atmosphere.

Behind him, the world was a wall of forest green. He turned to look at it; it was a huge wave cresting, about to crush him, drown him in Taharahnugi's dream; and he ran toward the darkness ahead, toward the stars and the limits of the dreams. He could feel the deadly mass of souls behind him, around him, pressing forward to grind him into the soul-of-souls.

"No," he shouted as he ran, as he jumped from island to islet. His head was pounding; he was seeing as if through a bloody haze. "Let me go."

And everything exploded into thought around him.

Dreams had overtaken him. Now they would overwhelm him.

"*Give up*," shouted the rocks, "*Give up*," sang the wind, "*Give up*," echoed the blue-gray air, and the clouds rained words: "*Giveupgiveupgiveupgiveupgive-upgiveupgiveupgiveup*."

Islands and islets, dust and debris, rocks and clouds were becoming conscious, turning into souls, converging upon Ned. Souls were leaching away his life, tugging at him, passing through him, catching him, drawing him back into the warmth of a single thought, bathing him in the bright light of common sight.

But his only thought was a scream of agony.

"*Let them in*," cried Ahasuerus. "*You've come to the end of the world, there's no place left to run. You're caught, accept it.*"

Souls were pumping Ned dry, making him invisible.

"*Merge the dreams*," said Taharahnugi.

"No," Ned whispered, trying to shut out the wash of sound bubbling, crackling, cackling, whistling, hissing inside his head. "I won't be a figment of your dreams." He took a step, carried the dead weight of a thousand souls that were feeding on him; but sleep and dreams were overtaking him.

I'm lost, he thought, willing his eyes to remain open. He looked at the starlit islands drifting ahead. And I'm so close. He took another step. He was buried under a mass of souls. His shouts were muffled, lost in dreams. He took another step. . . .

And he stepped off the edge of the world toward the stars, into the crack between dreams. The souls fell from him like rags.

He fell, regretting death, gagging on fear.

He saw the stars spread across a diamond vendor's velvet.

He was frozen in the icy depths of Hell.

He had confounded time. It was whirling too quickly for him to speak, too slowly for thought.

Then the stars blinked out, and Ned was wrapped in the heavy folds of darkness. But his shouts became long colored streamers, and he could think; it was as if once again time was a river carrying him forward toward unknown destinations.

So this is death, he thought. But it was not as he had expected; his life had not passed before him, rather it was blanked out, day by day, year by year, like stars being swallowed by a hole in the sky.

Darkness was a substance. Ned found himself falling, then swimming, then walking through it, breathing its miasma, pushing through it as if through viscid syrup.

The dreams haven't merged, he thought. He was alone, pushing through death's reaches, looking for a break in the darkness. All was silent, but a dim gray light began to permeate the layers of darkness, exposing a twilight world. Ned imagined he was walking through regions that had never felt strong sunlight nor known human life.

But there was life here, bursting all around him in silent agonies of birth and death. Shapes bled into one another. The ground shifted. Luminescent mountains banded the horizon. Smooth ice shapes and gem faces were slowly melting as they pushed higher into a starless twilight sky; but Ned could not be sure of what he saw, for Hell was a specious solidity, a palimpsest of shifting illusions. Ned could not keep anything in focus for more than a few seconds. It seemed that the mountains were subtly degrading; yet when Ned blinked his eyes, or shifted his attention, everything would be built up and solid once again—for a few seconds. It was as if Hell was remaking itself, remaining pliable until by trial and error or divine wish it could find a proper reality.

The mountains grew as he walked. Diamond peaks sparkled and cut into an empty sky while crests of tourmaline and chrysoprase rose beside crystal alps. Mountains of topaz and spinel sported opal towers and moonstone ridges; ivory lowlands sprouted amber flowers. And Ned could see, if he looked out of the corner of his eye, small fluorescing gem-spurs growing out of the ground near-by. The floor of Hell was bursting with inorganic life.

Above the mountains, the black sun was a dead ember in Hell's firmament. It was a pit with no bottom, a hole in the sky. And out of this hole flowed the very stuff of Hell.

Ned found the edge of Hell. It was a wall of searing bright light, as if a hundred years of afternoon sunlight were pushing against Hell's dominions. But Hell soaked up the light as it did sound; and Ned was several steps into this bright region, almost out of the dead clutch of Hell, before he felt its impact. For an instant, he was blinded. He felt as if the sun had exploded inside his head. Then, by degrees, he could see, but it was as if he was looking through a fish-eye lens: he saw the scrub and rock and pebble of tundra-land rising into a knoll, flattening out, then rising again to be met by Junction's grassy plains. Ned was sure he was looking at Bridgehead, but this time he was looking out of Hell.

A figure stood in the tall grass. Try as he might, Ned could not bring it into focus. He walked on, but it was hard going. Every step seemed an eternity; distance seemed to be meaningless, yet when he turned his head he saw that the mountains were now behind him.

Ned was pushing into an invisible barrier. It felt as

if the hands of Hell were holding him back. But he was so close. Just a few steps more. . . .

He pressed toward the grayness of the tundra. A country of clouds shadowed the sun, draining the landscape of color, leaving only ash to be dissolved in bright light. Better to be turned into ash than into a dream, he thought, pressing, pushing at the invisible membrane that divided the two realities of Junction and Hell.

Without a sound, he pushed through Hell into Junction—found himself standing upon firm tundra, drawing deep breaths, blinking at the sky, Before him was grass; beyond was Junction, still the same: prim, pretty, full of foul smells and fine citizens. Today it was a bit noisier than other days; only a thin whisper reached Ned, a grumble. The Desert Midland Bank reflected the afternoon sun like a nightbeacon flaring for sailing ships and shamelessly showed Junction's teeth to the creatures of Hell.

Perhaps I'll be safe here, Ned thought, looking at this familiar world. It was whole, unbroken by forest dreams and islands. Everything was clear, as if drawn in sharp pencil and neatly painted.

Once again, he espied the figure that had been watching him: it was a boy who had been chewing on a milky weed. The boy's mouth was open as if to form a scream, and the weed was falling to the ground. The boy was overweight and his face was soft and familiarly average. He had long blond hair that stuck to the sides of his face, small teeth set in a large jaw, a rather large, sensual mouth, and dark blue eyes that Ned knew would lighten to cerulean after the boy ate or made love.

Ned was watching a younger, more innocent version of himself; he was staring at his doppelgänger. He knew what the boy was thinking, for once he had had the same thoughts himself. He understood that he had entered a speculatory world, and he wondered if his mother might be alive in this alternate Junction; perhaps he would find her sweeping the porch, sewing his father's shirt, or kneeling in church.

Excited, Ned shouted at his doppelgänger, but the boy had closed his eyes and was screaming. Ned remembered his own reaction when he first saw Deacon in the guise of the birdbeast. I'm still trapped, he thought sadly.

There could be no merging, Ned thought, for every thought split the world; and he imagined the alternative pasts, the might-have-beens, distant presents, all the equally real worlds of the future. He turned toward Hell; it was a familiar ocean where shapes swam like thoughts. Where is Ahasuerus? he asked himself. Perhaps this world has no Ahasuerus, no New York, Ingrid, Deacon, nor Taharahnugi. No soul-of-souls, he thought.

Perhaps the hole in the sky will pass, or close up. Then Hell would melt away and end the dream-time. . . .

He shouted to the boy again, and the boy ran.

And Ned followed, peering out of one dream into another like a creature made of eyes.

Behind him, something green glittered among the roiling shapes of Hell.

Author's Postscript

The verses found in my text are extracts from: (page 72) an early 16th Century University Play: *Gammer Gurton's Needle* by a W. S.; and (page 72) *The Jovial Crew, or, The Devill turn'd Ranter: Being a Character of The Roaring Ranters of these Times, 1651* by "S. S. Gent" (i.e. Samuel Sheppard). On page 119 the second stanza is from *The Jovial Crew*, and the song on page 161 is an Old High German charm.

Magnificent Fantasy From Dell

Each of these novels first appeared in the famous magazine of fantasy, *Unknown*—each is recognized as a landmark in the field—and each is illustrated by the acknowledged master of fantasy art, Edd Cartier.

☐ **LAND OF UNREASON,** L. Sprague de Camp & Fletcher Pratt $1.75 (14736-0)
Fred Barber was too sensible to believe in Fairyland—until a gnome kidnapped him!

☐ **DARKER THAN YOU THINK,** Jack Williamson $1.75 (11746-1)
Werewolves are one thing— but a were-*pterodactyl* ...?

☐ **SLAVES OF SLEEP,** L. Ron Hubbard $1.75 (17646-8)
The vengeful Djinn not only cursed his victim—he framed him for murder!

THE FAR CALL

by Gordon Dickson

The people and politics behind a most daring adventure—the manned exploration of Mars!

In the 1990s Jens Wylie, undersecretary for space, and members of four other nations, are planning the first manned Mars voyage. But when disaster hits, it threatens the lives of the Marsnauts and the destiny of the whole human race and only Jens Wylie knows what has to be done!

A Quantum Science Fiction novel from Dell $2.25

Dell BESTSELLERS

☐ **TOP OF THE HILL** by Irwin Shaw $2.95 (18976-4)
☐ **THE ESTABLISHMENT** by Howard Fast........$3.25 (12296-1)
☐ **SHOGUN** by James Clavell $3.50 (17800-2)
☐ **LOVING** by Danielle Steel $2.75 (14684-4)
☐ **THE POWERS THAT BE**
   by David Halberstam $3.50 (16997-6)
☐ **THE SETTLERS** by William Stuart Long $2.95 (15923-7)
☐ **TINSEL** by William Goldman $2.75 (18735-4)
☐ **THE ENGLISH HEIRESS** by Roberta Gellis....$2.50 (12141-8)
☐ **THE LURE** by Felice Picano $2.75 (15081-7)
☐ **SEAFLAME** by Valerie Vayle $2.75 (17693-X)
☐ **PARLOR GAMES** by Robert Marasco $2.50 (17059-1)
☐ **THE BRAVE AND THE FREE**
   by Leslie Waller $2.50 (10915-9)
☐ **ARENA** by Norman Bogner $3.25 (10369-X)
☐ **COMES THE BLIND FURY** by John Saul $2.75 (11428-4)
☐ **RICH MAN, POOR MAN** by Irwin Shaw $2.95 (17424-4)
☐ **TAI-PAN** by James Clavell $3.25 (18462-2)
☐ **THE IMMIGRANTS** by Howard Fast $2.95 (14175-3)
☐ **BEGGARMAN, THIEF** by Irwin Shaw $2.75 (10701-6)

At your local bookstore or use this handy coupon for ordering:

DELL BOOKS
P.O. BOX 1000, PINEBROOK, N.J. 07058

Please send me the books I have checked above. I am enclosing $ ___________
(please add 75¢ per copy to cover postage and handling). Send check or money
order—no cash or C.O.D.'s. Please allow up to 8 weeks for shipment.

Mr/Mrs/Miss____

Address____

City _____________________________________State/Zip ___________